RAINIER ERUPTS!

THOMAS P. HOPP

A NORTHWEST TALES novel

ISBN: 1530557909
ISBN-13: 978-1530557905

This story is dedicated to volcanologists, who have warned us this threat is real.

"Rainier is one of the most dangerous volcanoes in the world."
     —United Nations Decade Volcanoes Study Group, 1990

THOMAS P. HOPP

Praise for Thomas P. Hopp's Writing

"Solid science and pacing that never quits."   —Kay Kenyon,
Philip K. Dick Award nominated author of *Maximum Ice*

"One shock leads to another."   —*Carmel Valley News*

FOREWORD

This novel is intended first and foremost to entertain and frighten. It is a disaster story. I make no bones about that. However, it is also intended to inform. This portrayal of a major outburst from Mount Rainier is not beyond the realm of what is possible. It is, however, well beyond the realm of what is expected to happen anytime soon. My purpose is not to alarm people who live within the blast radius of the mountain, but only to ask, "What if?"

I wish to state emphatically that no current or past public official is portrayed in this telling. On the contrary, I have avoided creating likenesses of anyone who holds, or has held, a position of public trust at the national or state level, or whose agency would be on the front line against the events I describe here. Those agencies include the USGS's Cascade Volcano Observatory in Vancouver Washington, the Department of Emergency Services at Camp Murray, Washington, the National Weather Service, the Federal Emergency Management Agency in Bothell, Washington, and other offices less centrally involved. In developing the characters portrayed here, I have avoided describing any living person and have used artistic license to create job descriptions and titles that are not exact matches to existing ones.

In researching this story I interviewed quite a few people who lived through traumatic experiences when Mount Saint Helens erupted. I also reached out to public officials in the organizations listed above. While some officials offered me general information available through their media outlets, few were willing to discuss my concept in detail. In part I feel they viewed it as sensationalistic. And in part I assume they were not prepared to discuss overwhelmingly disastrous contingencies simply because such events are so unlikely that their agencies have not spent significant time considering them.

That said, however, I will reiterate. This event could happen. The giant holes in the earth at Crater Lake and Yellowstone Park make that clear. The amount of ice, water, and hot volcanic rock contained within Mount Rainier is greater than all the other Cascade volcanoes combined. And the mountain is active. The only substantial area for disagreement is whether or not the events I describe will take place in the lifetimes of those now inhabiting the danger zone.

PART ONE

RUMBLINGS

CHAPTER 1

A steady wind blew across frozen expanses near the summit of Mount Rainier. It carried snow that had fallen in a light dusting the night before. It drove thin streams of snowflakes across fluted drifts under a dark blue sky. Glazed ice sheets glittered starkly in morning sunlight.

At nearly 14,000 feet of elevation, two teams of four climbers moved slowly upslope. Roped together at thirty-foot intervals, the teams went single file on a path of boot prints blazed by their lead guide. They were on their final push to reach the summit before 10 AM, a necessity to give them time to enjoy the views and then descend the same day from the brutally cold and hypoxic environment they had penetrated at the limits of their endurance. Laboring in rarified air, puffing out clouds of precious moisture with every exhale, each man or woman took a single step forward, lifting his or her body with a brief tightening of agonized thigh muscles. Then, leaning on ice axes planted on one side like canes, the climbers would lock the downslope knee straight, bearing weight without too much effort until searing pain in the thighs' overtaxed muscles subsided. When the resting step had quelled the pain, the other foot was lifted forward and upward, and the excruciating process of taking another ascending step repeated. Those ahead and behind in the rope lines moved in the same halting cadence, each climber separately bearing his or her own agony and fighting the urge to cry out, "I give up!"

No one wanted to let the group down—or let the mountain

win.

A few thin clouds swirled around the mountaintop, looking as though they might clear by the time the party covered the last several hundred yards to the Guide Rocks. Those monolithic stones marked the lip of the summit caldera, a volcanic cinder cone situated on top of Rainier, which itself was one of the mightiest edifices of ash, cinder, lava rock, and ice on the planet.

At the head of the lead team, guide Jake Swanson turned in his resting step to glance back at the two rope-lines of his expedition. His parka's hood, climbing helmet, and reflectorized sunglasses hemmed in his view so much that it seemed he was looking out from a space helmet. The wide snow-covered arc of the mountain massif was dazzling white against a sky so deep blue it added to the notion that this was a space vista. In dozens of climbs to the summit, Jake had yet to lose his awe at the other-worldliness of the approach to the top. Far below, to the left and the right and behind, the green lowlands faded into summer haze almost as if they were being viewed from orbit.

Jake knew that most team members were now so hypoxic that they were intent on simply following the steps of the person ahead of them. They had no desire to look anywhere but where their next boot-step would fall. "Keep coming folks!" he called back to them. "We're almost there!" Several team members gazed up at him, mouths hanging open, breath coming out in quick freezing puffs. Jake let a grin light his handsome face, animating the medium length brown beard that was bleached blond around the mouth by high-altitude sun. He knew nothing inspired bone-weary climbers more than seeing someone else looking fit and confident.

He turned and took another pace forward and upward. At this crucial phase of the climb, it was essential to keep his rope team moving, to avoid letting them dwell on their pain and exhaustion so near—yet far—from the summit. Ahead, the wide shoulder of the mountain began to level out. Boot-steps came easier as the elevation gain diminished. Finally, as Jake reached the Guide Rocks, the horizon became a full circle of smaller mountains and hills, hazy with distance.

He stepped off the snow and onto the rocky barren soil. Then he called again to his customers. "We're here! We've reached the crater rim!"

His rope team's response was typical of many he had led. As they came up one-by-one and joined him on the solid soil, each arrival was not so much a matter of shouts and dances of jubilation, but more a matter of simply ceasing to move. Puffs of freezing breath issued from every mouth.

But as their hard breathing subsided, the climbers began to look around themselves. Pairs who had climbed together shared hugs that were more like the leaning together of two half-toppled trees than active embraces. The second rope team, led by Hari Jindal, Jake's partner in the Summits Unlimited climbing guide service, reached the rim and joined in the muted celebration.

After a round of handshakes and congratulations they moved on. Crossing the relatively flat quarter-mile expanse of snow-filled East Crater, they reached the highest prominence on the rim, a bulge on the rocky circle called Columbia Crest. There at the true 14,411-foot summit of Mount Rainier was Register Rock. They opened a metal case fixed to the boulder and signed their names on a leger of those who had reached the top.

Now came a brief time to shed backpacks and enjoy the pride and delight of having ascended one of the tallest free-standing peaks in the world. Wandering short distances among wind-scoured rocks and cinders, they took in grand vistas of the Cascade and Olympic Mountain Ranges, whose myriad peaks seemed tiny in comparison to Rainier's majesty. They looked far down into the Puget Sound lowlands west of them, where the blue waters of the Sound were crisscrossed by networks of green islands and headlands. Dark-green forested flats edging the Sound were punctuated by dozens of glinting lakes. Here and there, the panorama of blues and greens was interrupted by gray spots—the metropolitan islands of Seattle,

Tacoma, and Olympia, each lying under its own plume of yellow urban haze. All this lay under a vault of dark blue sky. It was a heavenly perspective, one they would remember as long as they lived.

They paused for some time, sitting or standing on boulders that had once been red-hot volcanic bombs tossed onto the cinder cone's edge by titanic forces within the mountain. As hypoxia subsided, appetites climbed. People took sandwiches from backpacks, along with water, juice, or hot chocolate. Some snapped photos with cameras or cell phones—photos of individuals, couples, rope teams, and of the entire expedition shot with timed exposures while they posed in two rows, some standing, some kneeling, and all grinning with the pride of an ambition satisfied.

All this transpired before 11 AM. Thanks to good weather and stouthearted clients, the expedition was running ahead of schedule. This prompted Jake to add one more event to the day's doings.

"Anyone up for exploring an ice cave?" he asked.

At several points within the crater, volcanic steam drifted up from holes in the dished surface of the caldera snowfield. The openings were surface outlets for a great maze of tunnels melted out of the ice that filled the caldera to a depth of several hundred feet. For those team members brave enough, Jake offered to lead a descent into one of the steaming caverns.

The group was equally divided between those who said yes and those who chose to stay above with Hari, basking in the sun and taking in the grandeur of the scenery. The more adventurous group moved to a place along the rim where sulfurous vapors wafted out from under the edge of the snowfield. They descended over wet boulders into humid, subterranean grottos with scalloped ice walls and ceilings dripping melt water. Lighting their way with flashlights and helmet lamps, the group scrambled several hundred yards down into a world of steamy mists that bore a brimstone odor, as if they were approaching Dante's Inferno at the summit of a mountain. Melt water streamed down from the fluted ice ceilings in constant drizzles, pattering off their helmets and parkas. No one wanted to linger and get a soaking, so the group resurfaced within minutes, regaling those above with descriptions of the sights, sounds, and smells in the subsurface realm of what was most assuredly a living, breathing volcano.

Next on the agenda was the long and arduous descent to Camp Muir, which had to be accomplished before the sun's warmth softened the snow and increased both the difficulty of walking in deepening post-hole-like footsteps, and the already significant danger of avalanches.

"Time to move out, people," Jake eventually called as team members were finishing their preparations, tightening boot laces and donning backpacks and helmets. "Take one last look around."

Near him, Sophie Minto, a member of his rope team and one who had gone down into the ice cave, let out a gasp of amazement. "Look at that steam!" she cried, pointing to a fumarole on a distant part of the caldera. "It wasn't that big before!"

Indeed, what had been mere wisps of steam issuing from a vent near the northwest rim when they arrived, now was a burgeoning column of vapor forming a plume that drifted east on the brisk summit wind.

"I'm glad we got out of the caves when we did," she said. Her expression was hidden behind her gold reflective sunglasses and her pink climbing helmet, but her concern was visible to Jake in the tight set of her mouth as she asked, "Do you think it's safe to cross the ice field with that going on?"

He shrugged. "Never seen anything quite like that before."

To be safe, they skirted the caldera on its south rim, nervously eyeing the steam billows until they reached the Guide Rocks. There, they roped up again and began to descend the snowfield on the east shoulder of the mountain with Hari's team in the lead. Steeper slopes awaited where the ice field broke over the bergschrund, a large crevasse that divided the upper stagnant snow from the lower, moving snow of the Emmons and Ingraham Glaciers. On the ascent, negotiating the crevasse had been an almost unnerving challenge for some. They had crossed the seemingly bottomless aqua-blue ice gap by walking across the eight-foot span of an aluminum ladder laid flat with a slat of plywood on it. Now, as they neared the bergschrund's edge and the waiting ladder, Jake's satellite phone beeped. He fished it out of a breast pocket of his lime-green-and-blue parka and clicked the transceiver button on, holding up a hand to halt his team. Hari's team, ahead of them, continued moving downslope. "Over," he said into the phone. "What have you got, Scotty?"

"Ah, roger, Jake—" The voice of his business partner and sometimes dispatcher, Scotty Wilkerson, in their office in Tacoma, was scratchy with static. "Got an advisory."

"Weather?"

"No. USGS says they've detected a swarm of earthquakes up there. You folks feel anything? Over?"

"Negative, Scotty. At least I don't think so. The wind is gusty up here, so it might be hard to tell."

"Roger that. Just be advised. Over."

"We did see something odd," Jake said.

"What's that?"

He was about to describe the steam cloud, but paused when he noticed something new and alarming. Small pieces of ice and rock were tumbling by on either side of him. "Hold on, Scotty." He shoved the phone back into its pocket without pausing to shut it off. He glanced left and right—and shock accelerated his heartbeat as his worst fears were confirmed. Myriad cross-slope cracks had opened around him and his team. The cracks were just inches wide at first but they expanded quickly. As they did, the entire surface on which Jake stood began to move downhill.

"Avalanche!" he cried at the top of his lungs. "Ice ax drill—now!" Quickly, he and the entire expedition dropped flat on their bellies with legs spread downhill, spiked crampons on their boot-toes dug into the snow for traction, and the curved points of their ice ax heads driven in under their chests with both hands. This maneuver, rehearsed under Jake and Hari's tutelage before the climb began, was the climbers' best defense against an uncontrolled slide on an ice sheet. But nothing could defend against the moment when an entire slope gave way and moved downhill in an avalanche. And that was what was happening now.

The avalanche quickly built momentum, carrying both rope teams downslope at an accelerating pace. Amid panicked screams and shouts of desperation, the two groups slid as if they were following each other on some mad toboggan ride. Jake's group, much less experienced with ice axes than he, were carried below him rather than above, where they had started the crazy plunge. Knowing that their only hope of stopping now fell to him—he fiercely jabbed the ice ax tip down into the stationary layers of ice and compacted snow beneath him. He dug in with his outspread feet, hoping their crampon spikes would bite into the hardened layers. But they bounced off ice chunks rather than digging in. He forced the ax tip down with all his might, but it jarred loose repeatedly and the blade jabbed him mercilessly in the ribs. Ice blocks slammed into his belly, knocking the wind out of him. Crying out in pain and frustration, he bore down on the ax point until it finally bit into solid snow, caught—and held. Almost miraculously, his sliding stopped. The rope tugged hard on his harness and went taught, bringing his three rope-mates to a halt as well.

Tumbling chunks of ice and snow surged around and over him for a few seconds. And then the avalanche was gone. It continued downslope and swiftly left them behind. Jake clung to his embedded ice ax as thunderous noises reverberated from the slopes below for several minutes, concealed from his anxious gaze by clouds of swirling white snow.

Jake and his rope-mates lay on their bellies with ice axes planted for dear life until the rumbling fully subsided. Eventually, Jake lifted his head and looked around. Below him on the newly scoured snow slope, equally spaced along the taught rope line, were the other climbers of his group. Nina Mournay lay still, too terrified to even glance around. She appeared to be quietly praying, face down in the snow. Paul Wozinski looked up at him, awaiting his instructions. But Sophie Minto, the last person on the rope, was missing. And something else—he now noticed with a fresh jolt of adrenaline—was terribly wrong. Beyond where Sophie should have been was a yawning chasm. The bergschrund crevasse had grown. It now yawned twenty yards wide and spanned the slope below them horizontally for hundreds of yards. The entire edge of the bergschrund had collapsed. *And they were at the new brink!*

"Everybody stay still!" he shouted. He reached over a shoulder and pulled a long ice picket out of his backpack. Still lying flat, he drove the picket into the hardened snow with the flat of his ax until it was anchored deeply in solid subsurface snow. Then, working hurriedly, he tied the rope holding the team together to a carabiner clipped to a hole in the center of the picket. And then he roped himself to a second picket, assuring that, come what may, no one—including himself— was about to slide any farther. Then he rose to his knees and surveyed the situation more carefully.

Another jolt of adrenaline rippled through him when he realized the other rope team was nowhere in sight. That they had been swallowed by the new crevasse was a foregone, numbing conclusion. Hari Jindal's team had been farther downslope and had caught more of the avalanche's force. They had had less distance to recover from their slide—clearly too little to avoid tragedy. The thought made Jake's senses reel. An urge to vomit rose in his throat. He took a walkie-talkie radio out of a pocket on the other side of his parka from his phone. He clicked the transmit button and called desperately, "Hari! Hari! Do you read me? Over!"

There was no response.

He tried again after a moment.

Still no response.

His shocked mind was jolted back to more immediate concerns by a faint noise. It was the sound of woman's voice—Sophie Minto's voice—crying from beyond where the end of the rope disappeared over the brink of the crevasse.

"Help!" Her voice sounded incredibly thin, distant, and desperate. "Somebody help me, please!"

Jake heard a muffled sound in his left breast pocket. He snatched out the satellite phone and called into it, "Scotty! Thank God you're still there!"

"What's happening?" Scotty asked, coming through heavy static.

"Avalanche!" Jake cried. "Hari's team fell into a crevasse!"

"Oh, my God," Scotty replied.

"Get on the phone to Park Service Dispatch at Longmire and tell them to send help!"

"Roger that," Scotty called back. "What is your exact locat—?" He was cut off by a tone that announced the signal had been lost.

Jake thrust the useless phone back in its pocket. Then, moving carefully on the treacherous, icy slope, he went into a drill he had demonstrated to other climbers in the lowlands and practiced dozens of times on the slopes of Rainier. He clambered to and assisted the others in securing themselves with their own ice axes driven in deeply and tied off as belay points. Once he was sure Nina and Paul were safely anchored, he enlisted Paul's aid in a rescue attempt for Sophie. Paul was a relatively inexperienced climber, but he was a big man and easily the strongest among them. That made him the best replacement for Hari, who would have been Jake's assistant in this challenging task. Working together, the two of them set a deep ice anchor near the brink and boot packed it in solidly.

Leaving Paul at the brink minding the ropes, Jake went over the edge, rappelling on a doubled length of rope, toeing in with the tips of his crampon spikes and then pushing off and descending a few feet per bounce until he reached poor Sophie. She was suspended helplessly in mid-air via her harness, which was figure-eight knotted to the main rope. She hung belly-up and looked like she had tired in the twenty minutes it had taken to get to her. Her arms, legs, and helmeted head all dangled.

Her ice ax and right glove had vanished, pulled off by the jolt at the end of her fall. He looked for them below, but saw only vertical ice walls with swirling white mist obscuring their bases. The crevasse itself was immense—incredibly immense. It was nearly twenty yards to the ice wall on the far side. The chasm stretched across the mountain in both directions for distances that were obscured by the white mist, which billowed up from below and brought an alarming, rotten-egg smell with it. "Hari!" he cried as loudly as he could down into the mist. Nowhere in the mist-shrouded depths did he see or hear any sign of Hari or his team. "Hari!" he cried again. There was no answer. He hadn't really expected one.

When he turned to Sophie again, she gave him a faint smile. "Hi," she said weakly.

"How are you doing?" he asked, tilting his head to partly match the angle at which hers hung. "Can you sit up?"

"I'll try." She grasped the line with both hands, one gloved and the other not, and tugged weakly. He braced himself with feet spread wide and toe spikes dug into the ice wall, and then put an arm under her back and helped her get upright and seated on the leg-loops of her climbing harness. He noticed a trickle of blood on the left side of her chin, which bore a broad scrape mark where she had smacked against the ice wall.

"You okay?" he asked again, while arranging the pulley and rope that would lift her.

"Not really," she said, her head reeling woozily. "My left ankle is— I think… it's broken."

He glanced down and noticed that her left foot hung at an unnatural angle.

"We'll take care of that after we get you out of here." He clipped the pulley to her seat harness using a locking carabiner and clipped the lifting rope that Paul held at his station above, through a carabiner on her chest sling. Once he had her con-figured for hauling out, he said, "You're going to be okay."

"I know," she replied bravely.

Far below in the whited-out depths of the crevasse, a sec-tion of ice wall collapsed and rumbled onto whatever base of rock and snow lay below the obscuring fog.

Jake's ascent to the brink where Paul waited was an arduous, exhausting rope climb. He ascended with the help of a tandem pair of Prusik loops attached to his belay rope, one for his right foot and one clipped to his harness. He used the Prusiks to inchworm his way to the top of the crevasse, and then he clambered laboriously up and over the brink to rejoin Paul. The two of them then used the lifting rope and pulley to haul Sophie up to the lip of the crevasse. They pulled her to safety with one man on each arm. Once they had her lying on her back a few meters from the brink and secured by ropes to an ice anchor, Jake knelt beside her and gingerly examined her left leg. The foot lay cocked at an odd angle in the snow. She looked at him dizzily as he worked, moaning in pain when he touched the area just above the boot. He got out his phone, and was relieved to see two dots on its reception indicator. He punched a number and got a ring and an answer by a female voice. "Longmire Dispatch. Go ahead Jake. We've been waiting for your call. Over."

"We've got a boot-top fracture here. We're going to need a helicopter. Over?"

"We were advised by Scotty Wilkerson. One is on the way from Joint Base Lewis-McChord right now. Over?"

"Got an arrival time estimate? Over?"

"Ah. Negative. Maybe twenty minutes. Any sign of the other team? Over?"

"Negative."

Jake glanced at the brink over which Hari and the second team had fallen—and blinked in surprise and doubt. The white mist had grown into a large cloud billowing up forcefully from the crevasse. And it no longer resembled a mist so much as a column of steam—a huge column of steam. And it was accompanied by a rumbling volcanic hiss from the depths.

"Longmire?" he said into the phone.

"Go ahead, Jake," the dispatcher came back. "What have you got? Over?"

"We've got more trouble. A lot more!"

***

The geological monitoring station within the crater of Mount Saint Helens had been set up on a flat area beside a huge boulder of jagged andesitic lava rock, deep inside the maw of what had once been the mightiest volcanic eruption of modern times. It was an easel-like tetrapod stand of jointed metal pipes, anchored by concrete footings and piles of stones. It was painted brown, the better to blend in with the surrounding landscape, and was cluttered with attached equipment necessary to perform its volcano-monitoring functions. Most prominent was a flat rectangular solar panel more than a meter across, which faced south to absorb sunlight and power the other instruments that were attached to the legs of the tetrapod or linked by wires from locations on nearby posts or in underground recesses. These devices included a camcorder pointed at the mountain's steaming lava dome, a webicorder seismographic detector in a large box at the base of the station, a tiltometer, and a GPS locator antenna mounted at the top. The station, self-contained and self-powered, gathered information automatically in the absence of human operators and sent the data to the Volcano Observatory on nearby Johnston Ridge via a radio transmitter.

Today, the minicomputer that ran the station was due for a software update by one of two visitors. Andrew Hutchins, a field engineer in his early thirties, was experienced with such gadgetry. He was here with Lexi Cohan, a geologist in her late twenties, with the US Geological Survey's Cascade Volcano Observatory. Both normally worked in offices at the Observatory's Vancouver, Washington headquarters. But today they were in the field, dressed in summer weight hiking clothes, sunglasses, and ball caps with neck flaps to protect against the glare of high altitude sun. Andy busied himself with his assignment, while Lexi, the Observatory's newest staff member and a masters-degree student at the University of Washington, watched and learned. It wasn't in Lexi's job description to maintain monitoring equipment, but she had never had the pleasure of visiting a remote detection station, nor seen first-hand the astonishingly vast, dusty, hot, and dry center of the mountain's caldera.

Andy had brought a tablet computer and connected it to the station's computer via a USB line. It was a simple process to upload the new software. A few keystrokes on the tablet, and several minutes waiting while gazing in awe at the power of nature evident all around them, and the task was done. Before departing for the five-mile hike back to where Andy's brown USGS SUV waited at the Windy Ridge trailhead, it was essential to assure that the newly loaded software was handling the station's many assignments. Andy checked the outgoing antenna feeds from each of the monitors. He used the USB link to his tablet's screen to have a look at the output of the webcam, GPS monitor, and the tiltometer. The latter instrument, he could see, was reporting a very slight increase in slope, meaning the crater floor was swelling imperceptibly. But that trend had been continuing for months and he expected to see it. Next, he keyed up the feed from the seismometer. Its trace consisted of a series of horizontal lines with small jiggles on them, the computer-screen equivalent to the old days when a black ink pen marked a slowly turning drum of white paper. As expected, the sensitive trace showed many vibrations in the last hour due to their footsteps in its vicinity, and the jiggling of the station itself as Andy worked on it.

Lexi looked on from beside him and pointed at the computer-screen image. "What's that?" she asked. A dark scribble had appeared on the bottom, most recent line as it slowly traced to the right across the screen. A series of fat, jagged spike-clusters had appeared.

"Hold still!" Andy said, putting up a hand to signify that she should remain silent and stand still to assure that her own movements weren't setting the seismometer off. Instead of returning to baseline and holding steady, the trace scribbled more violently, marking an even larger event, far beyond any Andy had made while he was working.

"Is it a real quake?" Lexi asked.

"It sure is," Andy affirmed. He looked up at the lava dome and steep walls of the south crater rim looming above them, his face creased with sudden concern. "Maybe a rock slide?" he thought out loud. "A big one could be dangerous up here."

"I don't see anything," Lexi replied.

"Did you feel anything underfoot?" he asked.

"No," she said. "Did you?"

"No."

Another, even larger tremor appeared on the trace. But still there was no sensation of movement underground.

"I don't get it," Andy murmured, staring at the plot. "If it's not coming from Saint Helens, then where—?"

Lexi turned to glance behind them—and gasped. The view to the north looked out across the cinder-covered pumice flats at the base of Saint Helens' blown-out crater, and across the wide expanse of Spirit Lake where thousands of logs still floated after the 1980 eruption. Beyond the lake rose the crags of Mount Margaret, a large, non-volcanic mountain. And in the farther distance, framed in a clear blue sky, was— "Rainier!" she exclaimed, pointing at the snowcapped top of the mountain. "It's coming from Rainier!"

A single long white cloud clung to the top of the mountain and was drifting to the east on the prevailing wind. "Is that really an eruption?" she wondered.

"Impossible," Andy replied. He stared at Rainier for a long time, frowning. "Maybe it's just a weird-looking lenticular cloud."

He glanced at his tablet and its trace again. Another seismic spike had appeared while they were watching Rainier. This one was larger than the previous ones. It spread across the lines above it on the screen.

"That was a pretty good shake," he said, looking at Rainier again thoughtfully. "I'm surprised we can't feel it."

"You wouldn't expect to feel it," Lexi said. "Not if it was a long-wavelength teleseism coming from that distance."

"Good point, Miss Smarty-pants," Andy said, grinning at her gamely. "But Rainier has been quiet for years."

"Not anymore," she said with newfound conviction. "Look at that!"

The cloud at the summit of Rainier had taken on a new shape. The portion directly above the peak had surged upward in the shape of a small mushroom cloud. As they stared in silent amazement, it slowly dispersed and joined the rest of the cloud drifting east, like the latest chug from a steam locomotive's stack.

Andy disconnected the USB wire from the station and shut off the tablet computer. As he put it into his backpack, he said, "Let's get going. I want to get back to the car and get on the radio to Vancouver. Maybe they'll know what's happening."

As they moved off quickly down the dusty trail on which they had come, Rainier issued another chugging white puff.

***

Within an hour, a traffic helicopter had been diverted from monitoring the typically jammed freeways of Tacoma to a location near the lower slopes of Mount Rainier, to get film footage of the ongoing rescue attempt.

"This is Matt Ziegler aboard Chopper Twelve," said the newsman, framed in his front-passenger location in a shoulder-held camera shot by his cameraman Dan Ewing, who occupied the rear seat of the helicopter's cabin. Ziegler smiled as he spoke into his headset's microphone, while his image was projected back to the TV news station in Tacoma. "I'm reporting from as near the scene of this dramatic mountain rescue as we can get. An injured female climber is just about to be hoisted aboard an evacuation helicopter."

Ewing switched the video feed to a telescopic HDTV lens slung on a swivel mount under the nose of the news chopper, angled upward and focused on the drama being played out thousands of feet above their location. The powerful telephoto camera zoomed in on the Army-green rescue copter, a heavy-lift Boeing CH-47f Chinook with large rotors fore and aft. It hovered fifty yards above a place on the slope where the injured woman's climbing mates and a rescue team were gathered around to assist her into a stretcher-like litter that had been lowered on a cable to the snowy mountain slope.

"There she goes," Matt narrated. "They've got her in the stretcher. And now they'll hoist her up on the helicopter's winch."

The Chinook engaged its winch and the cable tightened. The stretcher rose from the snow. The video feed that followed the events was beamed via Chopper Twelve's radio transmitter to the news station's control room, where it was fed live to the news desk and the public, with Matt's commentary in voiceover.

"I am sure those other climbers will be glad to see their companion safe," Matt commented as the litter rose up to the open bottom hatch of the chopper. "But not everything is going to end well here. We are told that four additional members of the party are missing, and may have fallen into a freshly opened crevasse that you can see just below the party. That crevasse appears to have swallowed an entire rope team. So far, no trace has been seen of them. And a low cloudbank continues to block anyone's view into the crevasse."

The anchorwoman's voice inquired, "Matt, are we seeing clouds—or is that steam—coming from that opening?"

"I'm not sure, Amanda. We're limited by altitude in Chopper Twelve. We've got a three-person crew aboard and lots of video and radio equipment, so we can't risk flying over 8,000 feet. From this angle, and this far below the scene, I can't say if that's steam or just a cloud wrapped around that part of the mountain. We are not aware of any volcano alerts. Are you?"

"None reported here," Amanda replied.

"The climbing party," Matt went on, "is in an unenviable situation. They will have to leave the area soon without their missing comrades and hike down to a lower elevation. Otherwise they risk being stranded on the mountain at night, and that in itself could be fatal."

"They must be heartbroken—" Amanda began, but an outcry from Ziegler cut her off.

"Wait a minute, Amanda, I think we may have an answer to

your previous question. Look at that!"

Chopper Twelve's video feed had zeroed in on the rescue helicopter as it reeled in its human cargo and the crew wrestled the stretcher inside. Now, cameraman Ewing swung the telephoto from the Chinook to the crevasse and focused on a sudden outburst of black dust that billowed up and mingled with the white steam drifting off to the east.

"It's an eruption all right," Zeigler said. Before either the reporter or the anchor could say more, another larger fountain of black dust burst from the crevasse. This was a powerful outburst that carried rocks and boulders high into the air, tracing their trajectory arcs with streaks of gray dust.

"This looks like big trouble," Matt murmured inanely as a third surge of dust and rocks shot out, tracing even higher arcs of flying debris.

The three climbers and two rescue crewmen still on the mountain raced away from the brink as fast as they could run over snow and ice. They headed for the west end of the crevasse, hoping to escape the hail of rocks falling all around them.

The Chinook maintained its position only long enough for the crewmen to pull the stretcher fully inside its belly hatch. Then it wheeled to fly away from the crevasse. Before it had gone a hundred yards on its new course, the chasm unleashed another blast so huge that it enveloped the helicopter in a hail of boulders and dust. Stricken by dozens of flying rocks, the Chinook reeled wildly in the turbulent air, heaving from side to side. As the pilot struggled to regain the semblance of level flight, an even larger outburst erupted from the crevasse, sending titanic boulders spinning hundreds of feet into the air.

"Oh my God! What an awful sight," Matt gasped after a moment of speechlessness. "Those boulders are like an artillery barrage dropping around the helicopter and climbers!" The camera feed showed the climbers and rescuers running beneath a hailstorm of pelting rocks—none stricken down so far— while the Chinook tossed and yawed under the barrage. One particularly large boulder rose in a long arc that descended toward the helicopter while Ziegler, the news desk, and the audience held their collective breaths. The boulder's dusty path descended until it clipped a blade on the rear rotor system of the Chinook and the aircraft spun madly out of control.

"Oh, my God!" Matt cried again as the stricken helicopter plummeted. Fortunately, it had not yet risen far above the mountainside and consequently did not have far to fall. It careened onto the snow slope just below the crevasse, shedding its fore and aft rotor blades one-by-one. Then the fuselage crashed belly-down on the snow and tumbled over and over before sliding to a stop on its side a hundred yards downslope, where the pitch of the ice field lessened.

"Can you see what's happened to the people inside?" Amanda asked.

"I don't see how they could have escaped serious injury—or worse," Matt shouted in astonishment. "We'll try to get closer," he said.

"Please be careful, Matt," Amanda said.

A moment later, the clatter of myriad small objects could be heard on the metal skin of the news chopper, mingled with a surprised outcry from the pilot. The copter turned sharply in mid-air, shifting the camera view from the peak to the green lowlands below.

"We're getting out of here, Amanda," Matt said, almost mechanically reporting now, using his newsman's instincts despite fear that made his voice tremble. "There are rocks falling from the sky all around us. So far, just small ones." More clattering was audible over the news feed as a rain of small stones peppered the news chopper.

The video feed swung madly as Chopper Twelve's pilot banked the craft sharply left and right and raced away from the angry mountain. "I've got an engine warning light!" he called loudly enough to pick up over Ziegler's microphone feed.

"Sorry folks," Ziegler said, turning to face the rear-seated cameraman again, his expression taught but his voice controlled. "Discretion is the best policy under the circumstances. We'll have more for you as soon as—"

At the anchor desk, Amanda sat speechless for a moment when the newsroom camera flashed its red ON AIR light, telling her that her image was live again. She glanced at the outgoing TV monitor feed. Beside her perplexed face, the inset image from Chopper Twelve had vanished, dissolving into static.

"We'll— We'll be right back!" she stammered.

Viewers at home saw the video change, inanely, to a shampoo commercial featuring a smiling model running in slow motion with long, lustrous, bright-red hair streaming out behind her.

CHAPTER 2

The curving line of Day-Glo red floats marked the gillnet that arced across the Nisqually River just above its confluence with Red Salmon Creek, a lower tributary that joined it to meander through saltmarsh flats for several miles to the river mouth at Puget Sound. A dinghy with a small outboard motor clamped to its narrow thwart was tied at one end of the net's float-line rope. The small craft's skipper was an old weathered Nisqually Indian fisherman by the name of Jimmy Finch. Dressed in rubber boots, dungarees, a Pendleton shirt and a worn blue goose-down vest, Jimmy tugged a portion of the long gillnet into the dinghy. Entwined within it, he hauled aboard a Chinook salmon, also called a king salmon and with good reason. The fish was over a yard long. The dinghy listed precariously as Jimmy tugged the monster over the starboard gunwale. The Chinook didn't struggle much, having long since expended its energy trying to escape the net twined through its gills. Jimmy dispatched it with a well-placed blow of his fish club, a two-foot length of cedar ornately carved with totem animals. He laid the big fish parallel to two slightly smaller fish he had already brought aboard, and then he paused and wiped a lock of his long gray hair away from his face with the back of a rubber-gloved hand. He glanced at the sole passenger aboard his little boat. "They're all yours," he said with a friendly smile. "For a couple minutes anyways."

Carlie Hume, a young biologist with the Washington Department of Ecology, reached into her green backpack and came out with a small icepick-like device in her blue-rubber-gloved hand. She wiped the salmon's scaly side with a white sterilizing swab she held in her left hand, and then drove the needle end of the device into the flesh of the tail. When she drew it out, the hollow biopsy needle held within its core a small sample of the fish's flesh. She pushed a lever that dropped the biopsy sample into a purple-capped plastic test tube, which was half filled with a clear liquid that would dissolve the sample and preserve its trove of DNA and toxics. She did the same for the two smaller fish. "There!" she said eventually. "All done."

Finch smiled again with a forbearing, amiable look in his eyes. "Back in the old days, nobody had to tell Nisqually people if their fish was safe to eat. In the old days, we learned from nature what we could eat and what we couldn't. My ancestors taught us we should just eat what Bear eats."

Carlie shrugged. "Bear had better watch out these days. That fish just swam past the outwash of DuPont Chemicals' old industrial waste site. My job is to make sure they're within acceptable guidelines for toxic chemicals—and check the genetic diversity of the DNA to make sure your salmon stock won't go extinct."

Jimmy nodded. "I know. You gotta do your job. Bear's gotta do his. And I gotta do mine."

While Carlie stowed the sample in a small cooler of ice she had brought along, Jimmy untied the bow rope from the float-line. Then he moved to the stern and turned his attention to the small motor. He adjusted some levers and then gripped the wooden handle of the old, frayed pull cord that would turn the cylinder and fire up the spark plug. He paused and looked at her. She raised her eyebrows, expecting one of his bittersweet but humorous quips.

He inclined his head toward the line of red buoys, which were once again placidly rippling the outbound river current after their disturbance by his fish harvesting. "This here net runs right where my elders got arrested for fishing. Ever hear of Billy Frank Junior?"

"Of course. I read about him when I was preparing for this

project. And I think you've told me a couple of times already that he was your great uncle. Like maybe last time we were out here?"

"I suppose I might have." He grinned and tapped a fingertip on his temple. "Getting old, you know."

He pulled the ignition cord. The motor *plup-plupped,* but it didn't fire up. "This thing needs work," he said apologetically. The boat drifted downriver as he tinkered with the throttle and choke levers. Another pull ignited the cylinder and the engine revved. Jimmy settled it down to idle by adjusting the throttle, which was like those on motorcycle handlebars but located on the tiller that projected forward from the little old Evinrude engine. He flipped another lever, and the motor clunked into gear. The little boat began moving forward slowly. He sat on the stern plank seat with the tiller in hand, and began to turn the dinghy upriver. As he did so, Carlie, who was sitting on the center plank, turned to look ahead of them.

"Look at that!" she cried.

***

Big alder and cottonwood trees lined the channel ahead and Mount Rainier was visible between them in the distance. Framed by the trees' green foliage, Rainier had a long grayish-white cloud trailing away from its summit to the northeast.

"Is— Is that—" she stammered. "Is that *an eruption?*"

"Looks like it," Jimmy murmured. He twisted the throttle back and let the boat putt forward slowly against the light current, so that they could take in the impressive sight of Rainier smoldering in the distance. After observing the puffing steam clouds for a few moments, he said, "My ancestors would say Shuq Siab—the Great Spirit—was angry about something. It's a sign of trouble."

"I'd say it's a sign of hot lava," she needled good-naturedly.

"See it how you like. Nisqually people take such things seriously. Most of us, anyways."

"Your tribe experienced volcanic eruptions in the past?"

"'Course we have. We've been here since forever. We've

seen a lot of things. Not like you newcomers—you pahstuds."

"Us what?"

"Pahstuds. That's our word for Americans. It means, Bostons. You know, 'cause you folks started coming here mainly on ships from Boston. Whalers, settlers, invaders."

"Come on now. Don't start badmouthing my people again."

"Pahstuds took away our land—"

"By treaty."

"By treaties made when we was all sick with measles, mumps, smallpox. And then pahstuds broke their own treaties. They told us we couldn't fish in our own rivers. This one, for instance."

"I wouldn't have done that to you."

"No. You're a good pahstud. But my great uncle got arrested over and over again, just for fishing, till Judge Boldt said we had the right. Now I fish here when I please. And I catch all the salmon I need. Even if they ain't quite right according to you."

"Somebody's got to monitor them for toxics and disease."

"Thanks to the DuPont ammunition factories. We never asked them to dump their waste chemicals into our rivers. They just went right ahead and did it. Didn't care about no Indian fishing rights."

"And that's exactly why I'm here now. To try and make it right again."

He sat back and looked up at the mountain for a long time. "Wiaats, Tacobet!" He called to the mountain in a loud, oratorical voice. "Es hailtset chuff! O?"

He turned to Carlie. "You know what that means?"

"I have a feeling I'm going to hear."

He grinned. "I asked Tacobet how she's feeling."

"Tacobet?"

"That's her name in our Lushootseed language. It means, "Snow White Mountain. We also called her Nourishing Breast Woman."

"Really?" Carlie said. She looked again at the rounded form

of the smoking mountain. "Because it's shaped like a giant breast?"

"Yep. And because it's covered in white glaciers that look like milk running down. And if you go up there, you can see the ends of the glaciers pouring down milky white water."

"I've seen that. The water is white because it's full of rock powder."

He shrugged. "So that's how she got her name. Her waters come down the Nisqually River and nourish this land. We knew that from a long time ago. Her waters are pure and fresh, where they start up there. It's not till they flow past the DuPont dump that they get dirty."

He cranked the tiller handle. The engine raced and the bow came up. The old, underpowered dinghy began moving as swiftly as she could go, heading back to their point of departure a mile upstream at Frank's Landing.

***

The Johnson family of four humans and three pets was in the grip of the midsummer doldrums. Idling at home in suburban Alderton, Washington, most family members were scattered around the back yard. The father, Seth Johnson was stretched out on a chaise lounge on the deck, with a coffee cup beside him on a small table. A laptop computer was in its normal place in his lap. Shorts and a white T-shirt almost seemed too much clothing to wear on a scorching day, and the dark bronze skin on his temples was becoming sweaty.

Working on an important manuscript draft, he had pulled his chaise to a part of the deck that was shaded by the eaves of the house to avoid the direct sun. Though it was still early afternoon, the sun was already radiating like a hot coal on what was developing into a blazing day in the suburbs. Baking summer heat was especially common in new developments like this one, constructed on flat valley bottomland that had been cornfields until the developers' heavy machinery had arrived.

The Johnson home was one of the largest in the new development, and had been particularly appealing when the

Johnsons were house hunting, thanks to its capacity for people and pets, and the grand view of Mount Rainier from the back of the house and from a six-windowed octagonal study perched high up in its multi-roofed, three story structure. One appealing aspect had been the way the house mimicked the tall rounded form of the mountain, which loomed impressively in the near distance. Another appeal had been the relatively low price tag compared to houses just a few miles away on the bluffs above the Puyallup River Valley.

"Come on, Bella, fetch!" called Noah, Johnson's ten-year-old son, who knelt in the middle of the dark green, recently rolled out lawn. The boy, wearing bathing trunks and a blue-and-green Mariners baseball jersey, tossed an orange tennis ball from hand to hand, trying to engage the interest of the dog, a medium sized brown-and-tan female with markings of several breeds and a touch of gray on her muzzle. Bella lay flat on her side on the grass, partially shaded by the thin foliage of a recently planted cherry tree that would take years to grow big enough to offer any real shelter from the noonday sun. With one eye, Bella watched the ball's movement as Noah tossed it up and caught it, but she showed no sign of wanting to catch it herself.

"It's too hot to play fetch," remarked Amelia, Noah's thirteen-year-old sister. She sat on the steps that led from the deck to the lawn. Her blonded, tightly curled hair was tied back in a thick mass of long locks to keep it off her shoulders. Dressed lightly in a powder blue tank top and yellow shorts, she was petting a lazy, purring, tuxedo-marked black-and-white cat who was stretched out on his side on a step. "Isn't that right, Darwin?" she asked the cat, who responded with a big, tongue-curling yawn and a single peevish twitch of his white-tipped tail.

"Darn global warming," remarked Katy Johnson, the lady of the household, as she came out the open sliding-glass doorway from the kitchen with a glass of iced tea in her hand. Despite the cool drink, she had a light sweat on her brow and a pink flush across the freckled bridge of her nose and on her cheeks. Her straight, medium-length hair was pulled back in a tight ponytail for cooling purposes. "You could start up the sprinkler," she suggested. "That would make for some excitement."

"Naw," Amelia complained. "We did that yesterday. Can't we go somewhere fun today? How about Wild Waves? I want to ride the water slides."

"No-o!" Noah shrilled. "I'm scared of those things."

"You can ride the bay-bee slide," Amelia teased. "With all the other bay-bees!"

"Mom," Noah protested. "She's teasing me again."

"All right you two, don't start in. Don't you have friends you can play with?"

"Alex's dad took their family to Ocean Shores," Noah complained. "They won't be back till next week."

"Mia's at her grandmother's house," Amelia sulked. "I'm so bored."

"Sorry, kids. But you know your father is under a deadline. His article has to be emailed to the magazine by tomorrow. And I've got summer school students to teach Mondays, Wednesdays, and Fridays for three more weeks. Maybe after that."

"Aw," both children moaned in a harmonic song of distress that had started coming naturally to them.

"Give me a couple more hours working on this manuscript," Seth murmured, typing a few words into a document entitled A BRIEF HISTORY OF THE NORTHWEST WINE INDUSTRY. "Then maybe—"

"Boring!" Noah interrupted.

"Then maybe," Seth resumed forbearingly, "we'll go and see a movie."

"Cool!" Noah cheered. "Return of the Fantastic Galaxy Guardians!"

"No!" Amelia retorted. "I wanna see The Unicorn Girls!"

"Oh my gosh!" Katy cried in a sudden outburst that silenced their squabbling. "Look at *that!*"

She pointed up and over the neighbors' roof using the

index finger of the hand that held her iced tea. The familiar domed shape of Mount Rainier rose in majestic glory against a clear blue sky, a dominating presence when viewed at the close range of 25 miles as-the-crow-flies from Alderton. Usually a source of satisfaction and pride in their ownership of their home, the normally beautiful mountain had taken on a new foreboding look. A long gray cloud drifted east from its summit, raining down gray streaks of dust beneath it.

"Is that what I think it is?" she asked, trying unsuccessfully to disguise a note of fear in her voice. She flushed a deeper pink. Veins stood out on her neck.

Seth set aside his computer. "It—" he stammered in disbelief as he rose and took a good look at the mountain. "It sure does look like—"

"An eruption!" Noah exclaimed, his voice harboring none of the foreboding his parents' voices expressed.

All four Johnsons stared at the mountain for some time, wide-eyed and open-mouthed. A train-like puff of gray-and-white vapor joined the streamer of ash and steam moving eastward.

"Should we—?" Katy began but stopped as if her thought was too momentous to contemplate.

"Evacuate?" Seth concluded for her. He looked at her shocked face momentarily, with his own creased brow registering thinly veiled anxiety. "I— I don't know. The sirens aren't going off."

After more moments anxiously observing the mountain in silence, Seth murmured, "It looks like things have settled down—a little anyway."

"I'm going to turn on the TV." Katy said, hurrying inside. "Maybe the news can tell us something."

Amelia jumped up and followed her in.

Noah left the dog lying on the lawn oblivious to human concerns. He came to his father's side, took his hand, and turned to watch the mountain. By now, the eruption seemed to have abated. The dust and steam cloud was thinning as it drifted away to the east.

"How dangerous is it, Dad?"

"I'm not sure." Seth stared hard at the mountain.

"Could we get killed?"

He squeezed Noah's hand reassuringly. "No, son. If the mountain really erupts, we'll hear the sirens and get out of here in plenty of time."

"Where will we go?"

"Out of town on the evacuation route."

"And where after that?"

"I never gave it much thought."

"How about Yellowstone Park?"

Seth chuckled. "I think a vacation like that takes a little more planning—and packing—than we'll have time to do if the sirens go off."

"Aw, shucks."

***

"A barbeque it will be, then, Honey," Bram Boswell said to his wife. "A real Texas style affair like we used to have back in Dallas. And I want to invite the neighbors—all the neighbors, this time."

"Bill and Melinda? They won't come!"

"They will this time, when they get a whiff of that luscious barbecue smoke."

She smiled. "If you say so, Dear."

"Now, where's that waiter? My wine glass has been empty for ten minutes."

Bram and Honey Boswell were seated at a window table in the Tower Club Restaurant on the 76th floor of the Columbia Tower building in downtown Seattle. The real estate mogul, a balding man who wore the hair of his left temple combed sideways over the top of his head to cover its bare dome, was dressed in a black pinstriped suit that hung unevenly on his expanded frame. Boswell often shared luncheon with his debonair blonde wife at the Club, when her shopping trips brought her downtown and he could disengage from his world of meetings, conference calls, and aggressive, bombastic deal-making sessions, to share a few quiet minutes with her.

"Why don't you just pour a glass for yourself?" she suggested.

"It's the principle, Honey. For the prices I'm paying, the service ought to be perfect." When he was upset, his small mouth pinched up like a guppy out of water as he spoke.

"Oh heavens!" Honey scoffed, reaching for the bottle. "I'll pour it for you."

He moved as if to grab her wrist, and she desisted. "No, you won't," he said firmly. "Don't you touch that bottle!"

Boswell got up and went to where the waiter stood staring out the window. He tapped a thick finger on the man's shoulder. The waiter, a young, tall, refined-looking Creole who might have had family origins in Jamaica or New Orleans, wore a nametag that read DEWAYNE. He glanced at Boswell blankly, as if returning from distant thoughts. And then, surprisingly, he turned and looked out the window again, responding to Boswell's irritated expression with a question he voiced in a precise, almost Britannic lisp that gave the impression he may have studied acting. "Sorry, sir. But… did you see that?" He pointed out the window. Boswell followed the gesture and noticed that Mount Rainier had an odd-looking cloud over its summit.

"Is that smoke?" DeWayne wondered.

Boswell snorted dismissively. "Looks to me like we're gonna have some rain pretty soon. Now bring me my check. Considering what I'm paying for lunch, the service ought to be snappier."

DeWayne startled noticeably, realizing he had neglected his duties. "Sorry sir," he said. "The mountain, sir— Right away, sir." He turned and hurried off, his thin frame moving with poise and elegance that could have only looked more refined if he had carried a swagger stick.

Boswell returned to the table. "That idiot!" he muttered to Honey as he sat down. "He was staring at that mountain like he expects it to blow up or something."

"It looks beautiful from up here," Honey cooed. "Cloud or

no cloud."

Boswell looked at her and smiled. "You know what else is beautiful, Honey?" He covered her delicate, pale white hand with one of his thick-fingered mitts.

She batted the lashes of her big, model-perfect eyes and waited to be flattered.

"My money. That's what. And I think that boy ought to try a little harder if he wants a tip."

She had a way of glaring at him without appearing to actually glare. She pulled her hand from under his and took up her white napkin. She daubed daintily at the corners of her puckered mouth without mussing her perfect makeup and then tossed the napkin down dismissively, expressing the disdain for him that she kept bottled up inside. One day, she knew, it would burst out like a volcanic eruption.

***

In the spacious commons room on the fourth floor of the Earth and Space Science Building on the University of Washington campus, a series of vaulted, multi-paned windows looked out over carved stone sills to take in sweeping views of the south campus and beyond. The lower quadrangle buildings, built of red brick with ornate College Gothic style sandstone facades, lined a long gentle slope crisscrossed with lawns, formal garden spaces, and paved walkways, which swept down past the impressively tall spouts of Drumheller Fountain on southeast-trending Rainier Vista, laid out to give grand views of the shimmering waters of Lake Washington and Mount Rainier beyond. The volcano stood impressively tall on the cloudless horizon, its white glaciers and slopes dramatically lit gold or shadowed purple in the afternoon sun.

Donald Rutledge, PhD, professor and senior scientist with the Pacific Northwest Seismic Network, stood staring out one window, studying the mountain with a worried crease on his high forehead. He had come up from the Siesmography Lab in the basement of the adjacent Atmospheric Sciences-Geophysics Building expressly to peer at the volcano. With him was his graduate student, Lori McMillan, a newly minted bachelor in Geological Sciences from Montana State University and a budding seismology expert under Rutledge's tutelage. "Looks like this event is over as fast as it started," she remarked.

Indeed, the cloud at the mountain's top, which had been so portentous of trouble an hour before, had thinned and dispersed on a slow-moving wind.

"I wish I had your confidence," he replied. "The seismographs settled down almost too quickly, after giving such strong signals earlier."

"But that's good news, isn't it?" Lori asked. "I mean, we're basically back to normal already."

"But that's not normal at all," Dr. Rutledge resisted. "Usually there's a period of tapering activity before things settle down. Those were some powerful shocks. And they were positioned deep in the core of the mountain. I would expect activity for days afterward."

"So, what's the explanation?" Lori asked.

Rutledge scratched a gray-bearded jaw and stared at the mountain in vexation.

"Just when I thought we were going to have some fun," piped up Kyle Stevens, a postdoctoral fellow in Rutledge's group, who sat at a table nearby. He presented a striking appearance, even on a campus where personal styles were often extreme. With shaved temples, black, shock-topped hair, pierced earlobes sporting large black hollow ear spools, a small two-pronged nose-piercing ornament and a multicolored tattoo showing just above the collar of his black shirt, he looked the part of a man whom a volcanic apocalypse might suit well. And he sounded a little disappointed one was not in the offing.

Rutledge glanced at him dubiously. "Fun? I wouldn't call it that. Especially because you're not the one who has to face the press every time one of our volcanoes gets the shakes. Personally, I'd rather not see any more action out of that one." He nodded at Rainier. "It's just a bit too close to home."

"Too bad though," Stevens persisted while using a plastic

spoon to finish scraping out a container of cherry yogurt. "We could watch the whole thing right here from the comfort of a break room. We'd have ringside seats complete with soda and munchy machines and an espresso maker. What a great location for field work!"

"Watch out what you wish for," Lori cautioned. "You might get more than you expect."

"Suits me fine," he said with a smart-aleck smirk.

Rutledge ignored the exchange. Still staring at the mountain and wearing his perplexed expression, he said, "I've had a call from the Governor. She's got her emergency preparedness team in motion and she's cueing up a press conference—with me as the star."

"Cool," Stevens said.

Rutledge shook his head. "More like hot," he muttered. "I'll be fielding a lot of questions I'm not prepared to answer."

"Such as?" Lori asked.

"Such as, how did we get such a big outburst from a mountain that was completely quiet yesterday? Any ideas?"

Kyle Stevens shrugged. "You're the expert."

Lori McMillan asked solicitously, "What are you going to say?"

"I'm still working on it," Rutledge replied. After a moment more staring at the mountain he said, "Let's go have another look at the seismographs."

***

When Bram Boswell had finished signing his luncheon bill, he stood and helped Honey put on her light sweater. As they walked off together, he cast a glance over his shoulder and spotted the waiter, DeWayne, clearing their table. "There's a tip on there," he called back acerbically, "for what your service was worth!"

"Thank you sir," DeWayne called after the departing tycoon. He wondered at the odd tone of the remark until he picked up and read the check. Then he understood that the tip was as derogatory as the remark. The gratuity line was filled out in large numerals reading $0.02.

"Aw." He cast a peevish glance at the couple leaving through the foyer. "Thanks for nothing—sir," he muttered under his breath.

Sighing, he turned and looked out the window. The cloud had moved away from Rainier to the east. The streamers of gray dust below it had thinned.

"I'm glad that's all over," he murmured.

CHAPTER 3

The next morning, a second U.S. Army Reserve Chinook helicopter, number 247, was dispatched out of Joint Base Lewis McChord carrying a crew of five. By 11 AM they were hovering over the wreck of the first Chinook. On the steep snow slope near the crashed aircraft were the six original rescue crewmembers, all apparently unhurt, having spent an uncomfortable and anxious night sheltering from sub-zero temperatures and strong winds inside the wreck, and the three ambulatory mountain climbers. The subject of the disastrous rescue attempt, Sophie Minto, was already strapped into the fallen helicopter's stretcher-shaped rescue litter, wrapped in blankets to keep her warm.

The pilot of Chinook 247, Hans Clearidge, a big, square-shouldered and square-jawed man whose muscular frame stretched his army-green flight suit at the biceps and shoulders, handled his flight control stick gingerly. "Pretty gusty up here," he murmured into the microphone of his flight helmet. "Feels like there's quite an updraft. I think that steam from the fissure is sucking air up the slope."

"Roger that," Ramon Diaz, his copilot, replied. Diaz was turned in his seat to monitor the work of flight engineer Jason Shen, the rescue lift operator, on the rear deck. "Just a little aft, Hans," he said to Clearidge through his helmet mic. "Just a little more. A little to the right. There! Hold steady!"

"All right," said Shen. "I'm lowering the cable down the rest of the way... Okay. They've got it."

Below them, Rainier National Park Climbing Ranger Garrett Kiesling, the mountain expert of the first crew, caught the end of the hoist cable and tugged it the few feet necessary to reach the litter.

Shen let out some slack on the line and Kiesling quickly attached the litter's four straps to the big metal hook at the end of the lifting cable. Then he stepped back and gave a signal, twirling the index finger of a gloved hand in the air to signify winding the cable to raise the litter. Shen did as bidden and soon the litter, and Sophie, were swinging under the belly of the helicopter, buffeted by wind gusts but otherwise stable.

Within seconds Shen brought the litter up beneath the hatch on the belly of the Chinook, and with the help of Crew Chief Arlen Duffy, wrestled it inside and set it down on the metal decking.

The Chinook's Emergency Medical Technician, Roberta Dane, was quickly at the head of the litter. "Hi!" she called cheerily to a distressed and pale looking Sophie Minto, who was belted in tightly with crisscrossing restraining straps and wrapped, mummy-like, in red blankets covering everything but her pink-helmeted head. "How are you doing?"

"Not so good," Sophie replied weakly.

"You definitely look a little worse for wear after what you've been through. But you're going to be fine now."

Shen leaned near and gave Sophie a heartening smile. "We'll have you safe in Madigan Hospital in less than an hour." He moved around her quickly, making the litter fast to the decking with heavy buckle straps.

"Okay," he called into his microphone when finished. "Patient is secure."

"Roger," Hans replied. "Hitch some rescue harnesses to the cable and let's get those other guys off the mountain quick. It's getting windier. We could run into some trouble if things don't happen fast."

"I'm on it," Shen said. Working quickly, he detached the cable hook from the litter and attached three straps with large metal rings to it. Then he went to his companionway control console and lowered the cable toward the rescuers, who were waiting to be rescued themselves.

Moments later, the three climbers came up belly-to-belly in the harnesses and were assisted one-by-one into the passenger compartment by Shen and Duffy. Once they were all aboard, the process was repeated for the rescue crewmen. Once the full count of passengers was aboard, there were shouted thanks and back slapping all around.

Hans watched from his pilot seat. "You boys and girls have a seat and get yourselves belted in," he called. "I don't want to hang around here any longer than I have to."

***

The lecture hall in the University of Washington's Atmospheric Sciences-Geophysics Building hosted a news briefing at noon. Donald Rutledge was the lead panelist, as was typical. The tiered seating of the classroom was about half-occupied with pressmen and women. Two news cameras were aimed at a podium with multiple microphones attached to it, and a long table with another microphone on it. Rutledge stepped to the podium at the appointed moment and began the introductions. After introducing himself, he gestured with an outstretched hand. "My colleagues seated at the table to the left of me are from the Cascade Volcano Observatory in Vancouver, Washington. It so happens they were at Mount Saint Helens when the Rainier event occurred. Being near Seattle, Andrew Hutchins, and Lexi Cohan," he gestured at each in turn, "have been assigned by the Observatory to join us for this presentation. But first, I'll kick things off by giving you all some really good news. The Pacific Northwest Seismic Network can confidently state that there have been no new rumblings from Mount Rainier since the initial event subsided to background levels during the night. There is a good chance this one is over. But let's get some detail from the real experts here, the volcanologists. Who wants to go first?"

Andy and Lexi looked at each other and both shrugged. And then both began to speak. After a pause and some em-

40

barrassed chuckling, Andy said, "I'll start."

"No, let me," Lexi countered, twisting the tabletop microphone in her direction.

"Ladies first," Andy acquiesced.

"As Dr. Rutledge said," she began, "Andy and I were actually inside the caldera of Saint Helens when the event on Rainier occurred. And we can therefor confidently state that at least Saint Helens is quiet, or we wouldn't be here."

That brought chuckles from the crowd.

"And," she went on, "as Dr. Rutledge said, Rainier seems to have settled down quickly. In fact, we are both surprised by just how quickly things have returned to baseline."

"These things do happen," Andy said, turning the microphone in his direction. "Especially when a mountain is not really on the verge of coming alive again." He smiled at the press people, who sat in rapt attention or in a few cases snapped photos of him.

Lexi wore a less-than-complacent look. She reached for the mic to turn it her way, but Andy held it firmly. "We see none of the classic warning signs that we learned from Mount Saint Helens—no harmonic tremors, no pattern of repeated quakes deep inside the mountain, and nothing like the bulge that occurred on Saint Helens' side just before she blew."

Lexi tugged at the microphone stand, but Andy continued to hold it when a male news reporter called from the crowd, "So are you sounding the all-clear on this one?"

Andy leaned forward to speak, but Lexi pulled the mic from its holder and put it to her mouth.

"I wouldn't be too quick to say this one's all over. Not just yet."

"Why not?" asked the newsman.

"There is one odd thing we have been monitoring for some time."

"Odd?"

"It's called aseismic inflation," Lexi replied. Pens scribbled on note pads and the TV cameramen zoomed in on her face. Andy sat back, rolling his eyes as if he thought this cat should not be let out of its bag.

After a moment in which the audience sat in expectant silence, Lexi went on. "Aseismic inflation is when an area of land rises slowly in the absence of earthquakes. We have been monitoring just this sort of thing at Rainier for a period of what—?" she looked at Andy for confirmation, "—six months?"

"About that long," he affirmed reluctantly.

"So let me get this straight," the newsman said. "Mount Rainier has been inflating like a balloon?"

"Yes," Lexi replied. "Kind of like a balloon.

"And filling with what? Lava?"

"Magma," Lexi corrected. "It's only called lava when it comes out—"

"God forbid," Andy murmured.

Lexi paused as if realizing she had gotten herself into sensationalistic territory.

Andy held his hand out for the microphone and said softly, "Let me."

She handed him the mic.

"Realistically," he said, "aseismic inflation can happen without any significant eruption. We have seen it before at several volcanic sites that we monitor closely. As often as not, the aseismic inflation will just stop for no apparent reason, or even subside. So, in and of itself, the swelling isn't a clear sign of trouble. I wasn't even going to mention it." He looked at Lexi meaningfully.

"So," the newsman persisted, "is Rainier still inflated, at this point? Or has it—er—deflated again?"

Andy and Lexi exchanged cautious glances.

"We'll have to get back to you on that," Andy said. "It takes detailed analysis and we haven't had the time—"

"And these things don't usually happen fast," Lexi said. "So the mountain is probably still inflated."

"Just how much inflation are we talking?" asked the newsman.

"Oh, just a few inches," Andy said. "Maybe a foot. Not all

that much."

"But with a whole mountain going up a foot," the newsman said, "that means there's actually quite a volume of lava—er, magma—underneath it, right?"

"True," Andy admitted reluctantly. "But in most similar cases we have seen, it just stays there until it cools."

There was another moment of silence, and then a female voice piped up. "Can either of you explain why there were no evacuation sirens going off in the communities surrounding the mountain yesterday? There was an eruption, after all."

"Let me handle this one," Andy said to Lexi without getting an argument. "Volcano evacuation alerts are a very serious matter. They aren't issued for just any event. They require a series of steps before an actual alert or full evacuation order will be given. First of all, there are automatic mudflow sensors on the mountain and in the valleys leading from it. The simple fact of yesterday's event was that there was no mudflow from it. So no sensors were triggered. And no alarm was given. That's the way things are supposed to work. If the alarms had gone off prematurely, think what a mess it would have been to have tens of thousands of people fleeing their homes."

"But isn't it a question of 'better safe than sorry'?"

"Not in this case. Our system worked as planned. The sirens were ready and waiting for signs of a lahar. But none was detected and so they stayed silent. That's a good thing."

"Lahar?" the reporter said. "Can you explain that term for us?"

Andy had replaced the microphone in its holder. Lexi turned the stand to face her. "I'll handle this one," she told Andy. "A lahar occurs when you get volcanic heat mixing with snow and ice on the mountain. This causes a massive runoff of melt water, which in turn picks up soil and rocks to make a mudflow. If the flow is large enough, it can carry off large boulders and even trees. So, lahars can be quite dangerous if they get big enough. But again, there is no need to worry. We saw no sign whatsoever of a lahar—large or small—yesterday."

"And the mountain's insides have calmed down pretty well

today?"

"I'll answer that," Rutledge spoke up from the podium. "The mountain's activity has abated surprisingly fast. In fact, much quicker than expected."

"So, all's well that ends well?" the reported prompted.

"Exactly," Rutledge replied. And then he looked at his wristwatch. "And on that positive note, I think it's time we called this meeting to a close. We've only been given a brief time for TV coverage. So thank you, ladies and gentlemen of the press, for coming. We'll have updates for you in coming days. As of right now, the watchword is 'all-clear'."

As the crowd filed out and the press crews began breaking down camera equipment, Rutledge turned to Andy and Lexi. "You guys did a great job. And you seem to get along pretty well."

"Sure we do," Lexi agreed. "When he lets me have the microphone for a while."

"And when you don't go shooting your mouth off," Andy countered. "Boy. I thought you were going to set off a firestorm of questions. Aseismic inflation! Jeez."

"Well, it's a real phenomenon."

"Yeah. Real scary, to the public. I thought that reporter was going to turn purple."

"Anyway," Andy said to Rutledge. "We've worked pretty closely since Lexi joined the group six months ago."

Rutledge took on a humorous expression. "So are you guys comfortable with sleeping together?"

Lexi's jaw dropped. "What?"

"In a tent," Rutledge went on.

"What?" she asked again, more critically.

"I spoke with your bosses in Vancouver just before the conference. We agreed that we need a new seismic station near the base of Rainier. But someone has got to go up there and spend a couple of days installing it. They suggested you two could do the job. Are you up for the challenge?"

"It's exactly the kind of thing I usually do," Andy said.

"And I'm not opposed," said Lexi. "I want to get some more on-the-mountain time. I've had way too much deskwork lately."

"Good," said Rutledge. "We'd like to get a seismometer right over the area where that aseismic inflation is greatest. Sorry if I said anything embarrassing. You know, about sleeping together."

Andy smiled. "We know what you meant."

"Oh, I don't know," Lexi said rather coquettishly, pointing a thumb at Andy. "I've been thinking about getting him in the sack for quite a while now."

There were laughs all around. And when Andy glanced carefully at Lexi, she gave him a smug smile and raised an eyebrow. "Nights get awfully cold up on the mountain," she chirped.

Rutledge watched the exchange with an amused expression. "Well, then," he said. "I guess that's all settled."

CHAPTER 4

Katy Johnson had been watching a news report on the kitchen TV while she prepared a lunch of ham-and-Swiss sandwiches at the island counter. As the segment ended, Noah, who had been helping her spread mayonnaise and mustard, wiped his condiment splotched fingers on a paper towel. "Are we going to have to evacuate, Mom?"

"No, Dear. They said the mountain settled down last night."

"Shucks. What was all that other stuff they said?"

"Oh, just some scientific talk about—whatever. And, what do you mean, shucks?"

"I'm bored. Maybe if the mountain blew up, at least we'd have something interesting to do."

Amelia was seated in a chair on one side of the island. She had been listening with a disdainful expression on her face. "You call running for your life interesting?"

"Anything is better than sitting around here all day staring at your ugly face," Noah jibed.

"You take that back!" She took a slapping swing at his arm and missed. He dodged behind his mother, squealing.

"Noah," Katy said sternly, "you take that back. Your sister has a pretty face. Don't tease her."

"Ugly face! Ugly face!" Noah shouted, maneuvering to the opposite side of the island for safety. "Ugly, ugly, ugly face!"

Amelia rose and went for him. He screeched and circled the island at a run. Amelia began to pursue him, but Katy caught her by an arm.

"Ow! Mom!" she cried. *"He* started it!"

Noah had turned like an animal at bay. "I hope the mountain *does* erupt," he hissed at her. "All over you!"

"That's enough!" Katy shouted loudly enough that dishes in the cupboard rattled. She closed her eyes momentarily to sooth what was developing into a brutal headache. "Now, you kids cut it out or I'm gonna suspend cell phone privileges for both of you for a week!"

"Aw!" Amelia moaned, suddenly contrite.

"Texting too?" Noah asked. "Or just voice?"

"Don't get smart with me, or I'll suspend gaming privileges too." Katy walked into the living room and called up the stairs with an edge on her voice, "Seth! Lunch is ready! I need you to set the table."

"Coming!" he called.

She shook her head slowly as she went back into the kitchen. "Sometimes I think it would be better for all of us if the mountain *did* blow up."

***

Far above the suburban melodrama—in fact, fourteen thousand feet above it—there was motion inside the huge crevasse. Steam, which had never fully ceased, continued to puff up from the depths in rhythmic pulses. A hissing roar accompanied each billow as it was released, although no living human ear was present to hear. All climbing permits had been revoked and would remain revoked for the foreseeable future. Mount Rainier National Park's Paradise Visitor Center had been evacuated, and frustrated tourists and would-be climbing parties were turned back at the entry portal at Longmire.

Although the geologic forces within the volcano were relatively quiescent, the summit was adjusting to the effects of a new, superheated crack and the wide crevasse it had created. Steam-softened ice frequently split from the walls of the crevasse, enlarging it and tumbling onto hot rocks below to generate even more steam. On either side of the crevasse, once-pristine snowfields were cloaked in black blankets of ash that draped over one shoulder of the mountain and formed a broad streak down the northeast flank. There was no ash in the air. It had long since fallen or moved on with the high-altitude winds.

The sky above the mountain was clear and the summer sun illuminated the crevasse starkly, shining deep into its interior. There, four roped-together bodies lay strewn across jagged, massive gray boulders of andesite stone. The bodies were soaking wet, showered by melt water cascading down the sides of the crevasse.

Suddenly, a sharp jolt shook the boulders, the bodies, and the ice walls of the crevasse. A sizeable earthquake, this new temblor sheared off a huge wall of ice from one side, which collapsed onto the bodies and the steaming boulders and covered the crevasse's floor. There was a tremendous rumble and roar as thousands of tons of ice cascaded onto what had been a widening gap in the mountain's snow cover.

For a while, the boulders and the steam disappeared completely, quenched and buried under great masses of snow and ice. But soon the heat from below burst out, first in one place, then in several. And each new opening in the white cover belched steam with a dragon-like, hissing roar.

CHAPTER 5

Another press conference was scheduled for 4 PM the next afternoon. Hastily called and convened with equal haste, it hosted a larger contingent of press people than the previous one, although only one of the previous day's three experts was involved. Because Andy Hutchins and Lexi Cohan were preparing for their assignment on the mountain, Donald Rutledge was on the spot for a solo performance. At the appointed time, he took the podium and explained that a new quake storm had begun the previous evening, and new steam and ash eruptions had broken out at the top of the mountain—although these, too, had now subsided.

"We are watching these new developments very carefully," he continued. "We have been in frequent contact with the Governor and we agree with her that limited evacuations near the mountain are in order. But we still continue to hope that no greater threat will arise. Let me give you some details regarding what we know so far."

Behind him, a large drop-down screen showed a cross section of the tall, rounded form of Mount Rainier. He aimed the red dot of a laser pointer at the center of the image.

"Most of you are familiar with the internal structure of a volcano like Mount Rainier," he said. "But I would like to make some specific points, so let's review. The entire mass of Mount Rainier is built up of layer upon layer of lava and volcanic ash from many eruptions over a long period of time—half a million years or so. Overall, the mountain has the shape of a scoop of ice cream that has partially melted and spread across the land around it. That isn't a very apt description in the sense that nothing has melted at present, but nevertheless it gives one a sense that this volcano is less pointed at the top than many, and also a sense of how it has spread out, in some places covering entire mountains around it with lava flows, ash-falls, and lahar mudflows. As with most other volcanoes, new lava rises up a central throat within the mountain, originating from a huge, deep chamber of red-hot magma, which appears in this cutaway view as a large swelling beneath the base of the mountain. The magma chamber is miles wide, and is under great pressure from the weight of the mountain and the Cascade Range surrounding it. This pressure forces liquid lava to come up the central conduit until it either reaches the top or breaks out on one of the mountain's sides. Regardless of where it comes out, it may either blast out as ash, as we have recently seen, or pour out as non-explosive lava flows—or both. The explosiveness of any given eruption relates to the amount of water contained within the magma that gave rise to it. And it is our particular misfortune here in the Pacific Northwest that our mountains, including Rainier, receive copious moisture in their magmas from subducted ocean floor that is pulled under the root of the Cascade Range and melted. So the lava is apt to be quite saturated with water, and because it is red hot, quite explosive with superheated steam. This makes us extremely wary of any rumblings. The other unknowns at present are, how much lava is moving up into the throat of the volcano, and how high has it already risen?"

A hand went up from an eager young newsman down front. "Can't you tell that from your seismographs?" he asked.

"Normally, yes. But this activity started just three days ago, so in this case we have precious little seismic data to work with. And so far, this is not a very typical event. If it were, there would be more frequent earthquakes, and possibly some stronger ones. That would help us better understand what is going on deep inside the mountain—sort of like reading an ultrasonic image of a pregnant woman's belly."

"So when will we know if it's a boy or a girl?" another newsman called from the back of the crowd, getting chuckles from the crowd.

Rutledge went on good humoredly. "What I'd like to know is how well-behaved this baby's going to be. Right now, all I can say for certain is that the new flurry of quakes yesterday evening was a small and short-lived event. There was more steam vented, and a small amount of ash as well—but less than the first outburst. That's encouraging. Things may be settling down again. If so, we can hope the volcano will go back to a long quiescent phase like the centuries-long lull before all this started."

"But that's what you said before," called the newsman in the back. "And now we've had more quakes."

This caused a buzz of conversation within the group, which in turn caused Rutledge to put up both hands in an appeal for quiet. The man down front raised a hand again and Rutledge acknowledged him.

"How much danger is there to Seattle and Tacoma if the mountain doesn't settle down? What if it erupts big-time?"

"I'm sorry," Rutledge said flatly, shaking his head. "I am not willing to speculate on that."

"I don't think it's speculation he's asking for," the reporter in the back resisted. "Citizens have a right to know if they are in danger."

There was silence in the room for a moment, except for a few whispered side conversations.

"Isn't it true," the man in the back pressed on, "that certain worst-case scenarios could threaten the population of Tacoma with large mudflows, and maybe Seattle too?"

"I am not prepared," Rutledge said with a scowl, "to discuss such extreme worst-case scenarios. Don't forget, there is a very extensive network of lahar-warning systems on and around the mountain. We have worked out evacuation plans that can take effect quickly if the need should arise."

"How quickly? Minutes? Hours?"

"Minutes," Rutledge stated confidently. But his eyes darted

around the room nervously, betraying that he might harbor at least a hint of doubt himself.

A cell phone beeped at his hip. He drew it out and looked at the caller number. "I'd better take this," he said, raising an index finger to beg the audience's forbearance while he stepped away from the podium and its microphones. He listened a moment, asked several terse questions, got answers, and then clicked the phone off and put it back on his hip.

"I apologize," he said into the microphones. "That was a call from the seismology lab in the basement. Apparently, the quakes have started again."

"Just earthquakes?" the young pressman asked. "Or is there ash too?"

Rutledge glanced down at the podium, and keyed something into the laptop computer there. A moment later, the screen image changed to a video camera view down Rainier Vista. The mountain looked placid and unchanged in the distance. "See for yourself. The answer is, neither steam nor ash."

"How can that be?"

"Apparently, these new quakes originated deeper within the mountain. Down here." He switched the screen image back and pointed his laser at the bulging magma chamber in the diagram.

"That sounds like a bad sign—isn't it?" asked the young reporter. "Is something new going on down there?"

Rutledge scratched his beard and pursed his lips nervously. "Well," he replied uncertainly, "it isn't good."

"How much concern is called for now?" the newsman in the back asked.

"I'm not sure."

"That's not very reassuring."

Rutledge tugged at the knot of his tie and loosened the collar of his white shirt. "This situation is all pretty new to us," he explained with a lame grin. "The mountain is acting erratically, to say the least. It's not following any pattern I am familiar with. We need more time to study it."

"But does the public have time to let you study it?" the man in the back crowed with an almost triumphal tone in his voice. "Wouldn't it be better to evacuate those at the greatest risk and be safe rather than sorry?"

Rutledge's brows knit. He stared hard at the reporter. "That's the Governor's call, not mine. Evacuation is a pretty drastic measure. It would disrupt many thousands of lives. Meanwhile, we are by no means certain anything big is on the way at all!"

"So, when will you be certain one way or the other?"

Rutledge gestured with both hands spread wide. "Unknown!" he said with an air of finality.

Half a dozen hands went up. It was clear the press corps was in no mood to let him call a halt to the proceedings.

In Olympia, Washington, Governor Sheila Long sat with members of her cabinet and other functionaries, around a large oval boardroom table in a situation room. They were watching the conference on a wall-mounted TV with expressions of deepening dismay.

"That didn't go too well," she murmured as Rutledge left the podium with a dozen questions from his audience still unanswered. The screen blanked.

"It's a tough balance between too much and too little caution," said her Secretary of State, seated across from her. The tall bald man's domed forehead had begun to perspire visibly despite the air conditioning. "Call for a general evacuation, and you'll immediately have the entire western half of the state in chaos—and a predictable hue and cry from your political opponents."

"The economy could suffer a melt-down," said the Director of the Department of Commerce, a short, heavy-set man seated on her right. "There would be an immediate economic crisis if everyone in the metropolitan areas stopped working and quit their daily routines. And then imagine what will be said if the mountain *doesn't* erupt! How long are people supposed to stay away from their homes and jobs? Those quakes and ash-falls could go on for months!"

"We've been over this a dozen times," the Governor said with a note of exasperation. "But if a big event happens, those same people you're talking about might be killed!"

"Public safety versus public interest," murmured her Chief of Emergency Services, a trim man in a black fireman's uniform, on her left. "This is where the two come into conflict."

The Governor's lips puckered. She looked down and fidgeted with a brass button on the sleeve of her dark blue suit. "Get me some more experts," she said assertively, looking at a different person with each statement as she went on, "You call the State National Guard and put them on full alert. And you call the Emergency Operations Center at Joint Base Lewis-McChord. Tell them to come up to full staffing, all leaves cancelled. And you get me FEMA on the phone. We've got to turn up the heat on this situation to match that mountain!"

***

"Mom! Dad! Come quick!" Noah rushed up the back steps and into the kitchen. "It's smoking again!"

Katy and Seth Johnson had just finished cleaning the counters and loading the dinner dishes into the washer. They followed Noah as he rushed back onto the deck where Amelia stood transfixed by the sight that confronted them. The mountain was lit by a beautiful sunset pink glow, but the usually entrancing sight had taken on a sinister caste. There was black-and-gray cloud drifting off to the east side. This one was twice the size of the one they had seen before.

"Still no sirens," Seth murmured. "That's a good thing."

"I guess it is," Katy replied.

Noah pointed at the mountain. "Look!" he cried. "There's something up there!"

A barely perceptible dark dot hovered near the top of the mountain, seeming dangerously near the cloud and its downward drifting ash curtain.

"A helicopter," Amelia murmured.

***

"I say we abort the mission!" exclaimed Ramon Diaz, who was sitting in the copilot seat of Chinook 247, his mouth agape in astonishment and real fear.

"Easy Ray," Hans said, grinning a tense but determined grin. "I'm not gonna hang around for long. But the mission plan says locate presumed dead climbers and at least get photo recon of their disposition."

"Mission plan didn't say nothing about the mountain blowing up when we got here. I say we abort!"

"Arlen," Hans called, ignoring Ramon for the moment. "You getting anything on the scope?"

"Plenty!" said Arlen, who was using the Chinook's belly-mounted telescopic video camera to search in and around the erupting fissure for signs of the missing climbers. His face was lit with astonishment and perhaps a little dread.

"Man! The ash is blasting out of there like thunder!"

"You see any... bodies?"

"Negative, sir. Not a trace. But holy cow, what a sight!"

***

The crevasse at the top of the mountain had grown dramatically. Further collapse of its ice walls had extended it wider than a football field and exposed jagged, blackened rocks and cliff faces within. The climbers' bodies had disappeared, swept away by melt water or fallen into one or another of the myriad cracks that had appeared among the boulders and rock walls. The largest of these cracks was the source of the current eruption. Fiercely hot, steam-driven surges of black ash thundered up from the fissure's depths, billowed above the retreating sides of the crevasse, and coated the adjacent snowfields with blankets of black dust before blowing away to the east.

Deeper in the vent, thousands of feet below and unseen by the helicopter crew and their camera, the source of the ash was a constricted volcanic throat where red lava spattered the fissure walls, propelled by intensely pressurized gasses that exploded out of the depths with such violence that globs of glowing, red, semi-liquidized rock detonated into pulverized dust particles that were carried upward on a sulfurous, poisonous, incendiary steam blast that seemed to have issued from the gates of hell.

PART TWO

PREPAREDNESS

CHAPTER 6

At 10:45 AM the next day, a trap of sorts had been set. As FEMA Region Ten Deputy Director Rudolph Jones, traveling with several adjutants, debarked an Alaska Airlines direct flight from Washington DC, a reporter from KIRO TV was waiting with microphone in hand and cameraman recording over her shoulder. As Jones emerged from the gangway drawing a rolling carry-on suitcase and shouldering a backpack that looked like it might hold a laptop computer, she stepped in front of him holding the microphone between them. Faced with the options of colliding or stopping, he stopped.

As subsequent passengers halted behind him, the reporter tipped the microphone toward herself and said, "Hi! I'm Adriane Sariwa, KIRO TV News. Is it true Mr. Jones, that you left a FEMA national disaster-planning session to rush home and deal with this crisis?" She tipped the microphone toward his mouth.

Jones hesitated a moment, as if he hadn't anticipated being put on the spot so soon after arrival. A nattily dressed man in a blue suit, white shirt, and red tie, with close-cropped white hair and a high, intelligent-looking forehead, he cleared his throat and cast an uneasy glance at the camera. "I don't think I would characterize this as a crisis," he said.

Sariwa briefly tipped the microphone back in her direction. "What would you call it then?"

"Er—a situation. And yes, I did leave a FEMA planning session to come home and deal with it. Ironically, we were working on a regional emergency response plan code-named

The Big One, which deals with a massive earthquake and tsunami. Now we've got a volcano instead."

"So the situation, as you call it, is serious enough to make you cancel your plans?"

The cameraman zeroed in more tightly on Jones.

"The situation," Jones said, "is uncertain. My coming home now in no way reflects any sense of an immediate emergency. My specialization is in geological events—earthquakes, landslides, and of course, volcanoes. So it shouldn't be a surprise that I would fly home for this, er, situation. Remember, much of my job these days is emergency preparedness. That's exactly what we were discussing in the meetings I left to come here."

"Are you considering declaring an emergency?"

"That call would normally be made by the Governor. I'll be meeting with her later today."

"Have you seen the mountain?"

"In fact we just flew over it. Impressive."

"Don't you mean frightening?"

"Let's stick with impressive for now."

"How soon will you determine if there is to be an evacuation?"

"We will start with that question as our first priority when we meet with the Governor."

"When will you do that?"

"As soon as you'll let me go." He grinned, but his eyes met hers sternly.

"Why not fly to Olympia then?"

"Because the Governor is already here in Seattle."

"Where?"

"Columbia Center Tower. Governor Long has been given access to an empty office space with a good view of the mountain. I'm going there now to make preparations for an all-day meeting tomorrow with a group of advisors and business leaders. We will be discussing our options for appropriate preparations and responses if anything serious happens. Now, if you'll excuse me, I'll be on my way." He edged past her.

As he walked away, Adriane faced the camera with microphone to mouth. "There you have it," she said. "The one man most in the know about the state's state of preparedness, and he's not saying much."

Outside, a limo was waiting. As Jones and his adjutants got in, his cell phone rang and he answered while the driver was putting their bags into the trunk. It was the US Secretary of Homeland Security.

"Yes," he said. "Tell the President I said hello too. I'll be meeting with the Governor here in Seattle very shortly. She's arranging a conference with local business muckamucks to try and assess their reactions to possibly closing some of their operational areas for public safety. What's that? Yes, Mister Secretary, I am sure we will get an earful from them. Especially from the logging companies, which have operations all over the foothills of Rainier. And probably from the businesses that are located within range of the worst-case floods."

He listened to the phone for a moment while the chauffeur got in and started the engine. As the limo pulled away from the curb, he said, "Yes, the Governor's people have found us some excellent conference space in sight of the mountain. There is an empty suite on the 72nd floor of the Columbia Center. Should be an interesting day. She will hold a press conference at the end of the day and, based on our consensus—if there is one—she will order any evacuations or other preparations we deem necessary."

As the limo hurried along the airport's oval drive, Jones asked, "What's that, Mister Secretary? Yes. Yes, I do think we have the situation covered. No. No, I don't think the National Guard is required. The Governor and local law enforcement, and the Department of Emergency Services are handling things well, as far as I know. And I'll know a lot more, later today. Yes sir, I'll get back to you with an update."

***

An abandoned logging camp sat high on a ridge at Burnt Mountain, a substantial Cascade peak just north of the Carbon

River, which flowed down from Carbon Glacier on the north-west flank of Mount Rainier. Like many other logging camps in the Cascade Mountain Range, it had some features that made it attractive for setting up a geological monitoring station. Most importantly in this case, the camp's flat logging yard was an excellent place to set down a helicopter. A decade or two previously, the yard had been an assembly point where hundreds of huge old-growth evergreen logs felled on the slopes around it had been tugged in by heavy winches and loaded aboard trucks. Not only was the wide clearing free of trees, but the entire top of the ridge had been leveled off by bulldozers. Gravel riprap had been spread to accommodate logging trucks and heavy loading equipment. The logs had been stacked aboard trucks for a long downhill run to mills in Tacoma. Some of the ancient logs had been so stupendous in girth that a single giant trunk would fill an entire truck. Eventually, when the surrounding slopes had been stripped of trees, the empty yard had served as a campground for crews of reforestation workers, who had ranged over the clear-cut mountainsides planting a fresh crop of Weyerhaeuser Douglas fir super-tree seedlings, a homogeneous breed known for rapid growth and high production of new timber. The tree farm had sprouted in the intervening years into a thick young forest of twenty-foot-tall trees that cloaked the ridges and slopes of a one-mile-square parcel of National Forest land. Every tree was about the same height and nearly every one had a pointy top reminiscent of an overgrown Christmas tree.

The logging yard, hard-surfaced and inhospitable, had sprouted nothing to match the burgeoning new forest around it. Only scrubby bushes and grass had found a foothold, and no doubt this barrenness was intentional on the part of the land managers. Within a few more decades, the loggers would be back to claim their cash crop and plant another in its place. The flat expanse of the logging yard would be required again, so it made sense not to foster its re-vegetation.

For now, that history was part of a fortuitous set of circumstances. Heavy rains in previous years had washed out the access road several miles below the ridge and left the yard isolated and free of visitors. This, in turn, necessitated a helicopter lift to reach the remote ridge. Despite the difficulty of accessing it, this place, located uncomfortably near the fuming massif of Rainier, had been a logical choice for the Cascade Volcano Observatory to emplace a new geological monitoring station.

The quiet of the cool mountain air was interrupted only occasionally by the calls of camp-robber jays squabbling in the treetops, until the powerful thumping sound of the rotors of a Chinook CH-47F helicopter arose and swelled as the aircraft approached from the west. After hovering briefly, the big helicopter set down in the center of the logging yard. As big as the flying machine was, it seemed insignificant compared to Rainier, a stupendously huge eminence looming across one last intervening valley to the southeast of Burnt Mountain.

Within a half hour of landing, Hans Clearidge and his crew had helped Andy and Lexi unload a small mountain of geological monitoring equipment, plus metal pipes, fittings, and bags of cement sufficient to build a new permanent tetrapod-shaped monitoring station. There was a tent, as well, and a portable folding camp table, a stove, and a variety of other camping gear. It would take several days' work for the pair to set up and test their monitoring station. Furthermore, if the location proved valuable for first-hand observations of the mountain's seismicity—and if the volcanic activity forecasts remained non-threatening—their stay might extend to weeks.

"Anything else we can help you with?" Hans asked. "Otherwise we should be going."

"Nope, nothing else," Andy replied. He was already down on one knee beside his most important piece of equipment, the seismometer, which was set below grade in a heavy steel all-weather case that the well-muscled pilot and his crew had helped to half-bury in the sand and gravel of the logging yard. "Lexi and I can handle things now."

Hans glanced up at the mountain, breathtakingly huge from

THOMAS P. HOPP

such close perspective. The ash eruptions of the last several days had left angry-looking black rivulets discoloring the white slopes at its top. "Are you guys sure you want to stay?" he asked.

"Yep," Andy said without looking up. "We've got a lot of work to do, and then I want to monitor this station for at least twenty-four hours and make sure the signal from each piece of equipment is stable."

"Understood," said Hans. "But, personally, I wouldn't hang around any longer than I had to. You're awfully close to a pretty nasty-looking mountain. I keep thinking of that guy at Mount Saint Helens."

"David Johnston," Andy replied. "He was a volcanologist just like us. This is the kind of thing we have to do some-times."

Hans turned to Lexi, who was assembling a two-person tent nearby. "You too?"

"It goes with the job," she said with determination. Then she smiled at Andy and patted the green nylon side of the tent she had just put up. "And I wouldn't want to leave our little love nest too soon."

Andy smiled, but made no reply.

"Okay then," Hans said, looking from one of them to the other. "Good luck to both of you. I'll see you when you re-quest an extraction."

"Roger that," Andy said, returning to tinkering with the seismometer.

Minutes later, the Chinook lifted off. It rose a hundred yards straight up and then swung around and headed west toward Joint Base Lewis McChord.

Lexi and Andy stood together watching it go. "I hope I don't regret this," he murmured.

She looked at him sidelong with a smug expression. "You won't."

***

Sophie Minto had spent two nights in Madigan Hospital. That was more than was usually warranted by a simple boot-top fracture of the two lower leg bones. But it was justified by her unusually long delay in getting to the hospital. Now that the doctors were comfortable with the condition of her leg and her vital signs—which had been less than stellar when she was brought to them nearly two full days after her fall—they had agreed she could be released to the care of family and friends.

One of her newer friends, Jake Swanson, had been her frequent companion in her hospital room, and he had gladly volunteered to get her home.

Now, Jake drove his large, brown, crew-cab pickup truck with Sophie ensconced in a corner of the back with her foot up on the wide bench seat. Her calf, ankle, and foot were covered in a pink fiberglass cast with her toes sticking out.

Jake was piloting them among the rectangular gridded streets of an older South Tacoma neighborhood. She pointed to one of the houses ahead on their left. "That one," she said. "The blue one-story with the chimney in the middle."

"Nice place," Jake said as he pulled up in front.

"It's just a tiny little box," she said. "But it's alright for one person." There was a new white Tesla parked in a driveway consisting of two parallel long slabs of concrete that went past the side of the house to reach a tiny separate garage that looked too small to house even that small car.

When Jake shut off the ignition, there was a moment of silence. As they had driven the last miles to her house, their conversation, animated most of the way, had slowed. Having covered their harrowing helicopter rescue, they had turned to the loss of Jake's fellow guide Hari and his rope team. Sophie had only met the others briefly before the start of what was to have been a three-day climbing excursion up the safest ascent route on the mountain. She knew them all by name, but not much more. Jake, on the other hand, had gotten to know his customers well enough that his grief for those lost was readily seen on his face and heard in his voice. Each time he mentioned Hari, the quaver in his tone was unmistakable.

After a moment sitting still, he shrugged off his morose-ness, opened his door, and got out. "Let's get you inside," he said in a chipper tone.

He opened her door and assisted her in getting down from the crew cab's tall running board. Then he followed her as she crutch-walked her way up the narrow sidewalk that led from the street to her front steps, passing a summer-dried lawn of straw-colored grass. Seeing him looking, she said, "If I don't water it, I don't have to mow it in the summer. It'll be green in the fall."

"Good plan." He glanced around the neighborhood of modest houses, many of which had similarly dry lawns. "Looks like you're not the only one conserving water."

He helped her up the two steps and inside the front door, and then helped her get settled into her cozy little living room. Acting on her instructions, he rearranged some furniture so that she could sit on the couch with her casted foot elevated on a hassock with a pillow.

With further direction, he went into the little kitchen and made a lunch of tuna fish sandwiches and tea. While they sat in the living room eating, he asked, "Have you got people who can take care of you? Neighbors?"

"I just moved in here when I got my job at REI. I don't know many of the neighbors all that well. There's one lady a few doors down, but she's not answering her phone. Maybe she's out of town or something. And my boyfriend—well, he's my ex boyfriend now. But my parents live in Sedro Wooly."

"That's pretty far away."

"They're going to come down here tomorrow and fetch me back up to their place. I'll be okay until then."

"Are you sure?"

"Yeah. I've got plenty of food and supplies. And I'm get-ting good on my crutches. I'll be all right."

He got up and took their plates to the kitchen counter, cleaned them in the sink and put them in the drying rack. Then he came back into the living room and stood for a moment.

After an awkward silence, he shrugged. "Well, I guess I'd better be going."

She beckoned him to her with a crooked finger. When he came near, she reached up a hand, pulled him to her by the neck, and gave him a small kiss on the lips. "Thanks for lunch," she whispered.

He turned and went to the door, blushing slightly. He paused before going out and turned to face her. "Now, you're sure you'll be okay tonight with nobody here?"

"I'll be fine."

"I could…"

"No. I'll be fine. Thanks."

"See ya," he said as he went out, closing the door after himself.

She sat thinking for some time, staring at the closed door with its rumpled curtain over the window. When she heard his engine fire up, she sighed, took up her channel changer, and turned on the TV set. As he drove off, she began searching for news reports about the mountain. It wasn't hard to find one.

**

Rudy Jones and Governor Long stood at the wide floor-to-ceiling windows of a conference suite in the Columbia Center Tower. They were near the top of the loftiest building in town, and the sense of extreme height was dizzying from 72 stories. The perspective made tall buildings around the tower seem small and lowly. Beyond the city proper, the neighborhoods and rolling hills of the suburbs seemed almost flat when viewed from such a high place. The elongated waterways of Puget Sound on the west side, and Lake Washington on the east side of Seattle stretched for miles within the panorama. The only challenger to the tower's perspective of superior height was Mount Rainier. Although it lay fifty miles to the southeast, it nevertheless required viewers to raise their eyes to take in its immensity.

The big mountain was quiet for the time being.

"What a great venue for a volcano meeting and press conference," Jones said.

The Governor nodded. "There's room here for sixty-four delegates plus my staff, some experts, and the television people. Drs. Rutledge and Gage are at the podium right now, preparing a presentation on the mountain and their current assessment of the risk. Do you know them?"

"Oh, yeah. Rutledge has been working with me on The Big One earthquake project. Top-flight seismo-man. World-class. And you can't beat Gage for volcanology."

Rutledge, his gray hair and beard newly trimmed and dark-blue suit neatly buttoned, was busy at a podium set up on one side of the room. On the wall behind him a large screen was lit solid blue with a computer graphic reading, "Please stand by." He was preoccupied with typing on a laptop computer he had placed on the podium. As he worked, he carried on a quiet conversation with a tall, handsome, thirtyish redheaded man dressed casually in a red-and-black buffalo plaid shirt and blue jeans.

"And that's Howard Gage, beside him," said the Governor. "He's Deputy Director of the Cascade Volcano Observatory in Vancouver Washington. Have you worked with him as well?"

"We've met," said Jones. "But I haven't worked with him before now. No one thought Rainier would act up before a major earthquake happened."

"Both men have already advised me," Long said, "that they haven't got much to go on. The situation is too new. So, right now, I haven't got the faintest idea whether we should evacuate a large area, a small one, or none at all. I hope we can figure that out as we go."

Jones smiled ironically. "I hope so too. At our meeting in DC somebody said hindsight is twenty-twenty, but foresight is pretty damn close to blind."

"Thanks for the kind thought," she said with her own ironic smile. "Meanwhile, we do what we can. The main purpose of tomorrow's meeting is to try and get a sense of how corporate powerbrokers are going to react if their businesses are ordered to be shut down in the danger zone. I have a hunch it won't be pretty."

"I'm sure you're right."

"That's the main reason we've located this meeting in Seattle. We're reaching out to all the major employers in the area. Several dozen companies are sending high-level people to participate. There are some very big players—Boeing, Microsoft, Amazon, Starbucks, Google, Weyerhaeuser, Costco, Port of Seattle, Port of Tacoma, and a bunch more. We're allowing two participants from each organization. Most are sending a corporate Vice President of marketing or finance, and a chief legal counsel. I'm not sure if having so many lawyers in attendance bodes well, or poorly. What are they going to do? Sue us if they don't like what we say?"

"I guess we'll see. At least you've gone out of your way to treat them well." Jones glanced around the spacious room. Beneath elegant chandeliers, wait staff in formal black-and-white uniforms were setting up large round banquet tables with fine china and glittering silverware, tented napkins, and massive floral centerpieces. "Hopefully, they'll agree with you on your menu choices, at least."

"I'm sure of that. Just four floors above us is one of the finest restaurants in the state. We couldn't have better caterers."

"All this is covered by state taxpayer money, right?" Jones said with a chuckle.

"Yes—unless you're volunteering a national subsidy."

"No." His smile vanished.

She sighed. "I'm sure one of my political opponents in Olympia will accuse me of junketing up here in Seattle—living high and dining well at taxpayer expense."

"But I *do* get your logic," Jones said. "You want businesspeople to join you, not fight you. And Columbia Center is the place to meet if you're a power player in Washington State."

"Exactly. I'm sure I wouldn't have attracted anywhere near as much top brass if I'd invited them to a Holiday Inn Express in South Tacoma."

"And you've got the best possible view of... the action."

They glanced out the window at the mountain. It was quiet. Only faint gray wisps of dust drifted eastward from the summit.

"I got quite a view of that from the jet as I came in," Rutledge said.

"Me too," she agreed. "I flew up from Olympia in the Governor's airplane. That's quite a hole on top of the mountain."

They stared at Rainier in silence for another moment.

"So," he said. "Are you going to declare a general emergency?"

"Now that I have seen what's on top of that mountain, you'd better believe I'll do *something*. But I've still got a couple of hours before I make a decision as to what. The first press briefing is scheduled for 4 PM today. Rutledge and Gage are preparing a background presentation."

"That's good. But evacuations—yes or no?"

She shook her head slowly. "The devil is always in the details on these things."

"It's ironic," he said. "I was just sitting in a meeting with all the FEMA brass from California to Alaska, discussing how we would react to The Big One, a nine-point-nine Richter scale earthquake and tsunami on the coast."

"Why is that ironic?"

"Because an earthquake happens without warning. For FEMA, it's almost all a post-event reaction. But a volcano gives a warning, so you can plan ahead. We were planning on how to *react* to a major event, but not how to *prepare* for one. Which is what you're faced with now."

"You're right. The volcano is warning us that something might be about to happen. But the big question is, how bad will it be? So far, nothing too destructive has occurred."

Jones nodded thoughtfully. "Governor Dixy Lee Ray faced the same question with the 1980 Mount Saint Helens eruption. She was accused of being caught unprepared. On my flight, I read as much as I could about her preparations—or lack of preparations."

"I've been reading those reports too. Believe me, the way

things turned out back then makes me very nervous now. Dixie was blamed for reacting too slowly. A citizen lawsuit was even filed after the eruption, alleging negligence against the state."

"But the swiftness of a reaction," Jones said, "or its thoroughness, is a very subjective thing. Too little, too late, and you take a lot of flack from those affected. Too much, too soon, and you get constant heat from evacuees whose lives you've turned upside down. It's the same with hurricanes."

"Hence the need for tomorrow's meeting. I want to take the temperature of the powers that be before I make any big decisions." She glanced again at the quiescent mountain. "I think we've got time."

"I hope so. At least Mount Saint Helens was remote from major population centers. Rainier is almost on top of Tacoma and not too far from Seattle. The magnitude of the problem is much bigger."

"And that's what's making my life hell right now. Back in 1980, Governor Ray had the option of declaring a local state of emergency without disrupting too many people's lives."

"That seems like a prudent move for you to make, now."

"I know it. But consider the scale of things, and the timing. Ray declared the local emergency on the third of April, more than a month before the event. And she declared a red zone around the mountain on April thirtieth. Public access was banned and the local population was relocated by state troops, where necessary. She mobilized the Washington National Guard and used the State Patrol to reinforce the two county sheriff's departments in carrying out the orders. And she made violation of the evacuation punishable by six months imprisonment. Am I going to do all that?"

"You may have to."

"Thousands of people were evicted from their homes. And citizens couldn't visit a National Landmark they wanted very much to see. The public outcry was deafening. And it went on for more than a month. I dread being in that situation, but it could happen to me. Volcanoes just as often settle down again after venting a little ash and steam. So, if I displace hundreds of thousands of people needlessly—what do you think my chances of re-election will be?"

"That's not really a consideration at this point, is it?"

"No. Of course not. But I'm going to be the focus of a lot of hard feelings. The question is, how many people *should* I displace?"

"On the East Coast and the Gulf Coast, hurricane evacuation orders affect hundreds of thousands. It can't be helped."

"That's entirely true. But is FEMA prepared to provide funding and materials to house tens of thousands of people without an actual eruption taking place?"

Jones thought a long minute, and then shrugged. "We haven't really faced such a situation before. I don't know—"

"That's not very comforting. And another thing. Hurricanes are over in just a few days, no matter what. Mount Saint Helens, on the contrary, rumbled for months before anything big happened. Could FEMA house and feed people indefinitely under the circumstances?"

"It's hard to believe I could get approval for that. It would cost millions of dollars per day, over an indefinite period. Congress might get involved if we tried it, and not in a good way."

"But just look what *did* happen with Saint Helens. It could be that bad again, or worse. I read where Governor Ray's red zone restrictions were the only thing that saved twenty- or thirty-thousand people from being killed."

"I understand your problem," Jones said apologetically, "but consider my limitations without an actual eruption in progress—"

Long shook her head. "It's a nightmarish balance I have to strike. I'm sure I want to put a red zone in place as soon as possible. But how can I take care of all the displaced people? And how big should the red zone be? Just the mountain? Or all the way to Tacoma?"

Jones pointed at Rutledge and Gage at the podium, who had paused their preparations to gaze out at the mountain. "You've got your experts right here. Why don't you ask *them?*"

Gage saw the gesture in his direction. He walked away from the podium and approached them. After greetings and handshakes, Jones asked, "We were just wondering how bad this eruption might be—if it happens?"

"That's a tough question."

"We know," the Governor said. "But have you got any inkling about the possible size of the event? Even a rough guestimate?"

"Not really. It's more a matter of best or worst cases—the best being that Rainier settles down like it seems to be doing now. Maybe there won't be any more trouble."

"And worst-case?" the Governor pressed.

"I'd hate to speculate."

"But please do."

"Worst case, you might have to multiply the Saint Helens eruption by a factor of ten or twenty. Maybe more."

"And Dr. Rutledge's seismic data aren't giving you a hint of which it's going to be?"

"I wish they would. But we don't have enough data. This event is too new. We've got people at the mountain right now taking some big risks to set up another seismic station."

"When that's in place, will you be able to tell us more?"

"I wish I knew the answer to that question, too, Governor."

She paused to look out at the mountain. "It really does look like it's calmed down since we got here, doesn't it?"

"Yes," Gage agreed without conviction.

"But looks can be deceiving," Jones added.

"True," Gage said, this time with conviction.

CHAPTER 7

"There!" Andy exclaimed. "That should do it." He and Lexi had assembled the metal-pipe tetrapod framework of the monitoring station, and then attached the video camera, radio transmitter, GPS monitor, and leads from the seismometer box. He had just finished the last of the wiring work and everything looked to be in good order. "Got a signal?" he called to Lexi, who sat nearby at the camp table, watching the screen of a laptop computer wired via USB to a small radio receiver box that was set to the station's outgoing broadcast frequency.

"I sure do," she replied. "The video feed of the mountain looks—spectacular!"

Andy walked the short distance from the station to the camp table, and glanced at the screen. "The mountain's beautiful, even if it's dusted in black. But I'm more interested in the seismometer feed. May I?"

She scooted over on the bench and he sat at the computer and began typing.

After a moment, he said with satisfaction, "Okay! We've got a seismo trace!"

The screen was now white, with the small black thread of a fresh seismographic data line moving very slowly across its top. It extended to the right as telemetry from the seismometer came in via the station's radio signal. The trace was smooth, with only very small wiggles, some of which had been produced by Andy's footsteps as he walked from the station to the table. He looked from the screen up to the mountain.

"Rainier's pretty quiet," he said.

"That's fine with me," Lexi murmured.

Suddenly, the seismic trace jiggled sharply and then settled down again. "Did somebody fart?" Andy asked.

Lexi clucked her tongue at the crudeness of his remark but made no reply.

And then the seismo line jiggled again.

Andy cocked his head and looked up at the mountain. "Nothing's changed visibly," he murmured.

"There goes another one!" Lexi pointed at the trace as it jiggled and then settled down once again. "If those are harmonic tremors—" she began with an edge to her voice. "But, no. They look random so far."

"You're right," Andy affirmed, lifting off his brown ball cap and scratching his head. "They're randomly spaced. But that's an odd signal. Each event is so brief. Not much of a shake at all, really."

Lexi got up from the table, moving carefully so as to not disturb the seismometer. "You know," she said, "I've been hearing some odd noises from over that way." She walked around the tent and continued to where the flat surface of the logging yard disappeared over the brink of a deep, evergreen-forested valley. As Andy joined her, she pointed to a place about a mile downriver and murmured, "There's our answer."

There, on a gentle slope above the Carbon River was a logging yard like the one they stood in. Its flat surface had been cut into the hillside recently and was freshly graveled. On and around the yard, an array of heavy logging equipment was in operation. In the center of the yard sat a logging truck in need of a load, with its diesel engine idling a trail of blue smoke. Nearby, a huge yellow log-lifting crane on metal treads used giant pincer claws to encircle and lift a stupendous tree trunk, which was more than eight feet wide at the butt end and at least forty feet long. Swiveling on its treads, the machine swung the behemoth log over the truck's trailer carriage. When the pincers opened and released the log onto the carriage, the entire rig compressed downward as if it were being crushed—

but it withstood the impact. The loader rolled back and idled as two men in ball caps and Pendleton shirts emerged from the truck's cab and began lashing the giant trunk to the trailer, tossing wide orange straps over it and cinching them down on each side. Meanwhile, another empty truck arrived at the yard and stood by for its turn with the loader.

Just downslope from the logging yard, not far from where the loader and truckers worked, two men wearing yellow helmets stood at the base of a two-hundred-foot-tall hemlock tree. One was using a smoking chain saw to cut into the trunk. As Lexi and Andy watched in amazement, the sawyer stepped back, glanced up at the tree, and then he and his partner bolted away like jackrabbits over the brushy hillside. The forest giant swayed momentarily and then began a long, slow, graceful arc to the ground, trailing small branches that snapped off in the breeze of its fall. The mighty tree's impact shook trees around it, and was followed a moment later by a muffled crash just audible at so great a distance. A few moments after that, Lexi and Andy could feel the hint of a tremor in the ground under their feet.

"That explains it," Andy remarked sourly. "We'll never get a good baseline calibration with all that going on."

"How did they even get a permit to cut so close to the park boundary?" Lexi wondered.

"Maybe they convinced some bureaucrat the timber was at risk if the mountain blew, so they let them take it now."

"I wonder if we could go up the chain of command and get their permit revoked, at least temporarily, so we can get some clean readings?"

"I doubt it. Their permit probably comes from the National Forest Service, which is part of the U.S. Department of Agriculture. We're U.S. Geological Survey, part of the Department of the Interior. That's a long way around the national bureaucracy."

"Maybe so. But those guys are nuts. They could be logging somewhere far from here."

"But they wouldn't be getting old growth, would they?"

"That's old growth?" she asked, and then she took another look. "Those *are* some pretty huge trees, aren't they?"

"Looks like old growth to me. That's got to be one of the last uncut stands in these parts." He glanced around the mountainous countryside. "Other than inside the park, of course."

"Old growth!" she murmured. "How dare they!"

"That's the best wood in the world. Most of it sprouted before Columbus sailed. No branches on the main trunks, so there are no knots in the wood. They can mill it into premium grade plywood and two-by-fours. Each tree like that is worth a mint, if you can get it."

"Well, I *don't* get it," Lexi said. "How did those people ever get a permit to log old growth? I thought that went out with the Stone Age."

"Apparently not," Andy replied.

"And now greed is motivating them to risk their necks beneath a smoldering volcano? I wouldn't do it."

"Neither would I. But right now I'm more upset that they're ruining our data. Those thousand-year-old trees make quite a thump when they go down. I wish they would stop and let me get a good flat baseline. They're working late. It's nearly 4 PM."

"Greed, again. They're trying to get every stick they can, before the mountain—"

"They'll stop in a while and go home for the night," Andy said. "I'll get a good baseline then. Meanwhile, we should start thinking about getting the stove set up to cook dinner."

***

Alder wood smoke drifted above the smoothly flowing Nisqually River, carrying with it the scent of salmon barbequing Indian style. The sounds of native drumming and singing came from inside an old cottage on the banks of the river. The home, which belonged to Jimmy Finch, had space inside for little more than a living room, kitchen, bathroom, and one bedroom, but the smell of fresh salmon baking in the back yard filled the house with a delightful aroma. Family members, a few neighbors, and a several friendly moochers had gotten together to sing and play tambourine-like painted animal-hide drums with beater sticks. One of the two salmon Jimmy had caught this day had been cleaned and cut into two filets, and then handed out to neighbors who lived in the adjacent small houses. But the other fish—a big Chinook—was the source of the heavenly smell pervading the house. Outside the open back door, the cleaned fish was cooking tail-up with its sides spread like a sail by cedar-wood skewers that held it to a pointed cedar roasting spit that had been thrust into sandy ground beside the coals of a well-rendered alder wood fire.

Carlie Hume was guest of honor, of sorts, at this feast. Jimmy had gotten to know her in the course of multiple fishing trips, and lost his natural reluctance to have a pahstud in his home. He had invited her to share a meal and now, prompted by her questions, had gotten into a philosophical mood. As with many Northwest Native people, this made him want to sing and make speeches. He said in a droning, oratorical voice, "The mountain, Tacobet, she nourishes our life here." He used a slow, repetitious style of speech common to native orators and especially tribal elders. "The river flows from Tacobet like nourishing milk. It waters the land and makes a home for the fish we eat. But Tacobet seems a little angry, right now. People should remember, she can give life, but she can take life away, too."

Carlie listened attentively, as did a group of children sitting on the floor in front of Jimmy, as well as five other adults in the small living room, while two women quietly worked in the small kitchen within earshot of the tale-telling.

"My grandfathers spoke of the Great Spirit," Jimmy went on. "Some called him Shuq Siab, The Honored Man Above, others called him Sahalie Tyee. He had a lodge on top of Tacobet mountain. The mountain was off limits to people, back then. You couldn't climb up there. If you did, you died. Or you brought big trouble back with you. But the spirit people, the Skelalaytut, they went to visit Shuq Siab whenever they wanted to. Wha-Quoddie, the thunderbird, often visited the lodge. The changer, Dokwebalth, was always welcome there too. Seatco, the evil forest demon who steals away little children, he was never welcome." For emphasis, Jimmy made sweeping claw gestures at the children with one hand, which made the smallest ones squirm and shriek.

"Most of the time," he went on, "everyone was happy up there. And when everyone was happy up there, then everything was all right down here among the Squallie-absh—the Nisqually people. And Dokwebalth, who was a pretty good singer, he played his drum and sang his tamanowas spirit song for Shuq Siab. He sang, Hey-ay-yay-o-ay yay oh!"

As Jimmy sang, he beat his drum slowly using a feathered beater stick with a leather-padded mallet head. The other drummers followed his meter and joined him in singing his verse several more times. "Hey-ay-yay-o-ay yay oh!" Then Jimmy rapped his drum three times sharply and the room fell silent.

"That there song, that Dokwebalth sang, always made Shuq Siab happy," Jimmy continued. "But sometimes the spirits had arguments. Or sometimes people down here did something to make them mad. And that's when the trouble would start. Thunderbird wasn't too bad. He brought storm clouds and he made thunder from his wing beats. And lightning flashed from his eyes. But most of the time that was just to scare the little children and remind people they was doing something wrong." He punctuated this statement with theatrical glaring looks at the smaller kids seated in front of him. When he leaned nearer, scowling and wrinkling up his nose, they shrieked again in mock—or perhaps real—fear.

Jimmy continued, chuckling. "But Dokwebalth was another story. He was a trickster, and a transformer. He was the one who changed the salmon people into fish for bears and humans to eat. And he could change the mountain if Shuq Siab asked him to. He could make Tacobet pure white with snow. Or sometimes, like right now, he could cover her with ashes from the great lodge's cooking fire and make her top black. And that was a bad sign. And as he made these changes, he always sang his transformer song. It went, Hey-ay-yay-o-ay yay oh!"

Again, he and the others beat their drums and sang the verse several times. And again he rapped his drum three times hard and the room fell silent.

"Sometimes, if the people was really bad, then Dokwebalth could make the mountain explode. And then the sky would go black, and we'd get floods, and people's houses and the forests would wash away. And the animals would run away, and the people who survived would starve. Everybody was miserable."

The small children squirmed.

Jimmy grinned at them. "But then Shuq Siab would say, 'Boy, I guess I really got upset. Look what a mess I made of the land. And look at the people suffering, without food or no place to stay. I better make things right again.'"

"So he asked Thunderbird to bring the rains and wash the land clean. And he asked Tacobet, Nourishing Breast Woman, to pour clean water into the muddy river. And he asked Dokwebalth to tell the salmon people to please come back upstream, and the animals to return to the meadows, and the trees to grow again. And as Dokwebalth did each of these things, he sang his transformer song. It went, Hey-ay-yay-o-ay yay oh!"

Once again the drummers joined in until Jimmy rapped his drum three times. After a momentary pause, Jimmy smiled and said, "And that is all."

The children clapped their hands and the smallest uttered shrieks of delight, having been transported to a place of fear and then back to joy by Jimmy's performance. Several of the adults offered the northwest-native equivalent of applause by raising their arms with the backs of their hands toward Jimmy and repetitively sweeping their hands upward and toward themselves in a gesture that meant, "Thanks for what you have given us."

***

But Jimmy had more to give. He went to the back yard and

fetched the salmon on a large plank of split cedar wood. Working on a small kitchen counter barely able to hold the plank and giant fish, he served up plate-filling portions to all present, to which the women added bread, buttered corn-on-the-cob, and potato salad until the plates were about to overflow.

While they ate, sitting around the room with plates on laps, there were murmurs of delight about the taste of the fresh salmon and much praise for the fisherman-turned-chef. Then, the sound of car tires on gravel turned everyone's attention to the open front door.

"Oh-oh," Jimmy said in mock alarm. "Here comes the heat!"

A white SUV bearing the markings of the Nisqually Tribal Sheriff's office pulled up to the house. An officer in a tan uniform, smoky bear hat, and long black Indian braids got out and came up the house's creaky wooden steps.

"Hello Thomas!" Jimmy called to the young man, who paused at the threshold. "Come to bust us for fishing?"

It was an old joke and Thomas let it pass without comment. He nodded politely at faces around the room, maintaining a businesslike expression. "You folks have got to move," he said firmly. "Orders from the Governor—and the Tribal Council."

"We ain't moving nowhere," said a raspy-voiced older woman who had come from the kitchen. "White folks told my grandparents they had to move once a long time ago. Didn't move then either."

"Tribal Council took a vote. All you folks who live down here in the old village have got to come on up to the new village by the casino. There's new housing under construction there. It isn't quite finished, but you can stay in it till the danger's past."

"Ain't no danger right now," the old woman said, projecting an obstinate glare.

The trooper shook his head just once. "My job's telling everyone down here to get up there and settle in until it's safe to come back. Now, I've got other doors to knock on around here. If you folks will just pack a few belongings, we can arrange transportation for anyone without a working automobile."

Jimmy glanced at the people in the living room and let out a husky laugh. "That'd be just about everybody."

***

As Officer Thomas went from house to house, the people inside Jimmy's cottage finished their meals and left to go to their own homes, or in the case of the old woman, Jimmy's sister-in-law, to grumble and rummage about, gathering clothes and cooking utensils for the move.

"I'll run you up there tonight in my pickup, Verna," Jimmy said to her. "Then I'm gonna come back down here. I got lines out. I'll take 'em in, in the morning as usual."

"That might be risky," said Carlie, who had helped clear the dishes and now stood by feeling useless.

"I can still move pretty fast for my age," Jimmy countered. "Out on the water, I've got a good view of the mountain. You better go, though."

"No," Carlie said. "Strangely enough, I trust your judgment. And I'm supposed to test at least one fish every day that you go out. I've got my little trailer parked by the riverbank at Frank's Landing. I'll stay at least through tomorrow, then I suppose we'll both have to go if the mountain doesn't settle down."

Jimmy laughed. "*You* have to go. Billy Frank Junior and my grandfather fished here whether the cops told them to go or not. I'll pack up when I'm good and ready."

"You old fool!" Verna scolded as she put a cook pot into a cardboard box. Her fond expression suggested she didn't strictly disapprove.

CHAPTER 8

Katy Johnson opened the front door of her house to see what all the commotion was about in their cul-de-sac. She had been grading summer-school papers when the *whoop-whoop* of a police siren and a voice on a loudspeaker making a blaring but hard-to-understand announcement had caused her to stop and come to see what was the matter.

The noise came from a Pierce County Sheriff's Department SUV. It was slowly circling the cul-de-sac, while a loudspeaker blared from under its hood more audibly now that Katy was on the porch. "All residents are hereby notified to evacuate as quickly as possible. There is no immediate threat, but your co-operation is required. This is a twenty-four hour notice. By 6 PM tomorrow all residents must have vacated their homes and found accommodations outside the hazard zone."

Katy went down the steps and hurried toward the police car, prompting the officer to stop and roll down his window.

"Are you serious?" she asked him, her voice trembling with scarcely suppressed anger and a note of terror. "Twenty-four hours? To go where?"

"Yeah!" cried Amelia, who had come out and tagged along with her mother, as had Noah. "Are you serious?"

The officer, his green smoky bear hat straight on his head, smiled forbearingly at the girl's audacity. "Yes, I am quite serious," he said to her, still smiling. And then he looked more sternly at Katy. "I can't tell you where you should go, Ma'am. But all residents are required—"

"I heard you the first time," Katy interrupted. "I just couldn't believe it."

"Believe it, Ma'am. The Governor just put out a full Volcanic Eruption Alert. This entire valley is in the red zone—no one's allowed here after tomorrow."

Katy was so thunderstruck that she could do little but gasp in horrified astonishment. "But we don't have anywhere to go!" she cried, her eyes suddenly welling with tears. "We just moved here two years ago when I got my job at the school. We don't know that many people—other than ones who live right here!"

"Sorry Ma'am." The trooper sounded sincerely sympathetic. "But the Governor's orders don't allow any exceptions."

"What if we don't want to go?" Katy said with a note of anger in her voice. She looked for support at Seth, who had just come down from his office and joined them.

The deputy pulled off his sunglasses and looked at them both sternly. "If you refuse to go, we will physically remove you."

Katy put a hand to her chest. "Well—!" she gasped.

"That could include being arrested," the deputy went on, "and up to six months in jail."

Katy's face went from red to purple. She backed into Seth for support, sputtering and unable to say anything more.

Neighbors from adjacent houses came out and began asking the officer questions. Seth put a hand on Katy's shoulder. "Come on in," he said softly. "We'd better eat dinner and then start making some arrangements."

"Who with?" Katy said, trembling and unnerved.

"I'll make some calls. I'll try some of my professional contacts. Somebody will take us in."

Katy wheeled and called after the officer, who had begun to slowly roll on, "For how long?"

He stopped, a wrist draped over his steering wheel. "Until you're advised by the state that it's safe to return."

"That's impossible for me. I've got summer school students. I can't leave for days or weeks."

He glanced at her forbearingly. "Ma'am, they'll all be evacuating too."

"Yes," she murmured. "I suppose they will."

Inside the house, a glass terrarium sat on a stand near a sunny window in Noah's room. Inside the terrarium, Iggy the iguana stretched his two-foot-long green body and tail along a thick branch that had been laid in his cage, on which he loved to bask in the sun. He tilted his head and looked out the window, his attention attracted by the movement of a fresh small puff of steam rising from the summit of Mount Rainier.

***

At 8 PM the crowd in the Tower Club restaurant was beginning to thin. At a table with a good south window view, Governor Long, Rudy Jones, Howard Gage, and Donald Rutledge chatted over the remains of dinner and dessert. In the distance, Mount Rainier had taken on the pastel pinks and purples of sundown. Those tones were painted over glaciers, ridges, and valleys that were for the most part white, but which were blackened at the summit with a layer of fallen ash that trailed off down the eastern slopes. As for the steam clouds that had deposited the ash, there was not the faintest trace of one against the clear, purplish-blue sky.

The Governor took a bite of chocolate pie and chased it down with a sip of decaf coffee. "How's that seismograph doing?" she asked Rutledge, who was staring at the screen of his cell phone, held sideways for a wide view. On it was the white background and black trace of a seismographic feed re-layed from the University of Washington.

He smiled. "I couldn't ask for better! The trace has stayed flat-lined since you made the news announcement this after-noon. It's still running straight and smooth."

"Couldn't ask for worse, in some ways," the Governor murmured.

Rudy Jones smiled and nodded, as if he took her meaning only too well. "Isn't that how it always goes?" he asked philosophically. "You announce an emergency—and nature immediately starts making a fool out of you."

The Governor set her coffee cup down, put her forearms on the white tablecloth, and sagged. "What a day," she murmured, shaking her head slowly. "We've just had a press conference in which I ordered the complete evacuation of a dozen small towns and suburbs. I've put two-dozen other communities on standby for evacuation. The phone lines to the Capitol are already jammed. My staff is overwhelmed with calls that range from desperation to outrage and everything in between. And we haven't even heard the responses of business leaders yet."

Jones nodded sympathetically. "If it's any comfort, this is just the sort of reaction we get in the Southern states whenever a hurricane evacuation is ordered."

"No," she murmured, staring at the serene mountain with a glint of hatred in her eyes, "it isn't any comfort. And at the same time, I can't help worrying that maybe I'll regret not calling for a much *wider* evacuation."

"The devil is in the details," Jones said.

Long turned to Rutledge, still watching his flat-lined display. "Let's hope you see at least a few bumps on your seismographs before morning," she said. "Otherwise we're going to have a hard time justifying this to a roomful of powerful—and angry—businesspeople."

CHAPTER 9

The next day dawned clear over Mount Rainier. Although the snowy top of the mountain and its eastern slopes were thoroughly blackened with a coating of ash, the fissure on the summit was quiet, as it had been all night. A faint trace of steam rolled out and drifted east, but the crevasse was not a source of volcanic dust this morning.

This serenity could not last long. Sheer walls of ice lined the crevasse with their blackened vertical faces rising hundreds of feet on both sides. One of these ice walls hung precariously over steaming rocks that radiated enough heat to raise the wall's temperature. The ice surface was melting and streams of water drizzled down its face.

And then the ice began to crack from the base to the top of the wall. Suddenly, the entire eastern face of the wall crumbled and cleaved free, dropping into the crevasse. Huge blocks of ice, blackened on one side but white on the others, fell onto the superheated rocks on the bottom of the fissure. Instantly, a thunderous explosion drove steam and ash upward and outward, carrying giant boulders on the billowing front of its detonation. The force of the steam explosion shook the mountain.

**

Far below, in their camp on Burnt Mountain, Andy and Lexi sat side-by-side at their camp table, finishing a breakfast of eggs, pancakes, and coffee while occasionally gazing at the mountain.

"About last night," he ventured hesitatingly.

"You were an animal!" she said with a broad smile.

He was about to say more when the rumble of the distant explosion caused him to stop.

Lexi looked up and her eyes widened. "Ooo!" she exhaled over the rim of her raised coffee cup. "Look at that!"

A large outburst of mixed steam and ash was jetting upward from the top of the mountain. Although not so huge as to seem an imminent threat, it nevertheless was a stupendous sight from such close proximity.

Andy watched with her, wordlessly, as massive boulders tossed out by the force of the blast tumbled and slid down the blackened snowfields, triggering accompanying avalanches of mixed black-and-white snow. "Now, that's scary," he finally murmured.

"Sure is," Lexi agreed, setting down her coffee cup, the better to stare at what was transpiring high above them.

"I'll check the seismo feed," Andy said, opening the computer.

"That one ought to register," she said.

"Uh huh," he agreed. "Maybe we should start thinking of leaving."

A moment later, as they stared at a very large, very sharp peak on the seismometer trace, he said, "Yep. I think we should get out of here."

***

At about 10 AM, Bram Boswell walked out on a wide deck on the second story of his palatial Lake Washington house, still dressed in pajamas, slippers, and a maroon silk robe. He surveyed the lower deck, which ran the width of the house's waterfront side, where the catering company was already busy setting up tables, chairs, and banquet equipment. At one end two cooks were tending to a whole pig that was turning on a rotisserie above an oversized, blazing, gas-fired grill. He nodded his approval.

A movement caught his eye, and he looked up to the north.

Through an opening in a screen of trees and greenery, he could see his neighbors. Bill and Melinda Gates were standing on their own second story deck outside what he guessed was their bedroom. They were looking down at the bustling epicurean scene on Boswell's deck, probably attracted by the scent of roasting pork wafting on the light breeze.

He waved and, though the gap between mansions was great, caught their eye. Bill waved back. Boswell would have called out a hello, but the distance between the two decks was far too great for him to be heard if he tried anything less than a full shout. And there was a limit to what Bram was willing to do to capture their interest. He turned to his wife, who had come to stand beside him.

"See, Honey?" he said. "They're nice and friendly—when you catch a glimpse. They'll come today, you just wait and see."

"I'll believe that when I see it," she said. "How did you get an invitation to them, anyway?"

"Simple," he said. "I had our gateman drop off an invite with Gates' gateman. They know each other."

"But how can you be so sure they'll come?"

"Bill's secretary called my secretary at the office and confirmed."

"What an honor!" she murmured. Flushing red with excitement, she glanced to the north again, but Bill and Melinda had disappeared back inside the house.

Boswell chucked her lightly with an elbow, nodding at the railing now vacated by the Gates. "He comes across as a geek," he chuckled. "Even from a hundred yards away. But she's a real looker. A prime specimen."

"Oh," Honey scolded. "You old hound dog!"

Bram's cell phone rang and he pulled it from a pocket of his robe.

"Hi, Arnold," he said in greeting. "What can I do for y'all. What's that? *Is the party is still on?* Of course it is! Why wouldn't it be? The mountain? It's acting up again, is it? Well it's been acting up for days, so don't you worry about it, y'hear? Okay.

That's better. Lunch starts at 1 PM and goes all afternoon. Party goes all day and ends with a midnight buffet. And guess what. Bill Gates is coming. You don't wanna miss that! We're calling it Bram Boswell's Big Blowout Barbeque, in honor of the eruption. All right? Good! See y'all real soon."

***

"We're running late, Dear," Sophie Minto's father told her over the phone. "But we've got a good reason."

Sophie was sitting on her couch with her foot propped on the hassock. She had been watching news reports about her own rescue—and the continued lack of any sign of the other climbers lost on the mountain. "That's okay, Dad," she said. "I'm doing all right. You'll get here when you get here."

"We're going to stop and get a fresh salmon from the Indian fishermen at Conway for dinner tonight. We'll cook it in your oven, and then bring you home with us after a nice big salmon feast. Does that sound good?"

"Duh! Of course it does!"

"We've gotten to know an old Swinomish man up here. He always has the freshest salmon—and the biggest. But we have to wait for his boat to come in, and then we have to get it fast or it'll all be sold. We've got an ice chest in the trunk."

"I understand. Stop by the fruit and vegetable stand and get me some fresh huckleberry jam. I've almost used up of the jar you brought last time."

"We'll do that, Dear. Anything else we need to bring?"

"Just some hugs."

"You'll get plenty. Your Mom has been worried sick about you."

"Oh, tell her I'm all right. Just hurry once you've got the salmon."

"We will."

CHAPTER 10

Jimmy Finch's small dinghy putt-putted down the main channel of the Nisqually River at a modest but steady speed on a following current. Carlie was on the plank seat at the bow, staring at the water going by, mesmerized by its shimmering patterns. Jimmy had little difficulty keeping the small craft in the center of the wide river channel, and he casually glance at the scenery in front, to the side, and behind the boat.

"There's Tacobet," he said when he spotted the mountain coming into view behind them, appearing to be nestled between the tall cottonwood trees that lined the upstream banks of the river. "Looks like Shuq Siab is in a better mood today."

Carlie gazed at the mountain for quite some time while Jimmy steered the boat forward. Although she could make out a billow of white steam at the summit, with possibly a small amount of ash raining from its underside, nevertheless she agreed with Jimmy. The mountain didn't look anywhere near as angry as it had the previous day.

Jimmy piloted the small craft around a wide bend of the Nisqually where it meandered over the flat grassy floodplain of its delta. When he approached his line of orange floats, he killed the engine and the dinghy settled as it reached the first float. He tied his bowline to the float, and then tugged at his net line to see if he had caught anything. "Got something!" he said triumphantly.

As he began drawing in the net to claim his catch, Carlie glanced up again at the steaming mountain. "I guess this will be my last set of samples for a while," she said.

Jimmy tugged hard to bring a big salmon over the gunwale. As the fish—a grand looking Chinook—slipped into the boat, Jimmy sat down on the center plank. He paused a moment and then looked at her thoughtfully. He smiled. "I was just getting used to having you around."

"Yeah, me too," she said a little ruefully. "But once you get us back up to Franks Landing, I'll pack my gear aboard my trailer and go. An evacuation order is an evacuation order."

"Where'll you go?"

"Oh, I live up there," she pointed to the tree-lined plateau that overlooked the river delta from the south. "I've got an apartment in Lacey. That's out of the danger zone. And if that's not far enough away from the mountain, I can go to Olympia and stay with my parents."

Jimmy bent to the work of bringing in a second large salmon.

Making small talk as he worked, Carlie asked, "Do you have family besides your sister-in-law? Kids?"

Jimmy froze in mid pull as if she had stabbed a knife in his back. He didn't turn to look at her. "I was married once," he said slowly, as if painful memories were at work. He drew in more line. "My wife run the car in the ditch, down by Medicine Creek." He drew in more line. "Killed her… and my baby girl too." He knelt at the gunwale, immobilized by painful memories, his shoulders hunched, his normally robust frame looking frail and small.

"I'm sorry," Carlie said softly. "I didn't know."

Jimmy drew in a deep breath, let it out, and then hauled in another skein of line. "Long time ago," he said without looking at her.

***

Governor Long, Rudy Jones, Howard Gage, and Don Rutledge were panelists at a long table before a crowd of businessmen and women. Over the panelists' heads, the large screen showed the continuing trace of the newly installed seismometer on Burnt Mountain. Out the panoramic windows of the suite majestic—if dirtied—Rainier hove skyward fifty miles southeast of them. The viewing was excellent, the noon-time air was clear, and there were no clouds near the mountain or on it.

The conference space was filled to capacity. Functionaries from several dozen major corporations sat at the round banquet tables in a profusion of blue and black pinstriped suits, red, gold, and green neckties—or silk scarves on ladies' necks. The attendees were representatives of Boeing, Weyerhaeuser, Starbucks, Amazon, Microsoft, the Seahawks, the Mariners, and other large and influential corporations. None attending were CEOs or chairmen, but all were high-level people. Some were corporate legal people. All were adept at strong advocacy and winning arguments. TV cameras and recording equipment were set up at the back of the room but the film crew and reporter were absent, to allow a degree of confidentiality in the proceedings. By agreement, the television people would arrive at the end of the day to film the Governor's summary remarks about the meeting.

The formal wait staff was just setting down luncheon plates loaded with halibut or beef tenderloin or chicken breast with elaborate trimmings. Among them was DeWayne Pettijohn, who had gladly drawn an extra shift and overtime pay for tending to the needs of the participants. He had been assigned three tables near the front, as well as the panelists themselves. It was a customer load that kept him moving briskly.

Although the day's agenda called for a break and informal discussions at lunchtime, the debate was not by any means at low ebb. Rather, it was in full swing, without pause while the food was being served. The often-acrimonious discussion that had started with the morning call-to-order was continuing.

One tall man in a black pinstriped suit had the floor. He stood at a microphone on a stand and complained angrily, "I'm in the retail business. I've got over a dozen major stores within the evacuation zone you are proposing. How can you expect us to put all those operations on hold? I, for one, think such an evacuation would cripple this state economically. It's not even a question of how bad it might be. It will be horrendous. If you extend the evacuation order into the major urban areas, we'll lose millions of dollars in revenues every day. And some of us will lose tens of millions." He looked around the room for support and got it from quite a few nodding heads.

He went on. "I'm warning you. If you shut us down, we will be forced to lay off people by the thousands. That will be a political bombshell for you in the next election, Governor Long. So, before you make such a drastic decision—"

He paused a moment to consider his words, but he never resumed. Suddenly, the entire room was abuzz with low exclamations from every table. People began talking excitedly and looking up at the screen. A man near the back called out, pointing over the panelists' heads, "Look at that!"

"Wow!" cried DeWayne, who had just put a plate down in front of the Governor, "That's a big one!"

The four at the table turned to look up at the screen. The trace, flat only seconds before, was madly swinging up and down, scribbling the thick black surge of a powerful earthquake.

"Oh, my gosh!" the Governor exclaimed. "That does look bad!"

"Sure does," Jones affirmed.

The Governor glanced down the table at Rutledge. "How bad is it?" she asked under her breath to avoid exciting the audience.

"It's pretty serious," Rutledge confirmed softly. Gage nodded his agreement, looking grim.

They turned to gaze at the mountain. It remained visibly unchanged. Not even the hint of a steam cloud could be seen.

***

In the camp on Burnt Mountain, the green nylon tent had been rolled up and packed into its slipcase. It sat in a pile with other camp goods, waiting to be loaded aboard the evacuation helicopter when it came later in the day. Andy had walked a few paces from the table to look down at the logging operation on the valley slope below him. It was in full swing again. "Have they got special permission to be in the red zone?" he wondered aloud. "We're all set to evacuate, we've just monitored a major tremor, and they're down there acting like nothing's the matter. Look at 'em go. Like they want to get every last stick before…"

"Hey!" Lexi called to him. She was the table, staring at the laptop computer. "Come look at this!"

He walked over and put a familiar hand on her shoulder as he scanned the seismic data streaming from their station. In the upper right was the massive scribble of the big jolt they had measured—and felt—a few minutes earlier. Now, Lexi pointed at a series of smaller but still substantial bumps that had appeared lower on the trace. "Those surges aren't just rumblings from that logging operation."

"No," he agreed. "They're not. They're too big."

"And too regular," she added.

He leaned nearer the screen and stared at it closely. "Are you thinking what I'm thinking?" he asked.

"They look like full-blown harmonic tremors to me," she answered. "Something's moving inside the mountain. Something big!"

They looked at each other anxiously.

"Do you think this could be… *it?* The eruption?" she asked.

"I don't know. But I'm going to get on the radio to Lewis-McChord." He cast a worried glance up at the mountain. "I'm gonna ask them to move the timetable forward on that evacuation helicopter. I'll tell them we need to get out of here *right now!*"

***

In the living room of their home, Katy Johnson had set out four suitcases, two large ones and two smaller ones. They were open and all had accumulated loads of clothes and other necessary items as she shuttled back and forth from the laundry room and bedrooms.

She was arranging a neatly folded pink sweat outfit in one of the larger suitcases when Seth came in from the kitchen. "Okay. Thank you so much," he said into his cell phone. "Goodbye."

He clicked off the phone and stowed it in the breast pocket of his T-shirt. "That was Ollie, my editor at the Business Journal. She lives up north in Lynnwood. She says we're welcome in her guest bedroom for a while. Just the one room for all of us, but it's got its own bathroom. And she's real nice—for an editor."

Katy wiped a strand of hair off her forehead with a knuckle. "I guess that will have to do. What did she say about pets?"

"Oh. I forgot to mention them. I'll call her back." He reached for the phone.

"No!" She put out a hand and stopped him with a gesture. "Don't."

PART THREE

THE BIG BLOWOUT

CHAPTER 11

Bram Boswell's preparations were progressing well. Dressed in his party clothing—a Hawaiian shirt, Bermuda shorts, and sandals—he was out on his bedroom deck again to get an overview of how the caterers were coming along.

"Ah," he said to Honey, who had come to have a look too, despite not having every detail of her hair and makeup done just right, "That little piggy is browning up just fine. And the jambalaya and potato salad and fritters and cornbread and the mint julep bar, they all look like they need some customers. I think I'll go down there and taste-test them personally. Wanna join me?"

"Oh, you old hambone," she said dismissively. "Everything looks like it's just fine to me. Don't pester them while they're working."

A doorbell chimed distantly on the lower level, prompting Bram to look at his wristwatch. "Noon. A bit early, but I suppose everybody can't be fashionably late. Let's go see who it is."

Honey walked back into the bedroom and went to her vanity. "Let the help get it," she said, sitting down and taking up an eyebrow pencil. "Whoever it is, they're early. The invitation said twelve-thirty."

"Oh, heck," Boswell said as he made for the bedroom door. "Let's don't stand on ceremony. That might be Bill and Melinda down there right now. We don't wanna keep *them* waiting."

"You go on ahead," she murmured, leaning near the vanity

mirror and making deft strokes on a brow with the pencil. "I've still got my lips to do. If it's Bill and Melinda, make my apologies. And tell them I'll be there shortly."

***

"This is Matt Ziegler aboard Chopper Twelve with cameraman Dan Ewing and pilot Cal Winslow, reporting from east of Tacoma. Have we got a sight for you!" Ewing's telescopic camera zeroed in on the top of Mount Rainier, while Zeigler did a voiceover description. "The ice crevasse at the top of Mount Rainier has expanded quite a bit overnight, unobserved by anyone, with the possible exception of a spy satellite with infrared detectors."

"The bare ground has widened so much that it covers almost half the summit! I guess it no longer fits the definition of a crevasse. I wonder where all that melt-water went? Amanda, just look at that mountaintop! It's a ragged, jumbled landscape of pinnacles, cliffs, and sheer rock faces. The stand-out up there is that central pyramid-shaped block of gray volcanic stone. I don't think it was there yesterday. It looks almost as if it was thrust upward by pressure underneath it. It's got to be several hundred feet tall, at least. I've never seen anything like it, except maybe the lava dome inside Mount Saint Helens' caldera."

"It's an awesome sight!" Amanda at the anchor desk confirmed. "Is that steam or clouds around it?"

"Good observation, Amanda. Yes, it's steam all right. And to make things all the more ominous, it's jetting out on all sides, almost like the block is keeping a lid on things, and just barely. One gets the impression of raw, infernal heat boiling up from below. Look how its surface shimmers like heat mirages on a desert highway. That's a scary sight! Are you getting this at the news desk, Amanda?"

"We sure are, Matt. And you're going out live to the TV audience. We're all sitting here with mouths agape."

"We are too," Zeigler replied. "Wait! Dan, can you zoom in on that block?" The video feed zeroed in on the monstrous triangular form reminiscent of a Giza pyramid bathed in a welter of steam. "Amanda, it now appears a crack has opened on one of the pyramid's faces. There are huge boulders tumbling down the side of it. The crack appears to be opening wider, right before our eyes!"

Zeigler fell silent as the entire lava-rock massif shuddered and began to disintegrate. The two halves of the split-open block crumbled and immense pieces tumbled down into the gap between as violent forces below widened the new fissure with incredible speed. In a matter of seconds, the entire block disintegrated into hundreds of titanic, collapsing rock fragments. At the same time, jets of black ash-filled steam appeared, bursting upward between the tumbling blocks of stone.

"My God!" Zeigler cried. "It's hell on earth up there!"

Zeigler fell silent again an instant later when the top of the mountain leapt upward in a titanic detonation that obliterated the summit and hurtled out huge blocks of stone that trailed streamers of black ash behind them. A moment after that, an even larger detonation of black ash shot straight up into the sky as hyper-pressurized steam within the mountain's core boiled out—just as if the cork had been released from a demonic bottle of champagne.

***

Andy Hutchins and Lexi Cohan stood beside a pile of packed bags and boxes of equipment that had been their camp. Even the folding table had been broken down, the better to accommodate a swift "extraction," as the helicopter men called it.

But there was no helicopter in sight. Andy's call had prompted the dispatcher at Lewis-McChord to say, "We'll see what we can do," but so far, no Chinook was in view as they anxiously eyed the air to the west of them over nearby mountain ridges. They held hands, the better to share the fear rising inside them. Quakes from Rainier were nearly constant now, shaking the ground noticeably under their feet. A particularly strong jolt prompted them to turn and face the mountain.

Lexi screamed.

A huge detonation of black rock and dust was arcing through the sky over the top of the mountain. Lower down the slope, the snowfields were still intact and glistening white. But below the maelstrom of ash and steam, a barely perceptible wave-front of wind was stirring up swirling wisps of snow and dust on the slopes of the mountain as it descended from the summit at supersonic speeds.

"A shockwave!" Andy cried as the front raced toward them at unbelievable speed.

They had almost no time to react before the shockwave hit them. Its impact was like a punch in the gut, except that it hit each of them all over from head to foot. Its sound was a deafening bang that could be felt, as much as heard, within their skulls.

Stunned, they both reeled in crazy, staggering dances, but kept their feet.

And then it was past them. Leaves, twigs, and camp dust had been stirred up all around them. The debris drifted down while the mountain roared at a less deafening, but still almost intolerable level. They stepped into each other's embrace and hugged tightly to steady themselves and drive away their mutual terror. Tears wet the corners of Lexi's eyes.

Andy called into her ear, "It's gonna be alright."

"Is it?" she called back. Still clutching him tightly, she turned her head to look up at the black billows blasting into the sky above the mountain. It didn't look to her like things were going to be alright.

CHAPTER 12

"Three big salmon!" Jimmy Finch exclaimed as he pulled in more of his setline. "Three!" He grinned widely as he tugged the last of his prizes aboard the dinghy. "That one's gotta be twenty-five pounds." He beamed with satisfaction as it came in over the gunwale. "Hoo-wee!"

While he wrangled the third fish aboard, Carlie was busy taking a sample of the second. With practiced hands, she had the needle in and the biopsy out in seconds. She dropped the little piece of meat into the sample collection tube, capped it, shook the extraction fluid inside, and stashed the tube in her little cooler. Then she watched as Jimmy arranged the third salmon along with the previous two on the bottom of the boat. "There's hardly room for our feet!" she said.

"They'd sink us if I caught any more—" he began, but his words were drowned out by a sudden immense *boo-oo-oom!*

Like an airplane's sonic boom but ten times louder, the powerful concussion physically impacted the boat and its passengers. Jimmy did not so much sit on his plank seat, as get knocked back onto it by the force of the shock wave.

"What in blazes—?" he yelled over the roar, but he didn't finish. Hearing Carlie scream, he turned and followed her thunderstruck gaze—and was struck dumb when he saw that the summit of Mount Rainier had been obliterated by a huge black explosion. Massive outbursts were jetting skyward at impossible speeds, tossing out arcs of billowing gray dust and rock propelled by titanic forces from deep within the mountain.

"My gosh," he finally said in a small, overawed voice as the roar from the mountain subsided a little.

Watching the billows expand with incredible speed, Carlie at last found a coherent voice. "It's— It's finally happened!" she exclaimed.

"Sure has," Jimmy replied.

***

In the Columbia Center tower, the mountain's outburst went unnoticed for a few moments. Governor Long was at the podium microphone and had the attendees' attention. She pointed up at the screen behind her, which had continued tracing harmonic tremors non-stop through lunch, while she and the delegates had argued interminably about the balance between public safety and corporate cash flows. But the seismic traces had grown in amplitude, and many voices of dissent had fallen silent.

"By now," she said forcefully, "I hope you can see we're talking about a very urgent situation. I hope I can get a more cooperative attitude out of at least some of you. Now, we've still got all afternoon to work out details and try to make this as painless as possible for the businesses it impacts. But I want those high-powered minds of yours to start helping me, rather than fighting me every step of the way!"

She gazed around the room to measure the effect her words were having. Dissent and hostility had waned, but most delegates had simply shifted their focus to their luncheon plates, as the wait staff bustled to and fro removing stacks of finished plates or bringing the dessert course and coffee. No one seemed very intent on what she was saying. It was as if everyone had reached a point of saturation. Even Rudy Jones was whispering a side conversation with the waiter DeWayne, who had come to clear the plates on the panel table but lingered in what seemed an overly long discussion. He and Jones sparred in an almost flirtatious way that irked Long, given the seriousness of the matters at hand.

Suddenly a deep, thudding concussion bent the windows

inward and turned everyone's attention to the southeast view, in which a horrific sight loomed. The top of Mount Rainier had vanished, and in its place a black billowing detonation of ash and steam was rising into the sky like a nuclear explosion. People gasped. Several women let out shrieks of surprise and fear, including Governor Long. After a moment spent staring at the mind-boggling sight, Long's eye was caught by a movement on the screen behind her. The seismometer trace was scribbling violently, outlining a pulse of earthquake energy that extended from the top to the bottom of the screen. Simultaneously, the room rattled with the force of the temblor, which had rolled underground from the mountain to where they sat. The entire tower swayed in a seasick motion.

DeWayne had taken up a tray of used dishes and held them at shoulder level. Now, as he stood staring at the mountain, the tray slipped from his hands and fell to the floor. The cascade of clattering and shattering dinnerware added to the pandemonium of the moment. He went down to his knees on the carpet and hurriedly began collecting the mess, crying, "Oh my God! Oh my God! Oh my God!" His outcry expressed a feeling that was general throughout the room, although no one was watching him work.

All eyes, including DeWayne's were fixated on the exploding mountain. The billow at the top of the rising dust column was beginning to take on the shape of an immense mushroom cloud.

***

At the Boswell mansion, the early-arriving guests hadn't turned out to be the Gateses. They were a couple invited by Honey, folks from an ultra-elite charitable trust. The trust was so exclusive you had to be worth at least a hundred million just to join its rarified membership. Now, more guests were arriving by the minute. They crowded the lower deck from one end to the other. The barbecue shot out puffs of smoke as a man in a white chef's coat and toque hat used a long carving knife to slice off portions of the pig and pile them high on a large oval white serving plate on a table at his side. "Come and get it, folks," he called as he worked. A server stepped to the table with a two-tined barbecue fork in hand.

Bram Boswell stood nearby watching with satisfaction as folks lined up holding plates for the main course.

"Excuse me, sir,' said Boswell's doorman, who had appeared, holding an envelope in his hand.

"What's this?" Boswell asked as he opened the envelope and took out a card.

"From the Gates," said the man.

Bram read out loud from the card, "The Gates send their regrets. Sorry, but we decided we really had better go to higher ground." He looked up at the Gates mansion. There on the upper deck, on the bedroom veranda with suitcase in hand, was Bill himself. He waved a friendly goodbye when he saw Boswell looking. Then he turned to go.

Others near Boswell had joined him in looking up at the great man. Now, a heavy boom in distance made everyone turn and look down the lake to the south. The startling suddenness of the thunderous sound caused several women to cry out, but the view from Boswell's deck afforded no perspective on the mountain that now was on everybody's mind. The faint tremor of an earthquake passed underfoot, and water slapped around the pilings of Boswell's dock and against the sides of several yachts moored there. A moment before, the crowd had been chatting gaily and growing raucous on mint juleps. Now it went quiet. People exchanged nervous glances or conversed in hushed voices.

"No need to worry folks," Boswell called out loudly, wearing an overly congenial grin. "That mountain's over fifty miles from here. Mount Saint Helens only blew out for fifteen miles. I already checked up on that. So we're in no danger. Eat up! Drink up!"

After a moment's hesitation and some subdued chatting, the mood lifted. Laughter resurfaced. Smiles reappeared. Drinks were hoisted. Forks speared pork and fed it into mouths.

Boswell sighed in relief. Honey—who had made a glamorous appearance just minutes before dressed in a pink tennis outfit with a pink visor hat on her perfectly coiffed head—came to join him. She wore a concerned look on her gorgeous face. He raised a finger preemptively and said, "No need to worry, Honey. That old mountain ain't gonna ruin this shindig!"

She smiled, batted her perfectly lined and mascaraed eyes, and then took a strong pull on her mint julep.

Harley Newberg, a local banking magnate dressed in Bermuda shorts and a brightly patterned Hawaiian shirt that covered a wide belly, came their way. "I don't know," he said to Bram. "I think me and the missus might just take off. Play it safe, you know?"

"No. I don't know, Harley." Boswell said while nodding a hello to Julia Newberg, a small, thin, nervous-looking brunette at Harley's elbow.

"They say if it blows up real bad," Harley went on, "it could reach all the way to Seattle."

"Who said that?" Boswell scoffed. "Well, it's not what I say. They ain't never had any lava flowin' around here."

"Okay," Newberg acquiesced with a wry smile. "But if I get killed, I'm gonna blame you."

"Very funny," Julia said, clutching his elbow more tightly.

"Stick around," Boswell insisted. "We've got the Mariners on the big screen inside, and they're winning. And the Seahawks preseason game kicks off in," he looked at his watch, "just about an hour."

CHAPTER 13

"Come in JBLM! Come in JBLM!"

Andy had fetched the portable radio from the pile of camping gear and sat it on the wide flat stump of a Douglas fir. The same frequency that had carried Andy's earlier request for an airlift was now filled with crackling static, and no response from the military base. He put the hand microphone down beside the radio and glanced up at the cloud towering above the mountain. Lightning bolts snaked through the billows of black dust, adding their own crackling rumble to the general roar of the eruption. "That static is killing our communications," he said to Lexi, who stood nearby staring up at the mountain as if mesmerized.

She only half heard him. "It's plinian cloud!" she said in a voice choked with dread.

Andy looked up—and up again—at the towering column of dust and steam. "You're right," he agreed. The upward rolling billows had begun to spread horizontally in the stratosphere ten miles above the summit—or what had been the summit of the mountain. The cloud had taken on the classic shape of an anvil, first reported by Pliny the Younger at Vesuvius in 79 AD. A strong breeze came from behind them as air was drawn in from the surrounding landscape to join the upwelling air current within the hot ash column.

"You know what a plinian cloud does next?" he asked her as the wind intensified, buffeting against their backs.

"I don't want to think about it."

"But we have to. Parts of the cloud will collapse under the

weight of all that ash."

"I know."

"And then some of it will come down here."

"I know. That's what buried Pompeii. Are we going to die?"

"I don't know."

The descent of a pyroclastic flow down the side of a volcano is one of nature's most horrific displays of destructive force. At first, this one appeared to be merely a line of small billows at the base of the much larger rising ash column. But those small billows grew until they were vast ragged walls of gray surging down the mountainside toward Andy and Lexi.

"Do you think it will reach us here?" Lexi asked.

"I don't think so," he replied bravely. "There's a whole river valley between us and Rainier."

She nodded her head hopefully, but her eyes remained wide with fear. "Do you think that will be enough?"

"I pray to God it is," he murmured. And then his expression brightened. "Look! It's channeling into the river valley."

The pyroclastic flow had followed the contours of the mountain as it descended. Now it diverted into the depths of the steep Carbon River Valley and raced down it at full force, but seemed to pose no imminent threat to them. They walked to the brink, where they could see into the deepest parts of the valley, hundreds of feet below their vantage point on the lofty ridge of Burnt Mountain. The surge raced down-valley, a gray billowing nemesis carrying incandescent heat they could feel on their faces. Its stupendous energy was channeled along the meandering course of Carbon River, which burst into steam as it was overrun, amplifying the explosiveness of the flow.

Lexi pointed farther down the valley and cried, "The loggers!"

Straight in the flow's path was the logging camp where, incredibly, operations had continued until the mountain exploded. The loggers had by now abandoned their heavy equipment and rushed to their cars and trucks, and were racing away on the newly cut graveled road that had brought them to this place. The flow overwhelmed the logging yard within seconds, tossing the huge yellow loader ahead of it like a toy. Giant fallen logs tumbled end-over-end. And fleeing cars and trucks were swept up, one after another, in a maelstrom of gray dust and scorching gas.

"Oh, my God," Lexi murmured. She stared in wide-eyed horror as the lumbermen vanished into the flow front. The pyroclastic cloud scarcely slowed as it consumed men and machines, and then it continued roaring farther down the valley, carrying blazing wreckage of cars and trees and trucks—and men—with it as it went.

The front had passed by Burnt Mountain, but now the sides of the gray cloud billowed higher. Soon it had filled the valley from wall to wall, radiating still more hellish heat.

Andy and Lexi stepped together and put their arms around each other.

"It can't reach us here—can it?" she wondered aloud.

"Keep your fingers crossed," he replied.

A sound like the pattering of hailstones began around them. But the objects dropping from the sky were not made of ice. They were small red and black cinders of solidified lava, raining down all around them. They hugged each other more tightly as the little stones began striking them as well.

Soon the hail of stones grew to a torrent. They went to the pile of gear and fetched out a blue plastic tarpaulin and held it over their heads to shed the deluge of pelting stones. Miserable and terrified, they sat down amid their pile of gear to wait out the storm of cinders—if they could.

***

"Are you getting this, Amanda?" Matt Ziegler radioed from Chopper Twelve.

"We are!"

"From this angle, there's a gap in the dust cloud and we can see all the way to the top of the mountain. And what a sight!"

The camera feed showed viewers a gray anvil cloud

climbing miles into the sky, while the summit itself had become a newly excavated caldera almost a mile across. Within it, a vent was spewing out a tall fountain of orange-hot lava. Elsewhere, the summit was crisscrossed with fissures and fumaroles blasting columns of hot gas and dark gray dust from gaping holes that had not existed hours before.

"I don't think this is over yet!" Matt cried. "There's something more ominous than the lava and steam jets. Look at those blackened, glistening snowfields all around the outside of the caldera. They look like the beginnings of lahars."

Irradiated by the heat of the lava fountain, blasted by steaming gasses, and pelted by glowing volcanic bombs, the ice fields had begun to melt wholesale. They were transforming into streams of black, muddy water that ran down the mountainsides in ever-enlarging flows. "They're spreading in every direction and they're building up a dangerous momentum!" Matt exclaimed. "I hope people are prepared!"

***

The volcanic emergency siren in Alderton had been wailing for only a few minutes. But those were minutes that seemed an eternity to Katy Johnson. In the garage, she threw a suitcase into the open back hatch of the station wagon, and then tossed in more stuff after it—some of which was of questionable value, like a cooler she had meant to fill with food, but which landed atop the suitcase with a hollow thud. She grabbed some blankets off a garage shelf and tossed them in helter-skelter. Every move she made was punctuated by a grunt or growl of mixed horror and determination.

Visible through the open garage door, the towering, rumbling gray-black cloud over the mountain grew by the second.

"Come on! Come on! Come on!" she shouted at Noah who rushed from inside the house carrying Iggy in his cage. "Get in the car! Right now!"

Noah sat in the back seat and carefully placed the cage among the objects piled behind him.

Seth came out with a heavy suitcase he had shut with a

shirtsleeve protruding in one hand, and a transport cage with the cat mewing loudly inside, in the other. He dumped both in the rear and closed the hatchback.

"Where is Amelia?" Katy demanded.

"She's looking for Bella," Seth replied. "Can't find her anywhere."

"Amelia!" Katy cried at the top of her lungs. "Get out here right now!"

"I'll get her!" Seth called as he hurried to the door into the house. "She's coming with or without the dog."

Amelia came out the door at that moment, carrying a whimpering, trembling Bella in her arms. "She was hiding under my bed," she apologized. "Sorry I took so long. I looked everywhere else."

"That's okay," Seth said, ushering her by a shoulder to her seat in the back of the wagon. "Now let's get out of here—fast!"

Katy looked around the garage like she was certain she was forgetting something critical.

"Come on!" Seth shouted at her.

Galvanized into motion, she hurried to the passenger door and got in.

A moment later, the station wagon raced out of the garage in reverse. Seth shifted, cranked the steering wheel, and jammed the accelerator pedal to the floor. The wagon tore out of the cul-de-sac with its screeching tires throwing out white smoke.

***

Heavy thumping sounds came from twin rotors as the big Chinook CH-47F lifted off the tarmac of JBLM's heliport. Hans Clearidge was at the controls, his flight helmet and visor glinting in the sun of a day that had just one cloud in it—an immense cloud, forty miles to the east.

Beside him, Ramon Diaz was belted into the copilot's seat. "You sure about this, sir?" he said with noticeable trepidation in his usually military-brusque voice.

"No. But somebody's got to try and save those guys. Remember, we're the ones who put them there."

As the helicopter rose above the airfield and the crew got their first full look at the mountain, the Crew Chief Arlen Duffy, belted into the companionway seat behind the flight deck exclaimed, "Hot damn!"

His sentiment was echoed by the fourth member of the crew, seated aft. "Holy Moses!" cried Flight Engineer Jason Shen.

Only the very bottom of the mountain could be seen. Above that, multiple flat gray cloud layers hung at different altitudes, ringing the central towering ash column, which had spread into the stratosphere and flattened into an ominous anvil shape that was tailing off to the east on the jet stream and raining ash on the landscape below it. Lightning flashed around the base of the mountain and arced between the layered ash clouds. Even at a distance of forty miles, the rumbling of explosions and the roll of thunder were loud enough to be heard over the whine of the turbines and through the earphones of flight helmets.

Hans banked the helicopter in the direction of the maelstrom and eased the cyclic steering stick forward.

"Looks like we're flying straight into the jaws of hell," Ramon cautioned.

"Tell me something I don't know," Hans snapped back with determination.

CHAPTER 14

Jimmy Finch had taken the top off his old motor and was tinkering with it. "Lousy time for this thing to quit," he murmured as he worked.

In the distance, the cloud over the mountain had risen to stupendous heights and widened until it stretched halfway across the eastern sky from the too-close-for-comfort perspective of the Nisqually River delta.

Carlie watched Jimmy putter with a glum expression. "You know what a lahar is?"

"Nope." He paused and looked at her in squint-eyed good humor. "Some kinda joke maybe? Like har-dee-har?"

"Very funny," she jibed. And then she looked up at the mountain again and her jaw dropped.

Jimmy turned to see what had caused her reaction. His jaw dropped too. Until now, Rainier had retained most of its former shape—angled slopes rising out of the Cascade Range and climbing thousands of feet to a summit that had been hidden by the ash cloud. Now, as they watched in numb shock, the side slopes visibly rose up and then ripped apart, unleashing huge new outbursts of exploding steam and ash. It seemed the entire volcano had been lifted off its base and detonated into an expanding ball of smoke and dust, shot through with orange gouts of glowing lava.

They watched for many seconds as the solid form of the volcano transformed into a huge new plume of black-and-gray rock dust, blasting upward and outward. The spectacle wasn't accompanied by a sonic boom yet, but the notion that one was on the way was undeniable. In the interim, the awesome sight was accompanied by no new sound, only the rumbling that had preceded it.

"Maybe you'd better tell me what a lahar is," Jimmy said eventually.

"I think you'll be finding out the hard way," she said, "if you don't get that motor going."

**

Deep within the mountain, forces were being unleashed that had been contained by billions of tons of overlying stone. The explosion that had torn open the top of the mountain an hour earlier had only been a harbinger of what now was taking place.

The volcanic edifice of Rainier had been built up by half a million years of eruptions. Layers of rock that had solidified from flowing lava, alternating with strata of soft ash from gas-driven eruptions, and beds of cinders spattered by fiery fountains, had accumulated over the centuries into an immense geological construct that, although it had had the semblance of permanence, was nevertheless destined to be torn apart. Snows falling over many thousands of years had built up ice fields and glaciers, all of which had been melting on their undersides and saturating the rock and dust layers below them with water. Deep in the core of the volcano, the subterranean aquifers had been heated far beyond their boiling points, and had been charged with poisonous hydrogen sulfide and carbon dioxide gasses carried in magma that had risen from cracks deep in the earth's crust.

After the upper rock layers were removed in the first stages of the eruption, those deeper strata of water-saturated mud and stone were released from the trillion-ton lid that had kept them in check. Now, they exploded, layer after layer, down into the core of the mountain. Each new steam-driven detonation blasted its layer skyward with atomic-bomb power. The interior depths of the mountain lifted up, one layer after another, and converted instantaneously into wave after wave of super-sonically expanding rock fragments, dust, super-heated steam, and poisonous gas.

The stupendous explosions expanded upward, but also outward. Glaciers on the lower slopes were inundated with glowing debris from above. They quickly began to melt, crumble, and boil into additional volumes of expanding steam that carried huge chunks of rock, hot water, melting ice, and incalculable quantities of mud—the makings of lahars of incomprehensible size and devastating power.

**

Andy and Lexi stared up at a sight they both knew carried lethal significance. The rain of pebbles had ceased, but now a new and much larger eruption was bursting upward into the sky, swallowing the older plinian cloud in its entirety. At its base, the ragged edge of a new pyroclastic flow appeared. It was much larger—and far nearer—than the previous one had been at its inception. Incandescent heat radiated from the thick billows—a foretaste of heat beyond imagining that was moving rapidly toward them.

"We're going to die," she said, summoning as much courage as she could muster, just to say the words. Her chin trembled.

"Yes, we are," he concurred. "Nothing short of a miracle–"

The radio crackled loudly, audible above the roar of the mountain. "USGS Station," a strong male voice called. "We are approaching. Are you ready for pick up? Over?"

Andy took up the handset. "It's too late," he called into it leadenly.

"Negative, USGS Station," the voice said with surprising assuredness. "We can get to you. I can see your position."

Andy turned and looked directly opposite the horror looming above them. There was clear air along the northern horizon, bounded by mountain ridges below and the edge of the black cloud above. "I see you too," he replied. He could just make out a black dot in the distance, and the flickering movement of its twin rotors. Its apparent size grew as it came straight at them. The faintest quickening of hope touched his palpitating heart. And then he looked back at the pyroclastic cloud. Its lower edge was swallowing ridges and blackened snowfields, and had already covered half the distance to him. He shook his head. "You're too late," he called into the handset. "Better worry about saving yourself."

"Negative, USGS Station. I have visual on you. I'll touch down for just a second and you can jump aboard through the rear door. Go to the pickup point!"

"Roger that!" Andy called, feeling the thinnest thread of hope. "We will be there! USGS Station out!"

He threw down the handset without waiting for a reply. He grabbed Lexi by an arm. "Come on!" he shouted over the increasing roar of the mountain. "Maybe he can pull this off!"

She resisted his tug.

"What are you waiting for?" he cried, anger rising in him quickly.

"The end."

"Look there!" he shouted, pointing away from the mountain to where the spot had grown as it approached to take on the shape of a helicopter. "They're here! Let's get moving!"

She still resisted. "No," she said. "I'm gonna stand right here and watch."

"Watch? Why, for God's sake?"

She pointed toward the pyroclastic surge. Now a featureless onrushing wall of gray, it had already crossed the scorched Carbon River Valley and was only seconds away. "How many people have ever seen anything like this?"

"Not many," he concurred, staring at the flow, which he could see would reach them long before the helicopter. He quit tugging her hand and just held it. He calmed, as she had in the face of the inevitable. He stood with her to face the onrushing wall of death.

"I feel... honored to witness it," she said.

"Me too." He wrapped her in his arms, kissed her on the cheek, and pressed her closely to him as they both stared at onrushing death. The air around them grew silent, as if in anticipation.

"I love you," he said.

"I love you, too." She put her arms around his body and they hugged each other tightly. Both kept their gazes fixed on the gray billows moving toward them with impossible speed.

When the leading edge of the blast took them, its shock-front hit with such force that they were instantaneously knock-ed senseless. There was no sensation of their bodies being propelled through the air and tumbling over the rough ground, no sensation of the deafening concussive blast that rattled the very earth beneath them, no sensation of the holocaustic heat that engulfed them.

***

"Damn!" Hans, a man not given to cursing, cried as the base, less than a quarter-mile from them now, vanished into the oncoming cloud. Simultaneously, he yanked the cyclic stick hard to the left and forced it far forward. In response, the Chinook turned sharply and its nose dropped steeply. He pulled hard at the thrust lever to the left of his seat and gunned the twin turbines to full power. Silently, he cursed himself for his fixation on the two people he had intended to rescue. That fixation had drawn his attention too far from what now confronted him—his own death and that of his crew, in the hellish cloud that was roaring on their tail.

After Hans's single curse, no one spoke. There was no need for discussion or recriminations. It was a simple proposition. Either the Chinook would win the race with the oncoming wall of hot ash—or they would die.

***

Don Rutledge, Rudy Jones, and Governor Long stood so near the Columbia Center window that they were almost pressed up against it. "That is a monstrous eruption," Jones murmured, stating the obvious in his shock.

"I can see that," Long replied, shaking her head slowly in grim astonishment. "But what I need to understand is, how bad will it get?"

Howard Gage came to stand next to them. "I can tell you just by looking at it—it's bigger than the Saint Helens eruption."

"How much bigger?"

"Maybe ten times."

"But that's—" The Governor sputtered, and stopped, at a loss for words. The look of horror on her face intensified, as if she was only now allowing herself to think of the consequences she would be dealing with.

"How far can it reach?" Jones wondered aloud. "To Tacoma? To Seattle?"

"I have a feeling we're about to find out," the Governor replied. She had begun to tremble.

Gage had broken a sweat. "It's caught us so—unprepared," he murmured.

Rutledge shook his head. "Sometimes you just can't predict these things."

"But that was supposed to be your job!" the Governor moaned. "Both of you!"

"The mountain—" Gage said apologetically. "It didn't give us proper warning signals."

"Proper?" Long repeated. "What do you mean by that?" She stared into his face with anger simmering.

Rutledge said, "Usually there are dozens—hundreds—of warning signs. Earthquakes, steam eruptions, ashfalls, harmonic tremors—"

"You've seen all of those—haven't you?" She kept her eyes locked on Gage's.

"But it all came on so quickly!" he defended. "Usually there are days or weeks of seismic events. Months. But it's like—" he gestured at the mountain with an open hand, "—something deep inside just snapped!"

Rudy Jones cleared his throat, breaking the lock Long's eyes had on Gage's. "There will be time to figure out what went wrong later," he said. "Right now, we've got a developing crisis to deal with. We'd better get to it."

CHAPTER 15

As the blast overtook them, Hans Clearidge fingered the cyclic gingerly, getting ready to react to what was coming. Suddenly, the Chinook was enveloped in gray—and it was tumbling. It felt as if the aircraft was upended and turned completely over. Hans frantically tugged the cyclic stick fore, aft, left, and right, until the helicopter executed what he hoped was a half barrel roll to get right side up again.

The maneuver seemed to work. It returned them to a shaky but approximately level orientation in what had become a featureless space of swirling gray dust and near darkness.

Hans continued shifting the cyclic in response to buffeting winds. As he did, he noticed the air inside the cabin becoming hazy and filled with choking, sulfurous fumes. He felt himself getting dizzy. Whether it was due to the gasses or to a sense of mortal fear that was making his heart pound, he couldn't guess.

"Get us out of here!" a voice called over his headphones. The rumbling of the volcanic storm and the whining of the overstressed turbines nearly drowned out the cry and made it unclear who had said it.

Hans's mind raced. *Did he have any notion whether he was now flying away from—or toward—the volcano?* No. *Was he certain he was flying the aircraft upright, given the featureless gray air outside his windows?* Not really—but at least the artificial horizon display showed they were not too far from level. *Had the Chinook been driven down and lost sufficient altitude that it might crash into one of the ridgelines they had crossed?* He had no clue.

Those thoughts convinced him of what he must do next.

He leveled the helicopter the best he could against the turbulence and pulled the thrust lever to full power. "I'm going to try to get above it!" he hollered, not knowing if his crew-mates would hear him over the roar of the mountain, the whine of the turbines, the thump of the rotors, and a hellish static that had arisen in his headset.

And then they broke clear of the ash cloud and hurtled straight up into the sunlit sky above it. Hans breathed sigh of relief, but gagged on the choking stench in the cabin air. He pulled his cockpit window open as far as it would go and sucked in several deep breaths of fresh air. As he did so, the dizziness in his head cleared.

Ramon did the same. And then he suddenly pointed across Hans to his left. "Man, oh man!" he cried. "Look at that!"

Where Mount Rainier had stood several hours ago, now a stupendous anvil-shaped gray-black cloud reached, it seemed, right up into the vastness of space. Hans took the sight in briefly. Then he glanced around to get his bearings. He was flying southbound, parallel to the mountain instead of away from it. He made a right turn and scanned the Puget Sound lowlands for his new objective. "There's McChord!" he ex-claimed when he spotted the familiar stripes of the runways, distant but dead ahead on a bluff above the blue waters of the Nisqually Reach of Puget Sound.

He pressed his helmet microphone button. "McChord," he said, "this is Chinook 247 inbound. Over."

After a long pause, a voice came back. "We thought we might have lost you, 247. Mission status? Over."

"Bad news, McChord. Mission failed. We got here too late. There are no survivors. Over."

"Roger that 247. Sorry to hear it. What is the status of your aircraft? Over."

Hans listened to the turbines and scanned the instruments. One turbine—the left one he thought—was surging and balking. Confirming this, the gauges showed number one turbine overheating. He could feel the effect of its faltering power as the aircraft slowed with each rasping noise from the engine.

"Unclear aircraft status," he replied. "She's been through a lot. We'll tell you about it when we get back. If we get back."

The balking of the turbine increased. A long streak of black smoke began to stream out behind them.

"Hold together baby," Hans murmured.

"Look down there," Ramon said, leaning forward and pointing straight down. Beneath them, the still-expanding front of the ash cloud was obliterating their view of the ground as it enveloped forests, farms, and neighborhood developments that formed a patchwork across the Puget lowlands. "We're in a horse race with that cloud. Think we can beat it?"

"I've got us over 150 miles per hour," Hans said. "And we're losing, by a little."

***

Seth Johnson laid on his horn. The driver who was stopped in front of him didn't react. Neither did anyone in the line of cars that stretched up and over a low hill.

"Why bother honking?" Katy asked.

"Because it feels good."

"But it's getting us nowhere. Where did all these people come from?"

"Same as us. They live here."

"This is supposed to be the evacuation route, but it's worse than a rush-hour traffic jam."

"Maybe there's an accident up ahead. I can't see over the hill yet."

Despite liberal horn use by Seth and many other drivers, the traffic continued at a stop-and-go crawl on two-lane Highway 162 northbound. As they dragged along, other cars came up on their tail and joined the line. Two cars back, a huge red pickup truck with a row of searchlights across its cab and a long air horn on each side, used those air horns to make loud statements of frustration.

"What do you want buddy?" Seth growled, glaring into his

rear-view mirror at the driver of the big rig. "You want me to pull over and let you pass? Lots of luck with that!"

The sky darkened by the minute. High overhead, the gray plume of ash from the mountain spread across the stratosphere and lowered toward them, darkening as it came. An odd, pattering noise arose on the roof and hood of the station wagon.

"Is that hail?" Katy wondered, staring at the windshield in front of her, where small objects were striking and bouncing off in all directions.

"No," Seth replied. "It isn't."

The hail of pumice pebbles increased in volume until at was pounding on the top of the car like a full-fledged hailstorm. Everyone in the station wagon stared at the welter of volcanic stones as they barraged the windshield and scattered across the pavement around the slow rolling traffic. Intermittently amid the roar of small, pea-sized particles, came the thump of much larger pumice stones mixed in with the small.

Suddenly, the truck two places back pulled out of the line and roared into the oncoming lane, which was empty of anything except pumice stones. Gaining speed quickly with his accelerator floored, the grim-faced driver kept his eyes fixated on the road ahead.

"Jerk!" Seth growled as the pickup roared past. "He'll just cut in front of us again. And look at that!" The station wagon had finally crawled forward far enough for them to see the highway interchange. Where they had hoped for a fast-moving escape route, they saw instead long lines of stopped traffic, not only on the road ahead of them, but on the freeway on-ramp to Highway 410, which was itself jammed with cars and trucks, all of which weren't moving very fast, if at all.

"Four-ten's dead stopped—in both directions!" he moaned. "Where do people think they're going?"

"Where did you think *we* were going?" Katy snapped.

"I'm starting to wonder." As the pumice hail roared, Seth gripped the wheel so tightly his knuckles went white. He scowled as he watched the big red pickup force its way back into the line near the on-ramp by threatening to crush a small car if it didn't yield. "You know what would be the worst thing in the world?" he muttered through clenched teeth.

"What?" Katy asked.

"To be buried by a mudflow in a traffic jam, and preserved that way for all time."

"Don't talk like that!" Katy gasped, with her eyes going wide. "You're scaring the children." It was clear from her tremulous tone he was scaring her too.

"We're already scared," Noah piped up from the back seat.

Seth growled, "You'll be a lot more than scared if we don't figure a way out of this."

"But what can we do?" Katy cried. "Maybe the mud won't come this far."

"I'm not sticking around to find out." Seth cranked the steering wheel, gunned the engine, and pulled out of the line of cars.

"Are you going to do what that man did?" Katy cried, pointing at the pickup, which was still only halfway merged with dead stopped traffic ahead.

"No!" Seth said through gritted teeth. He circled around with his tires squealing and rasping on the pumice, and then straightened out going in the opposite direction. Katy looked at him incredulously. "What are you doing?" she demanded. "*The flood* is this way!"

"I'm going back to Pioneer Road."

"That's all the way back by our house!"

"I know it."

"You're crazy! There's a lahar coming!"

"Yeah, but I know a little gravel road that branches off Pioneer Road and goes straight up the bluff. It just goes to a little parking lot on the hillside. But as long as we beat the mud there, we'll be safe."

"And if we don't?"

Seth raced ahead, ignoring her protest. In less than a minute, a green road sign marking the intersection with Pioneer Road appeared on the right. Seth turned the station wagon onto Pioneer Road, but immediately hit the brakes and skidded to a stop on the pumice. A quarter mile ahead on the straight lane it appeared that a freight train was rolling across their path. But just as Seth was about to remark that he didn't recall any railroad tracks, a realization struck him with hair-raising certainty—*this was no freight train*. This was a stupendous mudflow as tall as a line of boxcars, moving like a train running at a fast clip.

"We're cut off!" Katy cried as the kids screamed in unison.

"What are we gonna do?" Noah cried.

Seth shifted the car into reverse and quickly backed into the intersection of Highway 162 and Pioneer Way, pausing there a moment to think.

"What are you waiting for?" Katy cried. "You've got to get back to the freeway!"

"Not to that traffic jam," he muttered. "They're all going to be buried in a minute."

"What about us?" Noah cried.

"I don't wanna die" Amelia cried.

"Shut up! All of you!" Seth clutched the wheel tightly, scowled, and gritted his teeth. His mental wheels spun. He contemplated bad option after bad option. He had stopped the car facing back toward their home. To his rear, the jammed traffic at the freeway entrance waited. To his right, the mudflow across Pioneer Road was surging faster and spreading sideways as well, eating up the ground in his direction. To his left, Pioneer Road continued its eastbound course. He glanced down it, but saw with deepening dismay that a separate lobe of the mudflow had crossed it there as well. That made his choice simple.

"We're going home," he said, stepping on the gas and going forward.

"What?" Katy cried. "You *are* crazy!"

Just ahead of them lay their neighborhood, several dozen recently built houses arranged around cul-de-sacs. Their house was the tallest among them. It rose in the middle of the clustered homes with Seth's turret-like, third-story office visible above the other roofs. A small rise in the land helped make it the tallest structure around.

He pressed the accelerator and the car sped forward, moving past one of the last remaining pumpkin fields in the valley, a normally placid space of green leaves and yellow blossoms, which was now peppered with pumice stones and being inundated on its far side by the encroaching flood. He looked farther up the valley, scanning the distance for signs of the mudflow. Rainier was hidden behind thick billowing dust clouds, lit occasionally by lightning bolts. Its rumble was audible over the sound of the engine. But at least as far up the valley as he could see among the housing developments, there was no sign of the mudflow in the center of the valley. The houses and street trees of the neighborhoods were peaceful despite the mountain rumbling over them and the flood passing by on either side.

As he turned onto the road that S-curved to their cul-de-sac, Katy warned, "I hope you know what you're doing."

"I hope so too."

***

After the initial boom, the air over Lake Washington had returned to its former clear, calm, quiet, and sunny condition. A vaguely formed arcing yellow cloud had appeared on the southern horizon but no other manifestation of the eruption could be seen or heard.

One entire wall of the great room that bordered Bram Boswell's lower deck comprised a set of glass doors that reached from floor to ceiling. The center doors had been pulled aside on gliders to create a wide opening. This allowed guests sitting or standing outside to look in and see the ten-foot-wide TV screen mounted above the elaborate bar. A Mariners baseball game was on. An away game somewhere in the East, it was less than thoroughly engrossing due to a runaway score.

Bram stood on the deck outside the doorway, holding a julep that he had reduced to little more than ice and a couple of mint leaves. "Well, I'm sorry to see you leaving," he said to two guests, a husband and wife who had been on their way out when he stepped in front of them. She had her purse slung over her shoulder and a shawl intended for night air tucked under her arm. Boswell stood as if he might try to physically restrain their exit through the great room.

"We have relatives who live near the mountain," explained the man, who looked like an up-and-comer, well groomed and dressed in high-end tennis attire. "We couldn't get through on the phone, so we need to go check up on them."

"Oh, that little old dust cloud ain't gonna hurt no one," Boswell said dismissively. His self-assuredness was born more from his desire not to lose his party crowd, than from any real knowledge or conviction. He paused a moment to eye the broadening cloud on the southern horizon.

"We'll be going, just the same," said the wife. She side-stepped Boswell and walked swiftly across the room, making for the door that led to the front parlor and the way out. Her husband followed, tossing back a quick goodbye wave.

"You're sure, now?" Boswell called after them. "The Sea-hawks' preseason game is about to start. I was just going to switch the channel. It's a gonna be a replay of the Super Bowl."

"No, thanks," the husband said as he followed his wife through the far door. "Bye."

Honey joined Bram. "Maybe we should let people watch the news. Everybody's asking what's going on."

"All right, all right, Honey. If people would rather watch the dang news than what might be the best pre-season game ever, I suppose I gotta let 'em."

He looked up again at the cloud. A new and much larger mushroom cloud had risen out of the first, dissipating cloud, and was vaulting higher into the stratosphere by the second. Although Rainier itself had never been visible from his deck due to distance and the intervention of a tree-topped shoreline, the huge cloud was more than making up for that absence this afternoon. "Folks!" he called loudly to the partygoers on his deck. "I apologize that y'all can't see the whole mountain from here. But you can see plenty of fireworks in the sky. Looks to me like this show is just getting good."

As if in reply a bolt of lightning crackled across the cloud from one side to the other. There was a smattering of applause and a few shouts of approval.

"Now, by popular demand, I'm gonna turn on the news inside."

There were a few catcalls of disappointment in response.

"So y'all can watch the fun inside, or outside, however you please. Now, may I suggest y'all get another mint julep? We've got a ringside seat to the greatest disaster ever!"

"Honey!" he murmured smugly, turning to his wife. "Do I know how to throw a party, or what?"

"You certainly do," she agreed. And then she glanced up at the cloud with the faintest hint of worry in her big, beautiful eyes.

He looked at the cloud too. But he wore a broad grin. He raised both his hands high like a football referee signifying a touchdown—with his drained drink in one hand. He cried out joyously, "Thank you, Lordy!"

***

"Are you okay?"

"No."

"Me neither." Andy had risen from the place where he had fallen—or rather, had been tossed by the blast from the mountain—and crawled on hands and knees to where Lexi was groggily rising from a drift of volcanic dust that had partially covered her. She sat up and for a long moment they each strained to recover their senses. Above them, hidden by a sky-enveloping cloud of ash, the mountain rumbled and roared at near-deafening levels. Andy felt himself over for injuries and strains, of which there were many, but none crippling or life-threatening. Lexi did the same. Caked dust fell off their heads, both of which bore bloody scratches and frizzes of partially singed hair.

"How did we survive that?" Lexi asked.

"I think the pyroclastic flow parted over the peak of Burnt Mountain. It broke to either side of us. Otherwise, we'd be—"

"Cooked?"

"Uh huh."

They sat still for a long moment, both choked with ash and dizzy from fumes. Meanwhile, the mountain continued to roar.

"What are we going to do?" Lexi eventually asked.

"I don't know."

The force of the blast had tossed them into a low wet area, an old ditch on one edge of the logging yard. Not far from them, sitting on the brink of the ditch, was a long metal lock box of the kind pickup-truck owners use for securing tools in the rear area behind their cabs. This box was shut with a padlock, and so had not attracted much attention from them previously. Now Lexi pointed at the dust-covered box. Stenciled on it from one end to the other in large red letters was the word EMERGENCY. "I wonder what's in there?" she asked.

Andy rose and, moving as quickly as he could on banged-up legs, went to where the camp's tools were laid out. He dug into the layer of ash and pulled up a heavy mattock with a pick on one side of its head and a perpendicular adze blade on the other. He went to the lock box and leveled a full-force blow at the hasp holding the padlock in place. A solid hit sent out sparks. The hasp and lock flew away.

Lexi tottered to her feet and lifted the box's lid.

"Oh. My. God!" she said.

***

When Seth Johnson drove into the cul de sac, it was deserted. Several neighbors had left garage doors open in their haste to evacuate. Seth had done the same. As he rolled toward the garage he said, as if trying to convince himself, "Our house is the tallest in the neighborhood. We'll be as safe here as anywhere we can get to."

"Or unsafe," Katy chided.

"Oh my gosh!" Amelia cried, pointing out her side window. "Look!"

The street that had brought them to their cul-de-sac, like many streets in new housing developments, snaked through the subdivision in an irregular winding S-curve, and so vanished among the neighboring houses not far behind them. What Amelia saw that made her cry out was a strange movement of the roof of one of the farthest visible houses. Viewed between the roofs of two nearer houses, it seemed to twist and then crumple, and then it vanished completely. At the same time, an awful scraping, grinding, crunching sound became audible. As the noise grew in volume, the two nearer houses both shuddered and began to collapse. And then the dark front of a massive mudflow rounded the curve of the street no more than one hundred feet away from the idling station wagon. As the Johnsons watched, wide-eyed, the lahar quickly grew into a wall of mud and debris twenty feet tall, carrying on its front a tangle of massive forest logs and the wreckage of crushed houses.

Noah screamed a long, high-pitch shriek.

Amelia cried, "Dad! I don't want to die!"

"We're trapped!" Katy cried. "What are we going to do?"

Grim-faced but silent, Seth gunned the engine and raced the wagon inside the garage. He slammed on the brakes and screeched to a halt just short of hitting the furnace and water heater.

"Everybody out!" he shouted.

"We've got to get away from here!" Katy shouted back at him.

"It's already too late. We can't outrun it. Everybody upstairs, quick!"

"Houses are being crushed!" Katy screamed, but she opened her door as he had demanded. The other doors flew open and parents, kids, and animals spilled out. Katy rushed and opened the inside door and Bella raced past her into the house. Amelia had opened the transport cage door and Darwin bolted inside after Bella, yowling in terror. Noah followed, carrying Iggy in his cage.

Katy punched the garage door closer button and as the door began to descend, Amelia paused to look at it. "Yeah, Mom!" she said. "Like that's gonna help."

Outside the closing door, the lahar loomed, a wall of gray mud now only fifty feet away and advancing rapidly toward them, studded with whole tree trunks, a section of someone's roof, and even an abandoned car. It inundated the sedate rockeries and landscape plantings lining the cul de sac as it surged toward the lowering garage door.

Seth shook himself from a mesmerized pause and shouted, "Everybody upstairs! All the way up to my study! Quick!"

Shaken from their own trances, Amelia and Katy turned and rushed inside with Seth on their tails. As they raced up the staircase with animals sprinting ahead of them, Noah, who had gone ahead, stumbled and lost his grip on Iggy's cage. The lid came off and the lizard spilled out. He leaped away and ran *down* the stairs.

"Iggy!" Noah cried, turning to go after him, but Seth immediately swept him up in his arms and carried him upstairs. "Iggy!" Noah cried over his shoulder.

"Forget the lizard!" Katy cried. "We've got bigger problems!"

"My study is the highest part of the house," Seth shouted above the growing roar of the lahar. "If anyplace can stay above this flood, it will."

They quickly reached the bedroom level on the second floor, and then continued up a second staircase that led to the study.

The Johnsons' house was a generally square structure with multiple gabled roofs and the study topping them as a third story of a wide and solidly built home. As the family rushed up the steps and entered Seth's workplace, they got a commanding view of the neighborhood through the octagonal room's six windows, and they were aghast at what they saw.

Everywhere were the wrecks of houses that had collapsed under the force of the advancing lahar. Some houses had gone down sideways. Some had collapsed from within. But all were in ruin. The Johnsons' was the last house standing thanks to its location on a rise of slightly higher ground. The family looked out one window and then another, watching houses on every side disintegrate. Finally, there was nothing to look at but encircling wreckage and flowing mud on all sides, under a hail of pumice pebbles raining down from the darkening sky.

That encirclement, and their higher location, paid a dividend. The flood could be heard grinding on the house, but it didn't knock the house over because it was crushing in from all sides at once. Everyone in the office shouted or screamed in terror as the crunching, grinding mass of the lahar thundered against their sanctuary. The floor of the study shuddered underfoot, lurching first in one direction, and then another as the first-floor walls buckled and broke and the flood entered the lower levels. Books cascaded from Seth's office shelves. His computer slid off the big oak writing desk and tumbled onto the carpet. Guest chairs overturned—and people and animals were jostled and thrown to the floor along with objects clattering from the desk and shelves. A window shattered. Mercifully, the glass fell outward.

And somehow, through it all, the top story of the house remained intact and above the deluge.

PART FOUR

MELTDOWN

CHAPTER 16

The news film crew and a female reporter had returned to the tower conference room. They were preparing for a live report with the mountain as a backdrop. Near them, Howard Gage was staring through one of two large telescopes that had been set up by the windows to allow delegates to observe the mountain. He had zeroed in the powerful scope's circular view on one of the lower slopes that remained visible at the base of the billowing monster the mountain had become. On the slope, he could see flows of muddy water—flows of stupendous size and depth, cascading over what had been the Carbon Glacier.

"My God!" he murmured. "It's the Osceola Flood all over again. But worse."

"Don't say that," Governor Long, who had paused a cellphone conversation and held the phone against her chest, said to Gage. "I just heard you lecturing this crowd this morning about the Osceola Flood. It washed over all of the Puyallup River Valley and most of the Duwamish River Valley, correct?"

"Correct. But that was a *prehistoric* flood."

"And now we've got the industrial parts of Tacoma and Seattle in those valleys."

"Correct again," he said, more grimly this time.

The Governor's face paled and her eyelids fluttered momentarily as if she might pass out. She raised the cell phone, on which she had been conversing with the Commander of the Emergency Operations Center at Camp Murray, and said, "General, I'll call you back." She clicked off the phone and stared out at the mountain. "This is beyond belief!" she murmured.

"Believe it," Gage said. "The entire top half of the mountain is gone. Nothing like that happened in the Osceola event—or Mount Saint Helens. This lahar might be a hundred times bigger."

"Don't say that," the Governor pleaded, covering her face with her hand.

"I think he just did," said Rudy Jones, who was standing near them. "And I've got more bad news."

The Governor shook her head, keeping her hand over her face as if she had no more room in her head for distressing words.

"I reviewed the status of the Volcanic Emergency warning system in those valleys, just last night," he said.

"And—?"

"And beyond the immediate vicinity of Mount Rainier, it's— well—"

"It's non-existent," Gage completed his thought for him.

Long removed her hand from her face and stared hard at Gage. "Is that true?" she demanded. "Is there no way to get a warning out? No evacuation sirens? No police patrols?"

Gage shook his head. "Not over an area as wide as that."

"Radio and TV announcements?" she glanced at the film crew.

Jones nodded. "The Emergency Broadcast System has been making announcements on all channels ever since the first explosion. I already double checked on that."

"That's something, anyway," Long said.

"Yes, but—" Jones said, pausing for emphasis. "Those broadcasts were never intended to handle this large an emergency. As far as I know, they have only been warning people to keep away from the mountain and evacuate low areas nearby. There's no contingency to deal with an eruption of this size."

"So, what are we supposed to do?" Governor Long's face had recovered its color and had begun to take on a puffy and purplish look, far beyond anxiety.

"What *can* we do?" Gage said, turning to the telescope again, "except watch and wish it wasn't happening?"

"Don't say that!" the Governor exclaimed.

"I think he just did say it," Jones muttered. "But what about these news reporters? They can help you get the word out."

"Of course!" she said. She raised a hand to get their attention, and then she paused. "But what exactly am I supposed to say?"

***

Inside the emergency box, Andy and Lexi had found forest firefighter equipment. As quickly as their injured bodies would allow, they took out a pair of fire shelters, heat reflective silvery metal insulation-padded blankets, which they laid side-by-side in the wet ditch. Into these, they placed the other great blessings the box had contained: two firefighter air-supply bottles with regulators and facemasks.

"Let's get buttoned into these shelters," Andy called over the roar of the mountain. "But don't turn on your air supply unless you're choking on gas. The air bottle won't last too long otherwise."

"I'm scared," Lexi shouted back as she sat and slipped her legs into the bottom portion of the mummy-like enclosure.

"Me too," Andy replied as he slipped into his own enclosure and began pulling it over his body. He paused and looked at her as she lay back to draw the top of the bag up around her face. Tears had run down her dusty cheeks, leaving black marks. He leaned over and kissed her lightly on one of those tear-streaked cheeks. "Be brave," he said. "No matter what happens."

"I will," she replied. And then she pulled the insulating blanket over her head and began sealing it. He did the same.

As they settled down side-by-side in the ditch, shoulders touching through layers of insulation that separated them, the roar from the mountain increased.

***

Sophie Minto lay back on her sofa, watching TV with her foot elevated. Alarmed by several concussions she had heard outside her windows, she had tuned her TV to a local news channel and watched as ever more horrific reports came in. Now, she was watching a shaky image transmitted by a helicopter that was obviously flying through turbulent air.

"This is News Chopper Twelve," the helicopter reporter called in voiceover. "Man, oh man, do we have a view! Just look at that eruption!"

Sophie gasped and sat up straight as the camera panned across Mount Rainier—or the place where Rainier should have been. The entire mountain had disappeared into a stupendous cloud of billowing ash. She barely had time to utter, "Oh, my God—!" before the screen went blue with the words BREAKING NEWS in the center.

The image switched to Amanda Lee at her anchor desk. She said, "We interrupt to take you live to Columbia Center where Governor Long is about to make a statement—"

The screen went black. The reading light on the end table beside Sophie went dark at the same instant. For a moment she stared at the blank screen in confusion. Then it dawned on her that her power was out. She picked up her cell phone from the end table and tapped her parents' number. She held the phone to her ear and waited through a much longer than normal silence, punctuated by hissing static. Then an announcement came on, starting with an alert tone. "Boo-bah-bee! Your service has been temporarily interrupted. We're sorry for any inconvenience. Please try your call again later."

She stared at the phone in dismay, and then set it aside on the table.

"Now what?" she wondered aloud. Another rumble from the mountain rattled her windows in reply.

***

At that moment, Governor Long was addressing the camera in

the tower conference room and speaking into a young male reporter's hand-held microphone.

"I've just gotten off the phone with the Emergency Operations Center at Camp Murray," she began. "I told them to declare a full state of emergency in all of Pierce, King, Kittitas, Yakima, and Thurston Counties, as well as a general alert for the entire state. I urge anyone in low-lying areas around Mount Rainier to move to higher ground immed—"

She stopped in mid-sentence when a round of gasps and outcries burst from the delegates, staff, and news-people. All were suddenly transfixed by an unanticipated sight—the clouds enshrouding the mountain were being torn apart by an even more stupendous explosion of gas and dust. The gray-black detonation filled such a large portion of the sky and burst upward so rapidly that rings of flat white condensation-clouds appeared above it as if the very atmosphere were being forced up beyond the edge of space. The entire mountain seemed to have converted into an expanding surge of pulverized stone, ripped through by arcs of lightning that encircled the maelstrom or discharged onto surrounding mountain peaks, which were dwarfed by the size of the detonation.

For a long moment, the conference room was almost silent. The cameraman swung his lens from Long to the expanding cloud. The people seemed to have reached a point of dumb, speechless horror. The windows made the only noise, rattling with sonic boom after sonic boom, generated by hyperspeed gas explosions within the caldera.

The Governor turned and to Jones, who stood a few steps away prepared to give follow-up remarks. "Can this possibly get worse?" she asked him.

"I think it just did." He made an open handed, helpless gesture with one hand. His other hand held a cell phone to his ear. "I just called Camp Murray," he explained, "but—" He touched the hang-up button and dropped the cell phone into a pocket of his white shirt. "Their line has been cut off. I hope nothing... happened to them."

"Impossible," the Governor replied. "They're in a hardened

facility south of Tacoma. I visited it yesterday before I came up here."

Donald Rutledge, who was standing near them at a telescope he had no need to use in order to take in the explosion, remarked, "South of *Tacoma*? I'd say anywhere *near* Tacoma is a bad place to be right now."

"The local power grid probably went down," Jones said. "But they've got their own generators. They'll get communications going again as soon as they can."

The lights in the tower flickered, and then steadied.

"Oh, no," the Governor moaned. "That's the last thing we need right now."

The crowd had thinned considerably since the first eruption. Now, threatened by the prospect of being 72-floors-high in a building without power, most of the remaining delegates began hastily gathering briefcases, putting on coats, and unceremoniously hurrying for the elevator landing.

Long shook her head as she watched them go. "I guess there's no point in their sticking around."

"No," Jones agreed. "I don't think they need any more convincing about how serious this situation is."

Rutledge agreed. "The mountain's done that for us."

***

The new explosion quickly spread a black cloud almost from horizon to horizon above the view windows of Seth Johnsons' study. The hail of pumice stones intensified. But the hail and darkness at mid-day held no horror that could compare to what they were experiencing underfoot. The house—or what was left of it—rocked and shuddered beneath them. Massive crunching sounds came from below as the lahar, which had slowed but had not stopped rising, continued to flow on all sides of them, jostling wreckage and tree trunks against the foundering remnants of their home.

Another window shattered. Through the new opening drifted a pall of volcanic ash bearing the hellish rotten-egg smell of sulfur. Although this new assault on their senses ought to have brought a strong reaction, the kids and Katy had already screamed themselves hoarse, and the dog had barked, and the cat had yowled, until all were emotionally exhausted.

Seth Johnson stood in a wide stance at the desk, steadying himself with both hands on its surface against the lurching motions that kept the others—animals and humans alike— huddling on the floor. He looked out the windows around him, watching a scene of unimaginable devastation. Not a house was standing where minutes before an entire development of suburban homes had filled most of the valley bottom. Somehow, the miracle that had preserved their home while others went down seemed like it might last. "Just maybe," he said above the volcano's rumble, "we might make it out of this okay."

Noah rose from his knees and looked out a window. "Do you really think so, Dad?"

"I hope—" Seth began, but he stopped when a new and more profound shudder went through the house. Beyond the cracked window Noah was looking out, the gabled garage roof, which projected out from the main portion of the house, sagged. And then, emitting horrendous cracking and crunching sounds, the garage twisted and disintegrated before their eyes. Katy and Amelia rose to crouch beside Noah at the window, watching wide-eyed as the garage tore free of the house entirely.

But it quickly became apparent it wasn't the garage that was moving. *The house itself* had torn loose of its foundations. It shuddered heavily under them and rocked sideways with a seasick movement as it began moving with the mudflow. They left the jagged wreckage of the garage behind, sinking in the torrent. As the house joined the movement of the lahar over what had once been a sedate neighborhood, it slowly turned 360 degrees. Born along in a mad surge of gray muck that carried whole trees and portions of destroyed houses, they moved slowly at first. But their crazy ride accelerated when the current that had swept them up merged into the main flow of the lahar, which was coursing down the Puyallup River channel at freight-train speeds. The house was racked with tremors and rocked from side to side, but it did not disintegrate as Seth fully expected it to. Although the first story had effectively vanished in splinters, the multi-roofed second story held together somehow as a unit. And as Seth shot glances on all sides, he could see that the house had become part of an immense raft of moving logs and wreckage. They were buoyed up by a tangle of giant forest trees lodged underneath and around them.

"Don't give up hope!" he called to the others.

A mile north of the Johnsons' neighborhood, an entirely different catastrophe was unfolding. The freeway they had tried to reach, Highway 410, was dead stopped, blocked by traffic accidents in both directions. People had gotten out of their vehicles to talk to fellow drivers, scratch their heads, and look up apprehensively at the spreading black cloud that had been the mountain.

When the leading edge of the lahar appeared to the south of them, there were shouts and screams, but there was little to be done. A few people ran away in hopeless races against a too-rapidly advancing force. Most got back into their vehicles and closed their doors.

As the flow overran the jammed highway interchange, people who had run were borne under. People who had waited in their cars, including the formerly aggressive driver of the large red pickup, were inundated where they sat by a wall of dark gray muck bearing giant logs and the wreckage of previously overwhelmed vehicles. Anything in the path of the lahar was crushed and consumed by its irresistible force. As it surged around and over the interchange, semi trucks on Highway 410—seemingly huge and immovable moments before—were swept up, overturned, and skidded forward by the leading wall of the lahar. One semi smashed into and rode up over another, and the two were propelled at freight-train speed into the traffic-jammed overpass of Highway 162 above 410. The overpass trembled with earth-shaking force and then collapsed into the torrent. Its fragmented pieces were carried away with what remained of the trucks that had brought it down, as well as the vehicles that had been stopped on top of it.

As the front of the surge passed, the once-jammed interchange became just another conduit for the multi-channeled, valley-filling mudflow. Carried on the rolling gray surface of the lahar, fragments of demolished homes careened past the interchange and floated down the valley toward the tidelands and waterfront of Tacoma. Largest among the home fragments was the roof of the Johnson house, still intact and supported on its logjam raft.

***

Chinook 247 flew in clear air, barreling straight for JBLM on a beeline course but trailing black smoke. Below them, the first pyroclastic flow had slowed and dissipated and they had ultimately outraced it. But behind them now, the sky was blackening rapidly from the much larger blast expanding from the new eruption. When the Chinook arrived over the heliport adjacent to the main runway, the new flow-front got there with it. Although the force of the blast had dissipated with distance from the mountain and its winds had declined to buffeting breezes of hot air that stank of sulfur, the stupendous volume of ash it carried was nevertheless a great hazard to the helicopter. By the time Hans pushed the thrust lever down and began to descend, dense, swirling dust had already enveloped the landing pad. Under the circumstances, setting the helicopter down would be a hazardous prospect.

"Chinook 247," McChord tower radioed. "Would not advise landing at this time. Visibility is nearly zero—"

"I see that, tower," Hans interrupted. "But no-can-do. We've gotta land. Got bad engine trouble."

"R— Roger that 247," McChord answered uncertainly. "Land at your own discretion. Over."

Ramon was craning his helmeted head around, side-to-side, and almost backward like an owl. "Madre de Dios!" he murmured. "It's getting black as night!"

"Don't distract me, Ray," Hans said. He gripped the stick carefully, delicately maneuvering to keep the stricken Chinook level in the buffeting wind. Landing lights outlining the heliport were barely sufficient to guide him down. When he was only a few feet off the ground, he hovered for a moment, preparing for the gentlest possible touchdown under the circumstances. At that moment, the left turbine gave a dying shriek and froze up. From the rear of the aircraft came sounds of metal parts snapping and clanking. The aft rotor system seized up completely and the Chinook plummeted.

Fortunately, it didn't have far to fall. It thudded down heavily on its landing gear of two long skis pierced by four rubber tires. It bounced once, tilting crazily as its fore rotor *whup-whupped* unevenly in the volcanic tail wind. Then it settled upright, and intact for the most part.

"Hoo-wee!" Hans shouted, cracking a grin of relief. "That was close!"

"Nice flying!" Ramon exclaimed.

Hans glanced back from the flight deck of the helicopter. Arlen Duffy and Jason Shen, strapped into their seats, had been silent for the entire return flight. Seeing Hans grinning at him, Arlen shook his helmeted head from side to side and let out a long breathy whistle.

Hans turned and keyed his transmitter. "McChord, Chinook 247 is on the heliport. Over."

***

The TV crew in the tower conference room was on standby, waiting while a reporting team elsewhere filed another breaking story. Meanwhile, Governor Long, Rudy Jones, Howard Gage, Don Rutledge, and the reporter were conversing off-camera.

The waiter, DeWayne, went to a telescope and looked through it. After gazing at the mountain briefly, he trained the telescope nearly straight down. "Oh my God!" he cried. "The football stadium is full of people!"

The others moved to the windows and glanced down. They

were momentarily stunned to silence, pondering the awful possibilities.

"CenturyLink Field is *packed!*" DeWayne went on. "The Seahawks are on the field. It looks like they were warming up for the game!"

"The lahar couldn't come all the way here!" Long protested to Gage in disbelief. "Could it?"

Gage looked at her with an expression of deep concern. "The Osceola lahar stopped just short," he said. "But I'm sure this one will be much larger."

"Oh my God!" Long gasped. She turned to one of her support people and demanded, "Get me a land-line connection to the stadium, right now!"

CHAPTER 17

The lower waterways near the mouth of the Nisqually River were placid. Despite the stupendous rumbling cloud filling the eastern view, the slow-flowing river was unperturbed beneath sunlit blue skies.

Jimmy Finch was still puttering with his unresponsive motor. Carlie Hume sat in the bow, nervously keeping an eye on events to the east. "Do you hear something?" she asked.

"I hear a mountain blowing up," Jimmy said without looking up. He was using a small screwdriver to adjust a setscrew.

"There's something else," Carlie insisted. "Another noise."

Jimmy sat back on his plank seat and cocked an ear. In addition to the distant rumble and thud of explosions on the mountain, a new sound could be heard. It was a far-off, ripping, grinding sound that grew in volume as they listened.

"What *is* that?" Carlie puzzled, not willing to accept what was coming.

Jimmy put the cover back on his outboard motor and began fastening it down. He murmured, "It sounds like Dok-webalth, the Transformer, is sending a big change our way."

***

The remnants of the Johnsons' house had floated past the half-submerged town of Sumner, moving with the logjam that simultaneously protected it and threatened to grind it apart. As the torrent proceeded, the house spun slowly around, giving the occupants of the study a changing view of a wide, gray flood that had spread out to span the entire Puyallup River

Valley. The house was borne on the flood over what had been farmland with interspersed mobile home courts, now swept away by the flowing, fuming morass.

None of this interested the Johnsons. What concerned them was the precariousness of their floating haven. As the logjam rode up and over the embankments of a segment of the now-submerged Interstate 5 highway, the house flexed, cracked, and rumbled. When one of the shed roofs of the house— the one that had been over Noah's bedroom—snapped in the middle and tore away from the other roofs, a fresh round of shouts and screams went out from all throats. But the remaining portions of the house held together as it was drawn along, out onto what had once been the mudflats of Commencement Bay but which now was a maze of warehouse buildings, sawmills, smokestack industries, and shipping wharves lining the dredged-and-filled waterways of the river delta.

Concrete box buildings succumbed to the force of the flood and collapsed as the house floated past them. Smokestacks toppled, disintegrating into cascades of red bricks that splashed into and joined the current of mud, trees, stones, and wreckage.

***

Jimmy Finch adjusted the choke on his motor and then gripped the pull-cord handle for another attempt at starting the balking machine. A dozen pulls into it, he doubted the next pull would do the trick. "I think it's flooded," he murmured.

Carlie had kept a sharp lookout upriver while he worked. Now she drew in a deep breath and pointed. "Speaking of floods," she gasped. "Here it comes!"

The first manifestation, beyond the roar and crash that had intensified for several minutes, could be seen among the tops of tall cottonwood trees—not the near ones, but the farthest. One treetop after another shook violently as massive objects struck its base, and then each treetop vanished, going down behind a screen of nearer trees. It was easy to guess what was happening but hard to imagine the scope of a mudflow that could level trees across the entire width of the river delta.

Carlie cried, "Oh my God! Oh my God! Oh my God!" as the front face of the lahar rounded a river bend and came into view. It was a roiling wall of mud-choked water thirty feet tall, in which freshly snapped-off cottonwood trunks bobbed, tumbled, and rolled like twigs. Too huge to be confined by the river channel, it smashed through the forests on either side, toppling tall trees like they were wheat straws. As the torrent of muck and timber approached, Carlie slowly raised her eyes to take in its full height.

Jimmy stood, braced his feet, and pulled the starter cord fiercely, using every ounce of strength in both arms. The cord snapped in two and he tumbled backward over his seat, landing on his catch of fish. But the engine sputtered, fired, and then raced at full throttle. Jimmy scrambled onto his seat and quickly adjusted the choke to settle the engine into a smooth purr. He cast a worried glance at the mudflow, which was a hundred yards away and beginning to loom above them, and then he pulled a lever that popped the motor into gear. He turned to face the bow and twisted the throttle grip on the steering handle, gunning the engine and racing the propeller. With a high-pitched buzz, the little dinghy took off in what seemed a vain attempt to outrace the rumbling torrent at their stern. The bow rose high as she accelerated, then came down and leveled out on smooth water ahead. Jimmy had to steer a curving course along the channel, and he glanced back nervously as the lahar steadily gained on them, surging onto the grassy flats of the tidelands. Soon, it formed a long front of cresting muddy water arcing from one side of the delta to the other, several miles away.

By the time the dinghy passed the estuary mouth and entered the open waters of Puget Sound, the lahar had caught up to them. Water at the base of the flood face was rising to meet it, and the stern of the dinghy was lifted on this slope. Now, in addition to the forward drive of the engine, the little boat raced downhill like a surfboard, with the crest of the lahar towering not behind it, but overhead. There was a deafening roar as roiling muddy water curled over and cascaded down the face of the mudflow, carrying splintered tree trunks that plunged on either side of them as the little boat sped on.

Jimmy struggled to steer a straight course out into the Sound. He handled the tiller gingerly, knowing that to be swept sideways by an eddy would mean rolling over and disappearing into the deluge. But the little Boston whaler's upturned stern and bow rode the face of the wave gamely at speeds the little buzzing motor could never have made on its own.

Carlie watched it all in silent terror, looking back from her seat in the bow. She gripped her seat plank with white-knuckled hands and stared up at the lahar, certain it was about to bear them under. But the moment of disaster never came. As the lahar surged into the open, deep waters of Puget Sound, it gradually sank into the depths and passed *under*, not over them. As the flood settled, its roiling face calmed and it became a smooth, giant swell that the little dinghy rode up and over like a roller-coaster car gliding over a summit. The surge moved beyond them and transformed into a tidal wave—a widening ring of smoothly rolling water about twenty feet tall. The wave no longer carried mud or debris with it. The detritus was left behind, swirling around the dinghy on flatter but still turbulent waters. Big tree trunks and with roots and branches still attached, which had tumbled so terrifyingly moments before, now bobbed placidly in the water around them.

Carlie and Jimmy stared in dumb amazement at the tidal wave that was leaving them behind. Where it moved along the shorelines to the north and south, it rose into roaring walls of white water that ripped down forests and annihilated houses built close to the beaches.

Jimmy throttled the motor back but kept it putt-putting, not wanting to go anywhere as much as to maneuver around dangerous snags and bobbing logs jostling in a strong current that was propelling them into the center of the Sound. Jagged wreckage of homes swirled around them, as did a few small icebergs—snowpack carried all the way from Rainier. Jimmy kept busy steering clear of harpoon-like jagged branches or clashing pairs of giant logs.

"How did we survive all that?" Carlie wheezed, catching her breath but scarcely believing she was still alive.

Jimmy shrugged and smiled at her. "Just dumb luck, I guess."

***

After trying vainly to call her parents several times, Sophie set the phone aside. "What am I going to do?" she murmured. "I don't have all that much food here."

A low, rumbling sound had been growing for some time. Mystified, she got up gingerly from the couch and used her crutches to go to a window. She pulled back the curtain—and suppressed a scream. Outside, a huge gray cloud of dust was swallowing her neighborhood. Frozen in place, she watched it overwhelm distant rooftops, barreling closer at a terrific rate. She wanted to tear herself away from the window and rush to some safe place. *But where would that place be?* Stunned, she watched the cloud engulf houses on her block one-by-one, and then swirl into her yard and overrun her window. Its impact on the glass was softer than she expected—only a gentle *whoomp!* Somewhere overhead, the wooden frame of the house creaked. The cloud had dissipated energy on its way from the mountain and had become just a strong gust of wind. But that wind brought with it copious ash, and Sophie could see nothing whatsoever outside except gray billows. She heard a constant patter as sand-sized grains of ash tapped against the window glass. She noticed he curtains on the other side of the room rustling at the bottom, where she had earlier lifted the sash to let some air circulate.

"Oh my God!" she cried, hobbling across the room on her crutches and quickly pulling the window down, though not before a huge dredge of ash got in and spread onto the carpet, graying it over much of the small living room. Along with the ash, something else came into the house—a sulfur-and-brimstone smell that quickly pervaded the room.

"Oh my God!" she cried again, fearing the smell was a harbinger of suffocation and looking around to make certain no other windows were open. Her mind reeled in shock. She began to tremble so violently that she could barely get herself back to the couch. She sat down, quaking with emotion and fearfully eyeing the translucent curtains. Outside them, daylight fled at an incredible pace. The unlit living room quickly dimmed to twilight darkness.

She eased her injured leg onto the hassock, and then laid her head back on the couch. She stared at the ceiling, above which the rafters creaked under the strain of buffeting winds and falling ash. Her chin quivered and she fought to control it.

"What am I going to do?" she murmured. "What *can* I do?" She began to weep softly.

***

The Johnson home—or what was left of it—was still moving swiftly on a current of mud and debris. A dense cloud of ash darkened the sky, smelling of sulfur and amplifying everyone's terror. The hail of pumice stones had moderated somewhat, but was continuing. As they watched, wide-eyed with fear, an anomalous apparition loomed out of the dusty clouds and towered above them: the huge electronic billboard of the Puyallup Indian Tribe's Emerald Queen Casino had somehow retained its electrical power. Rimmed by flashing green argon lights, its screen flashed images of happy gamblers holding up their winnings. As the Johnsons gazed at it, stupefied by its incongruity to the cataclysm surrounding them, the logjam on which the house rode struck the billboard's uprights. Suddenly the sign—perhaps eighty feet tall—was toppling toward them. Screams and shouts burst from every throat as the sign tumbled down, clipping one side of the house as it crashed into the flood. Its impact tore away another of the roofs that ringed the study and shattered the remainder of its windows. A portion of their logjam raft separated and floated away.

The entire roof tilted crazily as the sign tugged at one side of it. Mud sloshed in on that side until the heavy sign sank, leaving no trace other than a whirlpool eddy in the black water. Under them, the logjam rumbled, adjusting to its smaller dimensions. Their haven rocked dizzily from side to side as massive logs jostled into new positions in the tangle. Seth was knocked off his feet by the mad heaving of the room. He fell near where the others huddled with their backs against a low wall below one of the missing windows. He crawled to join the muddied trio, and Amelia threw her arms around his neck.

"Daddy, I love you!" she cried as gray gritty water splashed over them.

"I love you too, dear," he answered in a voice made raspy by searing sulfurous fumes that stank like hell on earth. He hugged her tightly.

From out of nowhere, Iggy the iguana appeared. He scurried across the muddy floor, climbed up Noah's arm, and then jumped off his shoulder and clambered up onto Seth's head.

"Taking the high ground are you, Iggy?" Seth asked with the briefest of smiles.

Suddenly, with a horrific crunching and rending sound, a huge muddy tree root rammed through the wall opposite them and projected three feet inside the room. There were more screams and shouts, and Iggy, as startled as the rest of them, jumped to a window ledge and vanished outside.

"Iggy!" Noah cried, reaching after him.

"Let him go!" Seth restrained the boy from following. "Maybe he can save himself."

"What about us, Dad?" Noah asked.

"Just hang on, son."

"To what?"

Seth reached out his free arm and put it around Noah's shoulders. "To each other."

He hugged both kids tightly and Katy joined in a four-way embrace. Darwin shivered in Katy's lap, and Bella nuzzled in to make it a six-way communion of fear and desperation.

***

"There they go!" DeWayne exclaimed, keeping an eye to a

telescope focused down on CenturyLink Field. "The Seahawks are leaving the field. So are the other guys. The crowd is starting to go out now, too. Wow. Look at them jam the exits. It'll take them forever to get out."

"And forever to drive out of the parking lots and garages," murmured Rudy Jones, who stood near the windows with Donald Rutledge, Howard Gage, and Governor Long.

"They don't *have* forever," Gage said firmly. He was looking through a scope too, but his was leveled in the direction of the mountain—or the stupendous boiling cloud of dust where the mountain had been. "I can see the lahar in the Kent Valley. It's huge and it's coming this way—fast!"

"Oh, my good Lord," said the Governor, who had just concluded a call with the Emergency Operations Center at Camp Murray, which was already sending out alerts to all TV and radio stations in the state via VHF radio link and internet communications. She stood at the window, looking down at the packed stadium and wringing her hands. "How much time do they have?"

"Minutes," Gage replied. "Maybe ten, maybe twenty."

"But that's impossible," Long said shakily. "Most of them won't even get to their cars by then."

"Probably not," Gage agreed. Then, choking with emotion, he said, "This volcano isn't playing by the rules. It didn't give us enough warning! Not for something as catastrophic as this!"

"I just had a thought," said Rutledge. "What if people stayed in the stands? They'll be high enough for safety, right Howard?"

"Er, yes," Gage responded. "If the stands don't fall down."

Everyone shared looks of shock.

"Will they?" Jones asked.

"I don't know," Gage replied. "Your guess is as good—"

"Get me that phone again!" Long interrupted, speaking to her aide. "I'm going to tell the stadium folks to get people to the highest parts of the stands."

"Good plan," Jones agreed. "If the announcers can get them turned around—and if the stadium can take the flood."

"I'll gamble on that," said the Governor as the aide brought her the landline.

While she carried on a terse conversation with the management of the stadium, Jones, Gage, Rutledge, and DeWayne continued looking out the windows through scopes or with the naked eye.

"Oh, my gosh!" DeWayne exclaimed. "There's a big jet landing at Boeing Field. Why would they want to go there now?"

Jones explained, "We've been using it as an emergency-preparedness transport center. We've got all kinds of military jets and heavy cargo planes going in and out of there. I hope they're ready for this!"

"I don't know." Gage swung his scope in that direction. "Nobody's lined up for takeoff. And, jeez! There are dozens of planes on the ground!"

"Oh my God," Long murmured, covering the phone receiver with a hand. "My airplane is on the ground there too, with the crew standing by. They'll be killed!"

***

Southcenter Shopping Mall, the largest in the Puget Sound area, was visible to the people in the tower only as a distant series of off-white, boxy buildings sprawled where the Kent Valley connected to the Duwamish River Valley. It hadn't aroused a significant level of concern among the observers simply because other even more grievous dangers had kept it out of anyone's thoughts.

But on the mall's multi-story enclosed promenades and in scores of shops and department stores, throngs of weekend shoppers strolled, carrying filled shopping bags or going from store to store searching for items to buy. Most were aware that Mount Rainier was erupting, but in the absence of any warning beyond earlier local TV and radio advisories to avoid the vicinity of the mountain, there had been little perceived reason to disrupt their Sunday errands and shopping. In fact, the crowd was unusually dense, perhaps drawn by a need for supplies related to the threat from the volcano. But the shoppers stopped in their tracks when muzak playing in speakers overhead abruptly ceased and a frantic young woman's voice came on the public-address system. "Attention shoppers! Attention shoppers! Mount Rainier exploded…big time! Really big, this time! You are not safe here. Get to your cars. Please hurry. And… have a nice rest of your day!"

The microphone clicked off and—incredibly, given the pandemonium of concerned and fearful cries echoing in the promenades—the muzak resumed its insipid, sedate toodling.

Shoppers and shopkeepers alike rushed out of stores to join swelling throngs of people hurrying for the exits. Women shrieked. Babies wailed. Young, long-legged men sprinted and dodged through the crowds, passing slower runners or bowling them over in their haste.

Outside, a Tukwila Sheriff's Department SUV moved swiftly through a parking lot. The officer called over his loudspeaker, "Everyone must evacuate immediately! A lahar is approaching this mall. Repeat. Everyone must evacuate the area immediately! Go to higher ground!" Having completed a circuit of the mall and fulfilled his duty, he turned into an exit lane and raced forward. But he immediately slammed on his breaks and screeched to a halt just short of rear-ending a car in front of him, which was stopped at the back of a traffic jam that had flared up since the officer's first announcements on this side of the mall. Ahead of him, cars were stopped in long lines stretching out the mall exit and into the maze of neighboring streets, which in turn were gridlocked tightly by hundreds if not thousands of cars. And to the south, the horizon was lost in a stupendous billowing black cloud that stretched halfway across the sky.

Like many other major shopping malls, Southcenter was surrounded by clusters of furniture stores, restaurants, hardware stores, bookstores, kitchen-and-bathroom stores, and dozens of other businesses occupying boxy buildings in strip malls or standing alone in parking lots that now were jammed with the cars of people all trying escape at once. Here and there, collisions punctuated the scene, where adrenaline-maddened drivers had run amok with their accelerators floored only to halt in tangles of bent metal and shattered windshield glass. Over it all roared a pandemonium of honking horns. But above that noise was another more ominous sound—a distant grinding, crunching, rumbling sound that grew in volume until it drowned out even the loudest blaring horns.

Then the maker of the noise appeared. The lahar was twenty-five feet tall. Forcing its way among the boxy buildings, it rolled over lines of cars with freight-train speed, inundating the traffic jam as a whole, flattening lines of cars beneath a torrent of thick mud and debris torn from buildings. People were borne under by the hundreds, whether they sat inside their vehicles or opened their doors to jump out and run a few paces before being overtaken.

Inside the mall, terrified shoppers rushed one way or another, unaware of the tragedy outside—and trying ironically to join it. When the surge of mud, debris, and wrecked cars burst through the wide glass doors at one end of the ground-floor promenade, it immediately consumed the nearest people. Then it swept forward to claim more victims as shrieking mall-goers ran madly for safety that was not to be found. Everyone who had not retreated up the escalators or stairs to the second story, regardless of their age or social station, was borne under by a sloshing wall of churning muddy water that showed mercy to none—while the muzak played on serenely overhead.

***

At Boeing Field, the Governor's airplane was indeed standing by. The Beechcraft Super King Air twin-engine aircraft had landed minutes before after a short hop from Olympia on a round trip to retrieve her to the capital when the day's meeting concluded. In the flight cabin, Washington State Patrol Special Services pilot Gil Claymore put a handset to his mouth.

"Ground Control, could you repeat? I did not copy your last communication. Over."

Just after the plane had touched down and taxied to its current position beside the runway, there had been a frantic call over the radio. It had been brief, unintelligible, and crackling with static. Officer Claymore stared hard at the tower windows. They glittered with a green anti-glare reflective surface, but what anyone might be doing inside was unclear.

He had been startled by the radio outburst, but Claymore was even more vexed by the lack of a follow-up reply. The newly landed cargo jet taxied near the terminal building, but halted short, awaiting ground personnel who had mysteriously vanished.

"Ground Control—" he started to repeat, but stopped when his copilot Trip Reed gripped his arm and pointed off to the right.

"Look there!" Reed exclaimed. "Is that—?"

"It sure is," Claymore said. "It's a lahar!"

In the community to the south of the airstrip, a flood of gray muck and debris was surging between, around, and in some cases through blocks of business buildings and streets busy with cars and trucks.

The King Air was parked perpendicularly to the south end of the runway, where Claymore had just pulled it in to await the Governor's arrival. Fortuitously, he had not yet shut down the twin engines and the big turbines were still running at idle.

"Boeing Tower!" Claymore radioed frantically. "Can you clear us for immediate takeoff? Come in, Tower. Come in—"

"Get us out of here!" Reed yelled.

Claymore dropped the handset and grabbed the control wheel and power levers. Quickly advancing the turboprops' thrust, he used his rudder pedals to steer the aircraft toward the end of the runway. Meanwhile, the lahar surged from between crumbling buildings to the south of the airport and poured onto the periphery of the field, knocking down a razor-wire cyclone fence like it wasn't there and coming at them with seemingly impossible speed.

For those viewing the unfolding catastrophe from the Columbia Center, the horror developed in what seemed to be slow motion. They had watched aghast as the lahar surged into the upper Duwamish Valley and moved toward them, mowing down trees and buildings. Now, as it overwhelmed the south end of Boeing Field, Governor Long cried, "I think that's my plane, right there!"

On the main runway, a lone, small, white aircraft was making a 90-degree turn at the south end of the tarmac. It rolled forward with what seemed excruciating slowness as the lahar front closed in on it. Nearby, the just-landed cargo jet was making a similar turn for the takeoff line.

The Governor stood with her forehead against the window, her face ashen. She clenched both fists and called out, "Come on, guys! Get out of there!"

Just as the ragged front of the lahar seemed about to consume the tail of the King Air, the propellers came to full power and the plane raced ahead. Gaining speed quickly, it lifted off, flying north in the direction of the tower. Meanwhile, behind it, the cargo jet was struck on its side with the full force of the flow. It tipped sideways and began to come apart, losing its wings and tail and tumbling on the front of the lahar. The other planes on the ground or standing at the terminal gates were quickly swept up by the lahar, the front of which became a tangle of fuselages, snapped-off wings, tail fins, and other wreckage.

As the King Air rose and sped out over Elliott Bay, the Governor cried, "At least *they* got away!"

The aircraft climbed into the safe blue sky to the north and west of them. When it passed the tower and flew on, the observers turned their attention back to the airport. The entire complex had been overrun by the mudflow. The airstrip, terminal, control tower, and other facilities all were gone, knocked flat and drowned in muck and debris.

***

In addition to Southcenter Mall, there were other places where business-as-usual had gone on despite concerns about the volcanic eruption. And in some, business was more brisk than usual *because of* the volcanic eruption.

Such was the case at the huge Costco building located in a sprawling business neighborhood south of Seattle proper, on the long-since-tamed floodplain of the lower Duwamish River.

Last-minute shoppers thronged the place. They swept up armloads of food, clothing, and other goods off shelves and dumped them into oversized shopping carts, which they then pushed to a long battery of cash registers, which had already accumulated long lines of worried, anxious, or angry shoppers. None were yet aware of the dire threat surging toward them.

Over a loudspeaker, a store manager who was also oblivious to what was coming, called, "Please be patient, shoppers. More checkout people have been called and are on their way."

The first inkling anyone had of trouble was when the mudflow rumbled against the concrete walls of the big box store. Quickly thereafter, the glass of the front façade shattered, admitting a towering wall of muck and debris, which overwhelmed the card watchers, tellers, and check-out lines before most even had a chance to scream. Within seconds, a tsunami of mud and debris swept down the merchandise aisles, consuming as it went frantic people running amid rows of discount-priced big screen TVs, tables of cut-rate clothing and books, and dry goods shelves. By the time the surge reached the produce and butcher sections at the back of the store, it filled the entire building halfway to its ceiling. Then the irresistible force of the surge pushed from both inside and out, and the tall concrete walls collapsed, bringing the roof plummeting down into the miasma of stinking mud and debris. Within seconds, the once-imposing building was no more than a set of ripples in the giant flow.

CHAPTER 18

In the tower conference room, there were moments of almost complete silence among those who stood at the windows. Rudy Jones and Governor Long had made numerous cell phone calls to the people and agencies they were concerned with. But in the face of the unmitigated destruction they were witnessing, there were frequent pauses to stand with mouth agape and stare out at the panoramic view of an unimaginable catastrophe unfolding.

As they watched with or without telescopes, the entire flat bottomland of the Duwamish River Valley was inundated, no matter that it was covered everywhere with buildings large and small. The oncoming wall of mud and debris completely engulfed the one-story structures in its path. It smashed old wooden-plank warehouses into matchsticks. It gushed around and between taller concrete and brick structures. Depending on their strength, many of these larger buildings succumbed as well, as one wall or another cracked, buckled, and collapsed into the flow, followed by the other walls and the roofs they held up.

The Interstate 5 Freeway and Highway 99, running north-south on either side of the valley, and the West Seattle high-rise viaduct and bridge running east-west just south of the city, were all jammed with stopped traffic. Although it seemed they must become scenes of mass destruction as well, they actually became the anomalies on this day of horrors. Over most of their lengths, the roadways were elevated on concrete columns sufficiently tall to allow traffic to move underneath them on surface streets on a normal day. Now, those surface streets were inundated, but the traffic stalled on the freeways was above the flood—although just barely.

The Governor murmured, "I hope the earthquake-hardening on those columns holds up." She referred to the retrofitting of every upright concrete support with a thick jacket of steel to harden them against cracking in the event of a major quake. Now, that same hardening protected the uprights from the impact of mud, logs, and debris that were swept into them by the lahar, forming immense debris-jams on the upstream sides of the rows of columns. None of the freeways succumbed, and thousands of people in cars and trucks were safe above the flood, albeit on roadways that now seemed to sit almost on the surface rather than standing tall. Even the lofty gray arch of the West Seattle High-Rise Bridge over the main Duwamish waterway seemed to stand a little less tall—but most importantly it still stood, its top laden with hundreds of cars and trucks.

Having crossed under the West Seattle Viaduct and bridge almost unabated, the flood surged into the city proper, inundating SoDo, the south-of-downtown business district in the same, inexorable way it had drowned the neighborhoods upstream.

"Good luck Starbucks," Don Rutledge murmured as the flood swept against the twelve-story brick-and-mortar building, which had once been Sears Roebuck's main center among the rail yards of old Seattle, but which had been purchased by the coffee giant to become its worldwide headquarters. Now refurbished, it was adorned with Starbucks' green-and-white mermaid logo gracing the old clock tower that rose from the center of its top story.

The group at the windows held its collective breath as mud and debris swirled on all sides of the building, flattening or obliterating smaller businesses on the street corners surrounding it. Kitty-corner to the inundated Starbucks parking lot, the single-story L-shaped warehouse where Amazon.com had gotten its start was overtopped and submerged by the flow. But as the flood surged onward, it became clear that the much taller and more substantial Starbucks building would withstand it—although the green argon lights outlining the mermaid logo flickered and went out.

The lahar advanced until the tower observers were looking nearly straight down. It became clear that Safeco Field and CenturyLink Stadium would not be spared. The surrounding parking lots were swept under quickly, including jammed lines of cars that simply vanished into the lahar's muddy depths. Within the stadiums, whose baseball-diamond and gridiron fields were visible to the watchers in the tower, the mud surged onto the playing fields—long since devoid of players—from all sides, rising like gray tides of muck that inundated row after row of seating. First to go were the high-priced field-side seats, whose occupants had long since scurried higher into the stands or gone to their deaths in the parking lots. As the deepening muck engulfed ever-higher rows, it forced back huge numbers of fans who had heeded the announcers' calls not to evacuate, but who now found themselves crowded high up in the already packed cheap seats.

"Come on stadiums," Long murmured. "Hold together—please!"

***

Inside CenturyLink Stadium, high in the nosebleed section among the cheapest seats of all, people were packed shoulder-to-shoulder, jamming the aisles and walkways between the rows of seats. Given that there was nowhere to go, the panicky crowd had little to do but try to keep calm and wait, knowing that either death would overtake them where they stood, or they would survive. The stands rumbled underfoot, as they did in the heat of a game when thousands of fans, collectively known as the Twelfth Man, deliberately stamped their feet to make noise. But today the rumble was produced by the lahar's load of debris scraping and crunching against the stadium's walls at street level.

"Gosh!" called out one little boy held in his father's arms

on a walkway between rows—a boy too young to understand the significance of the danger they faced. "Is that who I think it is?"

The father looked up at the row just above them, where a fully suited and helmeted Seahawk stood among the crowd. "Yeah," the father said. "That's our quarterback."

The quarterback was glancing around the stadium as if he were searching for someone. The scowling intensity of his eyes softened when the boy called him by name. He looked down at the father-son pair and smiled, partly to ease any anxiety the boy felt. He leaned down and stuck out a big hand, and shook hands with father and son in turn.

"I—" the father stammered. "I wish we could have met under better circumstances."

"Me too," the quarterback said. He straightened up again but still smiled at the kid's gob-smacked expression. He raised his left hand and looked curiously at what it held. Through all that had transpired, he had reflexively clutched a football the whole time. "Here!" he said, lightly tossing the football to the kid. "I don't think I'll need this today."

"Wow!" the kid exclaimed, catching the ball and holding it in both arms. "I'll never forget this day!"

"No," the quarterback replied with a rueful smile. "I'll bet you won't."

Their exchange complete, all three turned to look out over the stadium. The mudflow had risen quickly but now seemed to have crested at a depth of about twenty feet, which filled the playing field and much of the lower stadium level. Above, the stands were jammed with desperate, terrified humanity.

The father said, "I think maybe most of the people got away."

"I sure hope so," the quarterback replied. "And I see some of my teammates in the crowd."

***

The group in the tower had lapsed into mesmerized silence.

"Look at the docks!" DeWayne suddenly cried.

West of the stadiums, beyond a railroad switching-yard, in the eastern waterway of the twin Duwamish River outlets, sat a huge container ship stacked high with rectangular freight boxes. She was the Nagoya Maru, newly arrived with a load of Toyota autos from Japan, tied up with her bow facing upriver. The lahar came at her from in front and one side, rushing simultaneously down the river channel and across the wide, flat, asphalt-paved surface of the container terminal as well. Pushing before it a jumble of rubble, the front of the flow smashed into the giant port cranes that had been unloading cargo from the Nagoya Maru before the weekend had halted their work. Containers able to carry multiple sedans in one box, were stacked ashore for later attachment to trucks that would haul them inland. But these boxes were now pushed under the massive cranes' four tall pillar-like legs by the surge and smashed against the side of the ship—just as the river-borne surge impacted her bow.

The Nagoya Maru snapped her mooring lines and rode up high on the surge. Her bow pitched steeply upward, tossing containers off her decks and into the waterway. She rode over the front of the lahar and smashed down again, but the lahar had struck her at an angle and she didn't return to an even keel. Instead, she heeled over in the direction the surge had imparted. Slowly, against the great resistance of self-righting ballast deep below decks, she hove over sideways, splashing more containers into the roiling waterway. Her starboard list was so severe that she took tons of muddy water over her gunwale and quickly went down on her side, settling half-submerged in the middle of the channel. Around her, her cargo of red, orange, and blue container boxes floated by the hundreds. Most were slowly sinking as water leaked inside their metal seams.

"And, look there!" DeWayne cried again.

The others turned to look farther west, where Coleman Ferry Terminal was located not far from the foot of the tower. The flat asphalt surface of the waiting lot was jammed with cars trying to get across Puget Sound to safety. What may have seemed a good strategy at the sight of the first eruption, now resulted in traffic jam that filled the pier and stretched back into the streets of downtown Seattle. The ferry Spokane had been loading vehicles feverishly, her deck hands frantically waving two lines of vehicles across the metal-plank drawbridge and onto her multiple car decks. But now, as the ferry's captain got a glimpse of the oncoming flood, the Spokane's horn gave three sharp blasts, the signal that she was departing. Black diesel smoke belched from her stacks and she pulled away from the terminal without waiting for the draw-span to lift. This plunged several cars and a truck into the bay just as they were about to reach safety.

But the captain's decision to flee had come late—perhaps too late. As the Spokane was clearing the exit pilings of the dock, the churning lahar swept across the waiting lot, consuming hundreds of cars and trucks, and then surged over the loading ramp and poured into Elliott Bay immediately astern of the escaping ferry. Taking the fleeing Spokane from behind, the surge washed around and over her open-ended car deck, inundating the rearmost vehicles and driving the ferry into a dangerous listing turn that threatened to capsize her. Her stack belched even more smoke as the captain revved the engines fully and steered the ship against the lopsided impact of the lahar. Although she was swept hard sideways and heeled over so far as to dip the starboard edge of her second deck into the Sound, the squarely built ship steadfastly refused to capsize. Her captain at last managed to get her on an even keel as the lahar settled into the deep water of Elliott Bay and became a tidal wave, which smoothed out and rolled under the Spokane.

Rudy Jones put the fingertips of a hand on the window, as if needing to steady himself against the vertiginous height and the sickening view of floodwaters filling the Kent and Duwamish River Valleys from side to side from the dust-shrouded mountain on the horizon to the streets just below the Columba Center. "Do you think that can reach us here?" he asked no one in particular.

"I don't think so," replied Rutledge, who was standing beside him.

"Are you sure?" Jones asked.

"No."

"And look there!" DeWayne cried, pointing further to the west and north.

The lahar front, now transformed into a tidal wave, had begun to sweep out across Elliott Bay as a wide, smooth roller. Where it moved along the shoreline, however, it crested into a ragged and savage thing. It plowed into historic wooden piers and, one after another, reduced them to splintered jumbles of timbers and broken slats. It drove the resulting debris against the huge waterfront Ferris wheel, where a power outage had stranded sightseeing passengers by the score in large gondola cars. Although inaudible from the tower, the screams of people in the gondolas must have been hellish as the wheel was driven down on its side and covered by the wave. Farther north along the shore, a huge white cruise ship, the Alaskan Princess, had been moored lengthwise at Pier 66. She had cast off her lines and was leaving at full steam, showing her stern to the wave. But like the ferry Spokane, she had left too late. She was caught from behind and seemed to surf on the wave front for a time, but then she hooked to port and listed onto her starboard side. Thousands of Alaska-bound vacationers, who had been on deck for a departure party, were thrown around or pitched over the railings into the sound. Deck-top swimming pools produced their own blue tidal waves, which washed other hapless partygoers over the railings. Driven sideways by the power of the wave, the great ship rolled over completely, capsizing and coming to rest upside-down as the wave moved on to the north and west.

"Oh my God!" the Governor murmured. "The humanity!"

"We've got another Titanic on our hands," Jones muttered.

"Or a Poseidon Adventure," Rutledge said, "if she stays afloat."

"Do you think she will?" DeWayne asked. He had begun to tremble with the cumulative adrenaline effects of scene after horrific scene.

Jones put a hand on his shoulder to calm him. "Let's hope so," he murmured.

They stared at the cruise ship, transfixed with horror, until a staffer called from an east-facing window. "There's a tidal wave in Lake Washington too!"

All eyes turned toward the south end of the long lake, where a wave had appeared, similar to the one they had been watching on Elliott Bay. This wave, however, was taller because it was constrained by bluffs on either side. After it had inundated the city of Renton, the lahar had imparted its full energy into the lake.

"My God," the Governor murmured, watching the wave sweep northward. "What will that do to the lakeshore communities?"

***

The full impact of the disaster had not yet registered on some people in Seattle, especially those who were preoccupied with other matters or were in areas where nothing but the billows over the mountain could be seen. One such area was the racecourse of the Unlimited Hydroplane Racing Association on Lake Washington. In preparation for the upcoming Seafair races, a yellow hydroplane was roaring over the surface of the lake on a test run, circling an oval-shaped course marked with floating white buoys. The hydroplane's two-pronged bow crossed the ripples on the lake's calm surface at speeds nearing 200 miles per hour. Inside the jet-fighter-like cockpit, helmeted driver Jerry Gregson gripped the wheel tightly and steered the craft smoothly despite the fierce buffeting he was receiving from the lake, which went past in a blur of speed that amplified any slight imperfection in the water's surface into a jarring obstacle.

Gregson was on the water attempting to set a new course speed record in advance of the Seafair race. His boat, the "Miss

Happy-Go-Lucky," was functioning almost flawlessly. His speedometer registered speeds he himself could hardly believe. One-hundred-ninety-seven miles per hour, one-hundred-ninety-nine. Try as he might, he could not seem to get that extra mile per hour out of his sleek watercraft, which skimmed the lake surface like a cross between a jet fighter and a flying saucer with a hyperspeed propeller driving it at the stern.

"What'd you say?" he called into his helmet microphone. His shore communications man in the racing pits had said something, but it had broken up in static, which seemed particularly heavy. "Say again?" Meanwhile, he kept his eyes focused on the water in front of his twin bows and kept his hands clenched tightly on the wheel. One flinch at these speeds and his boat might roll over or flip end-over-end and disintegrate on impact with the water, which seemed as hard as concrete at these speeds.

As he roared down the straightaway and prepared for the difficult task of cutting a smooth, speed-conserving turn around the south end of the oval, his shore man shouted more words that were again made unintelligible by the static, and by the roar of his mighty piston engine. And then, too late, Gregson saw what his teammate had been hollering about. Coming around the evergreen-tree-lined point of Seward Park peninsula was a stupendous wave—a twenty-foot-high roller in the deep parts of the lake, and a crashing wall of white foam where it was tearing down trees on the point.

He took his foot off the gas pedal but his boat, built of super light materials and flat-bottomed to ride on a cushion of air, continued to skim over the lake at much greater than one-hundred-mile-an-hour speed.

"Ya-ah-ah-ah-ah!" he screamed as his hurtling boat and the giant roller quickly came together. Acting on instinct where no training could have helped him, he straightened out his curve at the last instant and the Happy Go Lucky shot straight at the oncoming swell, meeting the wave squarely. A tremendous jolt shook her as she struck the wave, and Jerry felt her rise quickly and launch into the air from the wave's crest. Incredibly, the well-balanced craft, which bore a horizontal stabilizer wing on her stern, flew like a thrown dart. She corkscrewed slightly but kept her nose pointed dead ahead and her bottom under her. When she inevitably dropped down to the lake's surface again, she hit the flat water beyond the wave with smoothly poised grace—and then skimmed on for another two-hundred yards before she came to rest.

Jerry craned his neck in time to see the shoreward side of the wave crash into the pits. It scattered other race boats— boldly painted in red, blue, white, and Day-Glo orange—like they were balsa-wood child's toys. It washed around three tall cranes that were used to launch the hydroplanes and retrieve them to their trailers. And then it surged up the lakeshore, still heading north.

"You guys all right?" Jerry shouted into his microphone. Among his crew he counted many good friends and more than one family member.

There was a long delay with no reply. Then a breathless voice came over the air. "Yeah! We're all okay. Everybody ran like hell to get up the hill above the pits."

"Great!" Jerry said with relief. And then he asked, "So, did I set a new record or not?"

***

The Boswells and their guests stood in clusters, drinks and plates in hand, on his wide lakeside deck or inside the adjoining bar-and-TV room. The party chatter had fallen silent. They watched the wide-screen TV with expressions of confusion and worry on their faces. Minutes before, the Seahawks pre-game talk show had abruptly stopped and the picture had gone blue. Bram Boswell had taken his channel changer in hand, trying to get the image back. When a new image appeared, it wasn't the talk show. The channel had segued to its local news desk where an ashen-faced anchorwoman read an announcement from a sheet of paper. "Repeating," she said. "This just in from the State Emergency Operations Center—residents are ordered to evacuate all river valleys and lowlands in the Seattle-

Tacoma-Olympia areas immediately and move to higher ground. Mudflows from Mount Rainier are extensive in all valleys surrounding the mountain—"

She paused and turned her head to listen to an off-microphone voice in the studio. And then she turned back to the camera wearing an even more stricken look. "I've just been advised that mudflows have already reached Tacoma and South Seattle."

The anchor sat silently for a moment, as if uncertain what to say next. The screen blanked and then went to blue with the words PLEASE STAND BY written in white letters.

In Boswell's crowd, women put hands to chests. Murmurs raced from mouth to mouth. There were gasps and stifled cries. Someone dropped a drink and the glass shattered.

"Wait a minute! Wait a minute!" Boswell shouted, raising both hands toward the panicky faces all around him. "They didn't say anything about Lake Washington. This here ain't no river valley." As he tried to reassure his guests, his voice lost its self-assuredness. "And— And this ain't no lowland. It's a lake, for Christ's sake. It can't come here. Can it?"

A woman on the deck screamed, and more screams joined hers. Boswell hurried outside and then stopped dead in his tracks. To the south, something was moving on the lake—something huge.

The wave was approaching the Interstate 90 floating bridge, which crossed east-west from Mercer Island to Seattle a mile south of them. The bridge was a gray concrete structure that lay flat on the water. Its wide three-lane roadways were mounted on a smoothly linked series of concrete pontoon floats. Although the bridge was surmounted by a stalled line of cars and trucks, the crest of a monstrous wave was visible beyond it—a smooth, glittering roller of water sweeping toward the bridge with the promise of death.

Boswell watched, mesmerized, until Honey came to his side and grasped his hand. "What is it—?" she asked.

"I don't know."

In a moment of intense shock, any human being's mind will

briefly deny what the eyes clearly see. For the moment, the Boswells and their guests stared in disbelief as the wave reached the bridge. Surging under the pontoons, it lifted the bridge one section at a time, starting at the Seattle side, where the wave was a little farther advanced. As each hundred-foot section of pontoon roadway was lifted in its turn, it tipped sideways and spilled its load of stopped vehicles into the lake. People caught in the dense traffic, dead stopped in both directions across the entire mile-wide span of the bridge, could do nothing except wait as doom approached in a slow-moving string of catastrophes. As each titanic section of the bridge tipped, it broke free of its moorings and floated loose on the lake surface after having jettisoned most or all of the vehicles on its surface. These floated briefly in the water around the pontoons but then sank, bearing their passengers to the lake bottom 200 feet below.

Many bridge sections, with their thick concrete walls breached, began to sink as well. They went down slowly, gushing out founts of white spray on their way to the bottom, starkly sunlit against the black cloud that now stretched entirely across the southern horizon.

Boswell and his guests watched with hardly a sound until the realization of their own peril seized everyone at once. Shouts and desperate screams went up all around the Boswells, and they joined in with terrified cries of their own. In an instant, everyone was running for the doors.

***

A second surge of lahar mud came down the Duwamish River Valley on top of the first, raising the flood to new levels. The small crowd gathered at the windows of Suite 7250 yelled and shrieked as the replenished lahar washed among the bases of the surrounding skyscrapers until it reached the foot of their own tower. As it impacted the bottom levels of Columbia Center, the whole building trembled. Governor Long screamed and men added their cries. Already unnerved, DeWayne let out a high-pitched shriek and turned to Rudy Jones, who happened to be standing beside him, and threw both arms around him. He pressed his face against Rudy's neck, unable to watch the horror of the lahar surging against the base of what had until then seemed an unassailable bastion. Surprised, Rudy hesitated, but then enclosed DeWayne in his embrace. They hugged each other tightly as the stricken building rocked dizzyingly and screams and cries came from all but a few of the bravest souls present.

"It's going to knock this tower down!" DeWayne sobbed. "With us in it!"

"Step back from the windows," someone shouted. "They might break."

Indeed, one floor-to-ceiling pane cracked directly in front of DeWayne and Jones, causing DeWayne to issue another blood-chilling cry. Jones drew the two of them away from the window as the shuddering and swaying of the building reached a magnitude that nearly knocked people off their feet.

"God, help us!" cried Governor Long.

And then the rumbling ceased. The building settled back to its normal, solid, upright configuration. People burst into agitated but relieved conversations. Some cautiously stepped near the windows and looked down again. Among them, Howard Gage called out, "The lahar is receding from the hill! We're safe."

"For now, anyway," someone replied.

Rudy Jones and DeWayne separated slightly, looked into each other's faces, and then hugged again.

Governor Long stepped to the window to reassure herself that Gage was correct. He was. She glanced around at the people nearest her. "I thought it was all over for us," she said, still holding a hand to her chest to calm her pounding heart.

Rudy Jones relinquished his embrace of DeWayne and went to the Governor. "Lucky we chose this place. It's just barely safe enough."

"Unless there is another bigger flow." She turned to Gage. "Do you think that might be possible?"

"I don't know," he said, gazing to the south, where Rainier—or what was left of Rainier—was shrouded in billowing gray clouds. "This is already so much worse than anything we ever dreamed of."

"So, will this be as bad as it gets?" the Governor wondered.

"I can't imagine anything worse," Gage replied.

The lights in the room flickered and then went out.

"And there you have it," Jones muttered. "Things just *did* get worse."

***

The entry road to the Boswell estate was a long stretch of pavement that wound down a bluff that overlooked the mansion. The Boswells and their panicked guests ran past the parking area at the base of the bluff and rushed up the long road, realizing that the seconds required to turn a car around in the crowded parking area would be more time than they had left. They raced uphill on foot, spurred on by the terrifying sight of the rising wall of water coming at them.

As they ran uphill in desperation, the wave hove up as it came into the near-shore shallows, and crested as it reached the mansion. Taller than the three-story structure, the wave curled over and came down on the house with a crashing roar. Substantial though it was, the mansion was no match for the force of the wave. It splintered into wreckage that was immediately swept forward with the wave, which continued uphill bearing a horrific jumble of jagged timbers and splintered plywood on its foreface. People shrieked as they ran, tiring but driving themselves on in hopeless desperation. The wave's energy, however, was far from exhausted. It boiled toward the hapless runners, now strung out on the road's uphill grade according to the length of their strides and their physical endurance. The angry waters engulfed the least fit immediately, sweeping them under a ragged, frothing front of water and debris. Then it rushed farther upslope to overtake the next.

Bram Boswell and Honey ran hand-in-hand, he in the lead

and half-dragging her as she shed one and then the other of her wedge-heeled summer shoes. They fell behind other runners as the wave neared, and he tugged her so hard that her feet came free of the pavement and she went down. Boswell, sometimes a tyrant but a doting husband at the last, turned to her and murmured, "Aw, Honey." He knelt to help her rise, but it was the last move either of them made. As she tottered unevenly to her feet, the wave overwhelmed them and swept them under a wall of froth bearing the wreckage of their home.

As the Boswells died, the wave surged toward the Gates mansion, which was the next in line. Unlike the Boswell home, however, the Gates mansion was built higher on the bluff. The wave ebbed just short of it, although it carried away the beach house and other lower buildings. Then it roared on toward the next house in line, rolling northward inexorably.

CHAPTER 19

The tidelands of the Puyallup River Delta—in ancient times a vast mudflat, in more recent times the realm of business and manufacturing buildings, lumberyards, smokestack industries, and dredged waterways with docks and piers—had been swept clear. It had returned almost to its former state, a flat landscape of mud, studded here and there with low hummocks of debris.

The city of Tacoma proper was located on a hill to the south of, and overlooking, the delta. The main downtown area therefore was relatively unharmed, much like hilly downtown Seattle. But Tacoma lay much closer to Mount Rainier and the ash cloud that had expanded from the third and most devastating explosion had enshroud the tall buildings in thick, choking dust and stinking fumes for the better part of an hour. Immense quantities of ash and cinders had fallen, coating buildings and streets and sidewalks with many inches of gray dust, giving the appearance that a stupendous blizzard had hit the city. Although the air eventually began to clear and anemic daylight reached the ground where almost total blackness had prevailed, ash continued to filter down from above.

Emergency lights were on in just a few of the tall buildings. Most buildings had gone dark and stayed that way.

Near the middle of the newly created mudflat, the multi-gabled roof of the Johnsons' house sat mired in the outwash of the lahar. It had settled in the midst of the desolation, grounded on wreckage beneath it, and washed on all sides by shallow, braided, multi-channeled streams that formed on the surface of the dissipated mudflow. Falling ash and cinders had covered the structure with dust several inches thick. Inside the study, which, through a succession of miracles, had ridden out the flood relatively intact—the family huddled against a wall. As if to emphasize that their troubles weren't over, a log, or part of a building, or some other piece of wreckage moved past in the stream channel outside, sloshing mud through a shattered window. Exhausted and inured to such assaults, no one cried out or rose to see what had been the source of the latest drenching. But the loud cracking of a thick beam somewhere down in the remnants of the house brought a whine from Bella, still cradled in Amelia's lap.

"Don't worry," Seth soothed the shivering dog. "The house is just settling a little."

"I hope you're right," said Katy, who sat beside him holding muddy and miserable Darwin in her arms.

Seth got up and stood on the sloping floor of their cock-eyed refuge and put his hands on a sill. "We're settling down alright," he affirmed. "The worst of the flood looks like it's past. Let's just hope the strain doesn't tear apart what little we have left."

"Oh! Our beautiful new home!" Katy cried. "This—" she choked, "is all that's left."

Noah patted a hand on the mud-spattered wall beside him. "Come on baby," he said. "Hold together."

Seth scanned the landscape, taking in a sight that was both encouraging, because the mudflow and ashfall seemed to have subsided, and terrifying, because the scope of the destruction around him was mind-boggling. Overhead, the ash cloud was thinning, but it still enshrouded the land in twilight. Only a weak greenish rim of daylight glowed on the northwestern horizon. Sheet lightning repeatedly illuminated the interior of the ash cloud with eerie orange flickers.

Katy stood up next to Seth, still holding Darwin. "What are we going to do now?" she asked, stroking the cat's wet, muddied head to calm him.

Seth shrugged. "I don't know."

"Can we walk across that mud?"

"I doubt it. It looks like it might be quicksand."

"So what do we do? Just sit here?"

"I guess so. Maybe someone will come along and rescue us."

"How soon do you think that will that happen?"

"I have no clue."

"We've got to do something. I remember watching the news about Hurricane Katrina. Those people in New Orleans, with all their houses flooded, some of them painted 'Help' on their roofs."

Noah stood up beside Katy and looked out at the nearest gable roof. "Too bad we don't have any paint. Do we Dad?"

"It's in the garage, wherever that is."

"So what can we do?" Katy asked again.

"I've got an idea," Seth replied, "and it just might work!"

***

Inside CenturyLink Stadium, as the roar of the second flood subsided, the crowd began to murmur. The stands were filled with a low rush of sound reminiscent of the reaction to an unexpected play. The quarterback smiled at the boy in his father's arms, who was still holding the football. "I think we're gonna be all right," he said.

"Yeah!" said the boy. "We're on the winning team this time!"

"Only thing is," the quarterback said, "I wonder how we're going to get out of here?"

"I'm hungry!" the boy announced. He turned to look in his dad's face. "Where's the hot dog man?"

The father shrugged. And then he gestured out over the swamped field and the stands packed solidly with people.

"That's a lot of mouths to feed," he said.

***

Jimmy Finch putt-putted his dinghy through the miles-long maze of huge trees, ice blocks, and debris that had been rafted into the center of the Nisqually Reach of Puget Sound by the force of the lahar. The water's surface had calmed, but Jimmy was kept busy making sure the little boat avoided what might be a fatal collision with a jostling log and an iceberg. As he steered generally eastward with the engine at low speed, he talked occasionally with Carlie. Neither had much to say beyond expressing worry for loved ones or making bleak speculations on the condition of society at large. Ahead of them, the huge cloud of ash over the still-rumbling mountain seemed to have thinned somewhat.

Jimmy had just completed steering around a giant log whose wallowing stump threatened to pierce the small boat with a jagged root, when the little engine chugged several times and then quit. He looked at the motor thoughtfully for a moment.

"Is it flooded again?" Carlie asked.

"Nope. Dry."

"What do you mean?"

He lifted the small red gas can that sat in the bottom of the boat and shook it. Then he set it down again with a hollow thump. "Outta gas."

"What are we going to do?"

Jimmy thought some more. And then he reached into a pants pocket, took out a pocketknife, and unfolded its blade. "Have some sushi," he said, reaching for the largest of the salmon.

***

The lights had come on again at the Columbia Center tower. In the conference room, Rudy Jones was in cell-phone contact with the FEMA Emergency Center in Bothell. Governor Long finished a conversation with her office in Olympia and then, responding to a hand motion from Jones, listened as he spoke to the person on the other end of his phone. "You can tell the President this is worse than Hurricane Katrina and Hurricane Sandy combined. The damage and loss of life are going to be, well, I'd say—a hundred times worse."

The Governor gasped, but didn't dispute his number.

"That's right," Jones said. "I said a hundred times worse. Now, I may be stuck here awhile. The streets are full of mud and traffic is stopped. I think it's best you go ahead with all phases of Response and Recovery without waiting for me to get there. But keep in constant touch with me. The Governor is here, so coordinating with the state should be easy. Are you in contact with the Emergency Operations Center at Joint Base Lewis-McChord? You are. Good. What is their status? Fully functional. That's excellent. Tell them to start rescue operations ASAP. And don't neglect Seattle as well as Tacoma. Already started? Good. I'll let you get to it then. Goodbye."

As he clicked off the phone, Don Rutledge and Howard Gage approached him and the Governor. "We may have another problem," Rutledge said edgily.

"What?" they both asked simultaneously.

"The weather."

"The weather?" The Governor shot him a questioning glance, and then glanced out the window. The sky was mostly clear with the exception of the dust cloud, which was thinning and slowly drifting northeast. "The sky is clearing and the ash seems to be blowing away. What's so bad about that?"

Gage pointed to the southwest. "See that long cloud line, low on the horizon?"

"It looks pretty benign to me," the Governor said, "compared to all this." She spread her hands to encompass the ruined valley and the debris-strewn bay, where the Alaskan Princess was in the last stages of sinking and two Coast Guard cutters were assisting wet and oil-soaked survivors.

"Don't be so sure," Rutledge cautioned. "The weather forecast for today called for a system coming in off the Pacific Ocean. That's bound to be it. The audio-visual guys are trying to get the NOAA National Weather Service feed up on the screen."

As he spoke, the image on the screen—a shaky seismograph feed from the Northwest Seismographic Network blinked off. A moment later it was replaced with a Doppler-radar precipitation map of Washington State.

"What's that?" The Governor pointed at a large comma-shaped arc of red and orange that swept across the map from Portland, through southwestern Washington, to the Olympic coast. "It looks like heavy rainsqualls."

"It's just what I was worried about," Gage replied. "We know volcanoes can affect the weather, and apparently this one has. The front was only supposed to be a weak onshore flow from the Pacific. You know—our usual weather this time of year—low clouds and a chance of sprinkles. But the energy of the eruption has completely altered the weather. Hot air rising over the mountain is sucking the whole weather system in and making it *much* more dramatic."

"I don't think I want to hear this," Long said bleakly. "How much more dramatic?"

"I don't think anyone really knows. Heavy rain, for sure. Maybe worse."

"What do you mean by worse?"

They looked at each other in silence for a moment. Then Gage shrugged his shoulders apologetically. "Strong winds? Power outages—more than we have now? Floods, in addition to the lahars? And I don't know what all else."

"Maybe it won't be as bad as all that," Rutledge suggested.

The Governor shook her head. "If this day has taught me anything, it's to prepare for the worst. So, I want to make sure every possible rescue operation gets moving before that front gets here. I just talked to the Emergency Operations Center at Camp Murray. They've already notified every police department, fire department, sheriff's office, state patrol—and of course we've got calls out to both the State and National Guards. But it will take time for them to get rolling. How long do we have?"

"An hour until it reaches Tacoma."

"An hour!"

"Maybe two till it gets here."

Long was speechless. Her eyes searched Gage's as if her mind was boggled by the news.

Jones had been following the conversation. He remarked, "That's not enough time to do much of anything."

Rutledge nodded thoughtfully. "I guess we all just have to do whatever we can."

The statement roused DeWayne, who stood nearby, out of an almost stupefied state of shock. "Would anyone like more coffee?" he asked.

The group looked at him like they thought it an odd question. Then after a moment Governor Long said, "Yes! Coffee. *Lots of it!*"

CHAPTER 20

Hans Clearidge and his crew were already flying again. Dispatched from Joint Base Lewis-McChord, their big Chinook—number 135 replacing their damaged 247—flew on a northeast heading that skirted the mountain. They were *en route* to the town of Bonney Lake, which, although only ten miles from the still rumbling crater, was situated on ground just high enough to have avoided inundation by the lahars that had wrecked the neighboring valley towns of Buckley, Sumner, and Puyallup. How Bonney Lake had escaped scorching and annihilation by one of many pyroclastic flows that had rolled off the mountain was a miracle that geologists would ponder for years. Right now, the task at hand was to deal with those whose luck had not been so good. Chinook 135's mission was to take on a full load of seriously burned and injured victims at the Pierce County Fire and Rescue Station at Bonney Lake, and airlift them to the emergency medical facilities of Madigan Army Hospital at JBLM, less than a mile from the helipad where the Chinook had just taken off.

Hans's aircraft was one of over three dozen Chinooks, Blackhawks, and Hueys that had been dispatched in all directions from JBLM as soon as Emergency Ops at Camp Murray had deemed the skies around the mountain clear enough to risk flying.

At the midway point of their route, the Chinook flew in smooth air, allowing the four crewmembers to look around at nature's horrific handiwork. The mountain itself was shrouded in billowing dark clouds shot through with lightning bolts.

High in the stratosphere, the jet stream winds were tugging the dust storm to the north and east, mercifully keeping its sandy precipitation out of the engine air intakes. Despite the cooperation of the jet stream, the foothills and valleys surrounding the mountain were thick with dust still settling from the explosions. Seen from above, the now-deserted highways and rural roads were blanketed with gray dust several feet thick and reminiscent of heavy snowfall. But in every river valley that descended from the volcano, thick lahars had smothered the bottomland from one side to the other with black muck, leaving behind buried landscapes from which the wreckage of smashed bridges, ruined buildings, or snagged-off trees jutted up here and there.

Bonney Lake sat on higher ground with just sufficient elevation above the valleys of the Puyallup, White, and Carbon Rivers to have survived intact through the flooding. But the ash looked to be anywhere up to two feet deep. Buildings with sloped roofs had shed much of the burden, but flat-roofed structures everywhere had collapsed under the weight of the ash.

When the Chinook arrived over the center of town, Hans hovered high above the dust-covered fire station and got on his radio.

"Fire Station Eleven, this is Chinook 135. Do you read? Over."

"We're here, Chinook 135," a voice came back. "Right below you. Do you see a large parking lot, just south of us? It's been cleared by snow blowers and marked off with yellow caution tape. Over."

"Roger that, Fire Eleven. You want us to set down there? Over."

"Affirmative Chinook 135. Is it big enough for you?"

Adjacent to the station, which was a relatively large facility, was a wide gravel parking lot surrounded with lines of fluttering yellow tape stretched between sandwich signs, stop signs, tree trunks, and whatever else was handy to mark out a safety perimeter.

"Looks a little tight," Hans said, "but we'll make it."

He brought the Chinook down toward the empty lot, but hesitated a hundred feet off the ground as a plume of gray dust billowed out on all sides from the helicopter's rotor wash.

"Wow," Ramon Diaz remarked. "Can't see a thing in that."

"Just give it a minute," Hans said, carefully tending his flight controls. He hovered the aircraft and watched dust stream out on all sides until bare gravel appeared. "That should do it," he said. He took the Chinook down carefully and landed gently in the middle of the open area.

Once on the ground, Hans and Ramon went inside the station while Arlen and Jason prepared the Chinook's interior seating and stretcher racks for a full load. The station's tall and wide drive-through parking bay normally housed three fire trucks, which were out on rescue missions on streets that had been cleared by snowplows. In the trucks' absence, the huge open area had become an emergency hospital. It was a beehive of activity. Emergency medical technicians had set up a triage center within the open area, and scores of victims were being cared for in chairs, on stretchers, or on blankets laid out on the concrete floor of the station house. Electric power, which was out in the rest of Bonney Lake, was provided by a mobile generator truck on one side of the station.

Local police and search-and-rescue units were helping where they could. Their trucks, aid cars, and squad cars were bringing in a steady flow of muddied and bloodied victims who had been retrieved from the margins of the areas of destruction.

"Glad to see you guys," said a man in a black fire-department uniform who hurried up and shook their hands. "Lieutenant Blakely. I'm in charge here. I've got a team of eight stretcher-bearers already working. We'll have you loaded and ready to go in just a few minutes."

"You guys have got your hands full," Hans remarked, glancing at the frenzied activity all around him.

"We sure do. But we've got great helpers. The local Red

Cross is assisting us in force, even though some of them have lost their own homes. People care. And they're pulling together to help where they can."

"Makes me proud to see it," Hans said, watching a pair of men, one young and one old, bearing a stretcher past him toward the helicopter. The victim aboard the stretcher was calm, despite being bandaged extensively for burns.

"Once you get these folks to Madigan," Blakely went on, "be sure to come back for more."

"You can count on it," Diaz replied.

"Nice to meet you both," said Blakely, waving at them with a clipboard as he hurried away toward a new patient being assisted by a woman who helped him hobble in through the front door. "Sorry but I've got to keep moving."

As two other stretcher teams carried victims out the back and several walking wounded accompanied them, Hans said, "Come on, Ramon. Let's get back in the cockpit. Looks like we'll be loaded and clear to fly before we're ready if we don't watch out."

***

"That don't look too good." Jimmy Finch gazed up at the long dark weather front approaching from southwest. He was in the stern of the dinghy, paddling with one oar while Carlie sat in the bow, pushing logs and ice away with the other. They were having trouble finding their way out of the giant logjam.

The raincloud approaching them from the southwest was nearly as black and ominous as the ash cloud to the east, with which it was beginning to merge.

"Here comes the wind," Jimmy said, facing into what was getting to be a gusty, cold breeze from the direction of the squall line, which was enveloping the headlands to the south and west as it rolled inexorably toward them. "Wind always comes before a big rain." He looked worriedly at the squall line, which was lowering down to touch the surface of the sound. The waters under it were covered in whitecaps. Everything else in that direction looked almost pitch black.

A large raindrop splatted on Carlie's cheek. She set her oar down and wiped it off. When she looked at her fingertips, they were coated in wet black grit. "What is that?" she murmured, although the notion that it was ash took only a second to register in her mind.

A drop splatted on Jimmy's shoulder and he wiped it away too. He rubbed it between his fingers. "Feels sandy."

"It's a black rain," Carlie said.

"I suppose so." Jimmy took another stroke with his oar, although any notion of outrunning what was coming was a vain wish. The inky squall line had by now closed off their view of more than half the seascape. Its gusty, chilling wind whipped froth over the little boat's gunwale.

When a peal of thunder emanating from within the squall line hit them with gut-rattling power, Jimmy set down his oar. He glanced around in all directions as if hoping for some means of escape, but he saw none. As black spatters landed on him with increasing frequency, he said to Carlie, "We'd better get ready for a mud storm."

"How do we do that?" she asked.

As Chinook 135 flew southwest toward JBLM, the black squall line came northeast to meet them. It was too tall to fly over and too wide to get around, so Hans saw no option but to fly through it. As the first huge black drops smacked onto the windshield, Ramon asked nervously, "You sure about this? We could divert north."

"Where to? We've got critical patients aboard and a medical facility waiting for them five miles dead ahead."

"We might be dead, ahead. You know what I mean?"

"Yeah. But there's a little gap underneath. I think I can hug the ground and get us through by dead reckoning."

Ramon crossed himself and said nothing more.

When they entered under the squall line, the Chinook's windshields were quickly plastered with black streaks of ash-soaked rain. The fuselage was buffeted by side winds. In the rear, people screamed in fear and pain, loudly enough to be heard through the crew's flight helmets.

Crossing the lahar-ravaged Puyallup River Valley, Hans had little to guide his dead reckoning other than a vague sense of where they were headed and the Chinook's compass heading, which at times seemed to change wildly.

"Hey, look!" Ramon called as Hans maneuvered low over a stream channel that had formed on top of the lahar deposit. Below were the shattered remnants of a house, isolated within the mudflow. "I see it," Hans replied. One roof of the multi-gabled structure had been cleared of ash. On its surface was a single word made from pieces of letter-sized white paper attached to the roof. It read, HELP. The bottom of the P was not quite finished. Kneeling beside it was a man attaching the last sheet of paper with a stapler.

Despite the difficulty and danger of maneuvering in the narrow gap between the cloud and the mudflow, Hans banked the Chinook and made a circuit of the rooftop. He said, "Get a GPS lock on this position if you can, Ray."

As he circled, he saw arms waving out every window of the only intact room of the house.

"Got it!" said Ramon.

"Good," Hans replied. Then, beset by side winds and an ever-thickening coat of muck on his windshield, he straightened out and pressed forward on his original course.

***

Seth Johnson waved frantically and shouted until the chopper disappeared.

"They didn't stop," Amelia moaned.

"Do you think they saw us at least?" Katy asked.

"I don't know," Seth replied. "They circled. That's something."

"Do you think they'll come back?" Noah asked.

"I hope so." Seth finished stapling the last sheet as black raindrops pelted him at an increasing rate. His shoulders and the top of his head were covered with a layer of wet black ash. The sign began to show the effects of the rain as well. Its letters, pure white moments before, took on mottled black-and-white tones.

"Come back in here, Dear," Katy said. "You're getting all icky."

"Wouldn't you just know it!" he moaned, sitting back on his haunches and looking glumly at his sign as the black rain drenched him and it. The sign's white paper was darkening by the second.

***

Sophie had sat on her couch for some time. Her emotions had been numbed by the extent of the catastrophe around her. Her mind was dulled by pain medications. Her senses were confounded by the sulfurous stench in the air. She laid her head back and closed her eyes for a moment. At least, she assumed it was a moment. But as she awoke she realized she may have dozed for a longer time. She got to her feet, hobbled to the window, and pulled the curtain back. The daylight that had seemed to be returning when she dozed had faded again to an even deeper twilight. A new, inky black cloud loomed in the southwest and large drops of rain had begun to spatter the window. As the drops ran down, they cut crooked black paths through a thin layer of dust coating the outside of the glass.

She took her cell phone out of a pocket, keyed her parents' number, and held it to her ear, but she didn't get even a service response. She checked the signal-strength display. There were no dots. She clicked the phone off, sighing heavily. *What am I going to do now?* she wondered.

A cracking noise in the rafters above the ceiling made her look up in alarm. There was a sudden fluttering in her heart. She was no architect or engineer, but it seemed obvious that too much ash on a roof could cause a house to *what? Collapse?*

She crutched over to the front door and opened it. Looking out through the screen door, she saw a neighborhood transformed. A layer of ash about a foot deep covered the street, the yards, the walkways, and the roofs of houses. Swirling in the wind, it had drifted higher in places, including against her screen door, which she tried to open outward, but found she could push it no more than a few inches before it stopped against compact, wetted ash.

"Help?" she called through the screen, tentatively. "Help!" she cried more loudly, glancing around at the other houses. All seemed dark and deserted. She realized with growing alarm that many of her neighbors had fled while she dozed under the influence of her pain medications. Tire ruts in the street where some had driven away before the ash had fallen too deeply were now just linear dimples in the deeper layer that had fallen on top of them. "Help!" she shouted as loudly as she could. Far down at the end of the block, she could see the backs of a family moving away on what had been the sidewalk. None of them turned at the sound of her call, although whether they heard her was moot, given the increasing noise of rain pattering on the dust. Each big drop impacted the dust with a loud *pock!* and, as the rainfall increased, the individual noises merged into a roar. What had started sporadically was becoming a torrent of huge black drops, which were beginning to soak the ash layer and turn it to shining black mud.

She tried to pull the screen door shut, but it stuck about six inches open. Standing with the aid of one crutch, she lacked the leverage to pull it farther. She stepped back and shut the front door. Standing in almost complete darkness now, she wondered again, *What am I going to do?*

The ceiling overhead creaked and cracked in an ominous reply.

Although Sophie had not been able to glimpse her roof, she had no trouble imagining it. No doubt dust had accumulated on the little, square, four-sloped roof as it had on the street, to a depth of about a foot. While each grain of dust was infinitely lightweight, the whole layer represented a heavy load on the house's two-by-four framework. And now, as the black rain roared down with increasing intensity, the dust layer was absorbing rainwater and holding it, greatly multiplying the weight overhead. The increasing burden made the Douglas fir rafters and trusses bend, groan, and pop within the space above the ceiling. *I've got to get out of here,* Sophie thought, *but where to?*

***

Jake Swanson had been at home in his condo unit in Parkland when the ash cloud arrived. He had looked out the glass sliding door that opened onto his covered balcony, but kept it shut against the dust and the stink of sulfur in the air. He had pondered rushing to his pickup and racing away, as some of his neighbors did. But he had decided that the deepening dust would snarl traffic in no time. So he had stayed put and watched the dust accumulate on his second-story deck, blowing in slantwise and forming drifts like gray powder snow. As the black rain had begun to fall he had tried to reach someone—anyone—on his cell phone. But it had quit working. He had wondered what effect a layer of dust and mud would have on the transmitters of a cell-phone tower. Not a good effect, he assumed.

Now, he watched in astonishment as a gray avalanche rumbled off the steeply sloped roof of his apartment and streamed past his kitchen windows, plopping in muddy globs on the ground below. And then he thought of Sophie Minto. He wondered if her parents had come as promised. That seemed a far stretch, given what must have become of the highways.

After some thought on the subject, he determined to go and check up on her, despite the arduousness of such a journey under the conditions. As the rain intensified, he realized it would rapidly make matters worse for driving, so he hurried out and down the muddy steps and across the dust-and-muck-blanketed lot to his big brown pickup, got in, and fired up the engine.

He lived just south of Midland, the south Tacoma suburb where Sophie lived. Soon he was not far from her, the big traction tires of his four-wheel-drive grinding through deep muck on an otherwise empty thoroughfare. The wet slop resisted, and the engine strained and roared with the effort of driving the tires through—rather than over—the mire. The pickup was the only vehicle moving in the neighborhood and perhaps, due to its large size and heavy engine, the only one that could. The straight north-south thoroughfare crossed a relatively flat plateau and then rose slightly as it approached Sophie's neighborhood. Under the circumstances, even this small slope became a great challenge.

The engine strained heavily. The thick black muck resisted until the big rig bogged down and almost stopped. Jake jammed the accelerator pedal to the floor, but the rear tires broke free and spun. The front tires clawed and dragged the vehicle forward by inches, and then they bogged down too. The pickup drifted sideways and refused to go any farther. All four tires were spinning.

Jake let off the gas, switched off the engine, and sat a moment. The black rain beating on his windshield had become torrential. He grabbed a green rain poncho from behind his seat and put it on. He pulled the hood over his head, got out, and stepped down into the mire, which swallowed his feet to a level well above the tops of his hiking boots. He looked at his mud-caked tires and let out an exasperated sigh. They would be going nowhere anytime soon. He looked around for a moment, getting his bearings while huge drops of black rain pummeled the hood and shoulders of his poncho. Sophie's house was just a few blocks away. He shrugged, shook his head, and began hiking up the hill. His feet sank in deeply, and his boots made sucking and splatting sounds with every step.

PART FIVE

WHEN THE RAINS CAME

CHAPTER 21

In Seattle, the ashfall had been much lighter than in Tacoma. Seattle had the key advantage of being thirty miles farther to the north of Mount Rainier, and with the prevailing Jet Stream winds blowing strongly to the northeast, only the edge of the stupendous ash cloud reached the skies overhead. The seismographic trace showed that the mountain had first erupted at precisely 12:53 PM, and then again at 1:59. The final and most devastating explosion had occurred at 2:26. The ash from that last explosion had begun falling like fine snow at about 4 PM, and continued into the early evening. The black squall line had approached the windows of the Columbia Center tower over a long period of time. As it advanced, it climbed the sky like a vast curtain that separated the world into a dusty but sunlit half and an obscured dark hell that no one could see into.

As the afternoon of horrors had worn on, the assembly of businesspeople and staff in the conference room had dwindled. People had grown increasingly restless and worried. Everyone had a home. Most had loved ones to look after. Over time, the businesspeople had trickled out in small groups to make their way down to the streets and find routes home in the most difficult of circumstances. Interstate 5 and Highway 99, the two freeways southbound out of town, were blocked by lahars and deep ash somewhere to the south. The two eastbound links, I-90 and Highway 520, were literally sunk. Traffic on the northbound lanes of I-5 and Highway 99 had dwindled to trickles due to the lack of vehicles coming from the south. Those routes, at least, offered escape to travelers headed north and northeast, albeit through palls of engine-choking ash that swirled up from the inches-thick accumulations at the slightest breeze or when vehicles passed.

The Governor and Rudy Jones received frequent cell-phone reports from the State Patrol and Camp Murray. From these sources, they learned that every road to the south of Seattle that had not been inundated was jammed with traffic, and little wonder. All major traffic arteries had been severed by lahars where they ran on the ground in at least three places: the Kent-Duwamish Valley, the Puyallup Valley, and the Nisqually Valley. These inundated stretches were like surgical slices dividing South Seattle in two, and separating Seattle from Tacoma, and Tacoma from Olympia. Stranded in the central section, the emergency response centers at Camp Murray and Lewis-McChord were co-isolated with Tacoma, but inaccessible to Olympia and Seattle. And currently they were grappling with inundation by heavy ash and the black rainsquall. Given the circumstances, Governor Long decided that the best option for her and her staffers was to ride things out where they were, sustained by communications with Jones' FEMA Command Center north of them in Lynnwood, which was still fully functional with only a dusting of ash and untouched by rain or mud so far. This arrangement worked passably well in the short term, and although the landlines had given out, a satellite relay link was open via FEMA to Camp Murray. However, much of what would happen in the waning hours of this long summer day was dependent on the weather—and the weather did not bode well.

"Things just keep getting worse," Long murmured, standing with her hands pressed against the window like a child. As the squall closed in, it obscured near objects like the still-jammed southern freeways and the crowded stadium. "In a minute, we won't be able to see a thing." She turned and looked with appeal in her eyes at Rutledge, Gage, and Jones, who had stayed despite the exodus of other meeting participants, knowing their expertise was well placed at her side.

"Not seeing it is a form of mercy," Rutledge said, "given

what's out there."

Long shook her head slowly. "But I *have to* know. We've only had a couple of hours of search-and-rescue activities. We've hardly even begun!"

As they spoke, the wall of blackness closed the final distance to them. At first, small taps of raindrops could be heard on the floor-to-ceiling windows. Then a bolt of lightning flashed blindingly near and a peal of thunder shook the building, loosening splinters of glass from the already cracked window that tinkled down onto the carpet. Larger drops of black rain began to streak the windows, rapidly becoming a torrent. The clatter of hail joined into the mix. More bolts of lightning dazzled the observers' eyes. Peals of thunder became an almost continuous roar.

"How bad is this going to get?" the Governor asked. "Are we safe here?"

Jones shrugged. "I'd rather not be *out there*." He tapped at his phone for a moment. "Uh-oh," he murmured. "The satellite link has gone dead."

Another blinding flash and simultaneous burst of thunder punctuated his statement.

"Atmospheric interference," said Gage. "The ash supercharges the air with electricity."

"Or maybe lightning struck the cell phone tower that's on this roof."

"Or both," Jones murmured. Wearing a sour expression, he put his useless cell phone in the pocket of his white shirt.

***

"This is not working out like I planned," Seth Johnson muttered. He leaned on the window frame and looked out at the paper HELP sign. It had been pelted heavily by muddy rain. Even though the staples held the pages in place, the sign itself had merged colors with the ash-spattered cedar shakes of the roof. It was all but invisible to any would-be rescuer passing overhead—not that any rescuers had come around since the helicopter had circled them.

Seth glanced at the rest of the family. They were huddled on the floor, leaning against the cockeyed wall, crowding together for warmth as the cool of evening augmented the chill of the storm. Everyone looked miserable including the dog and cat shivering in the kid's laps.

He glanced out what could be seen of the surrounding landscape, which was no more than the flat surface of the mudflow and the dark sky overhead. It seemed to him that the black rain was abating. And if his eyes weren't playing tricks, the southwestern horizon where the storm had come from had lightened to a shade of greenish gray.

"I've got to go for help," he murmured.

That brought Katy to her feet. "You've got to be kidding!" She looked out fearfully over the shallow streams woven all around the house.

"We can't just sit here. That helicopter has got other people to rescue. They might not be back at all."

Katy shook her head. "I thought you said it was all quicksand out there." She sniffed at the sulfurous fumes rising from the surface and made a half-disgusted, half-desperate face.

"I'll never know until I try." Seth crawled gingerly over the windowsill, avoiding jagged glass. The kids got up to watch with deep concern on their faces.

The mud surrounding what was left of the house had become a flat surface just below the second-story eaves. Scooting down the roof slope below his ruined sign, Seth reached out with a foot and tested the firmness of the surface. When it seemed to support him, he stepped off the roof and put the weight of both feet on the mud. Instantly, the surface transformed into a liquidized, bottomless morass. He quickly sank to his knees. Katy and the kids screamed in unison. He cast himself belly-down on the roof slope, clutching desperately at a vent pipe. He tugged hard at the pipe to keep from sinking further. Then, straining with all the strength in his arms, he drew his legs up and out of the muck, which made sucking sounds as his feet came free. He clawed his way up the muddy shingles and climbed back inside the room with Katy's help. Once he was back inside, muddied and minus one shoe, he plucked a splinter of glass from a forearm. Blood oozed where the glass had sliced in while he scrambled over the sill.

"And now we know," Katy said morbidly. "We're not going anywhere."

Lightning flickered and thunder rumbled through the black clouds overhead as if to underscore her statement.

"At least the rain is letting up," Seth murmured as he brushed mud from his clothes.

***

The rain was not letting up elsewhere. Thunder and lightning were more intense on the remaining slopes of Mount Rainier. Black torrents roared down with incredible intensity on the ring of crags that surrounded the new, stupendous hole in the ground where Rainier had once stood. Muddy rain spattered rocky outcrops and the remnants of melting glaciers. Where those glacial lobes had gushed streams of white water like Tacobet's nourishing milk, now vile-smelling black sludge issued instead. Illuminated dimly by greenish light from the horizon and occasionally lit by lightning flashes, streams of this thick runoff poured from the edges of shrinking glaciers and adjacent rocks, then merged into rivulets of muck, which coalesced into larger torrents under pounding sheets of black rain. Downslope, the torrents merged into wide flows, which cascaded down jagged rock faces and combined into even larger black cataracts. At the mountain's base, those larger streams merged into fast-moving rivers with raindrop-pelted rapids on their inky surfaces. Riverbanks collapsed, adding their mass to the surging dark waters. Saturated by the deluge of rain, entire hill slopes came alive and rumbled down to join the flow. It seemed nature was unsatisfied with the destruction wrought by the lahars and was determined to add the new peril of rising floodwaters.

***

When Jake arrived on what he figured must be Sophie's block, the black rain had moderated, but it was still pelting down. The preceding torrent had left a heavy layer of rain-soaked muck on every house and yard. Like some evil, wet, stinking snow-blanket, the layer made it difficult for Jake to be sure this was indeed the right block. As he sloshed along the buried sidewalk and passed under a mud-burdened bigleaf maple tree, he heard cracking noises and rushed ahead just as a huge branch snap-ped off. It thudded onto the muck-covered sidewalk and missed him by a matter of inches. Hurrying farther down the block, he came to a muck-covered car in a driveway and guessed by its outline that it was Sophie's white Tesla, now black with mire. But if this were Sophie's car, then her house didn't make sense to him. It had entirely the wrong shape.

A jolt of adrenaline raced through him when he realized the cause of his confusion. He wasn't looking at the front of Sophie's house, but at its collapsed roof. The little square house had crumpled under the weight of ash and rainwater and the front wall had buckled. The rear of the house still stood, causing the square, low-peaked roof to incline toward him until it touched the ground. He was looking at the roof itself, loaded with wet muck and peppered by bricks scattered from what had been its central chimney.

"Sophie!" he cried. His heart began to pound in his throat. "Are you in there?" He moved to the crumpled and splintered side of the house. Leaning inside the crazily misshapen frame of a shattered window, he called again. "Sophie! Are you here?"

"I'm here!" Her voice came to him faintly. "I'm here!"

He climbed inside carefully, avoiding broken glass that lined the window frame.

"Where?" he called.

"In the kitchen," she called back.

"Where's the kitchen?" He looked around at the crazily deformed walls and half-collapsed doorways of a house whose ceiling stood at its normal height in the back, but which angled down until the living room was crushed to a vanishingly small wedge at the front. Details were hard to discern in the interior, which was only dimly illuminated by twilight coming in from outside.

"Here!" she cried again.

He followed the sound of her voice, crouching under the low ceiling. Rounding a pile of bricks that had been the central fireplace and chimney, he worked his way deeper into the wrecked structure. In the gloom, he silently cursed himself for not bringing a flashlight. Easing through the remnants of a partially collapsed doorway, he entered the kitchen. Its ceiling had sagged but was supported by the refrigerator, range, cabinets, and counters. And there, sitting with her back to the oven door in a dust-splotched coral pink sweats outfit, with her casted leg stretched out on the dusty linoleum in front of her, was—

"Sophie!" He went to her and knelt down. They hugged each other tightly.

"Are you okay?" he asked, pulling back to look at her face in the gloom. Her cheeks bore black streaks of tear-wetted dust that made her look like she'd had a bad accident with mascara.

"Okay? Are you kidding?" She attempted to smile. "But yeah. I'm okay. No new injuries. Not yet, anyway." She looked up nervously at the ceiling that angled over their heads. Something in the roof cracked and the ceiling dropped several inches. Behind Jake, more fireplace bricks crumbled. The house settled more, and the space Jake had come through shrank to a splintered mass of two-by-fours, torn plywood, and broken wallboard. They held each other close, each fearing the worst. But the ceiling ceased—or at least paused—its downward collapse.

"Now we're *both* trapped," Jake muttered.

"Maybe not," Sophie said. She pointed at a twisted slab of painted wood near her. "That's part of the basement door. I couldn't get past it."

Jake turned and gripped the plank with both hands. Straining with all his might, he wrenched off the lower portion of the splintered door, revealing a black gap under it.

"You want to go *down there?*" he asked as he stared into the inky, claustrophobic-looking recess.

Another rending sound came from overhead and the ceiling descended several more inches.

"You want to *stay here?*" she retorted.

"No."

In the vanishingly dim light inside the hole, Jake could see a wooden staircase leading down to a dank-smelling basement. He thrust both legs through the opening and got his feet on the staircase. "Come on," he said. "I'll help you get that bad leg down here."

She moved to him, gingerly trailing her injured leg. With his help, she went through the hole head-and-shoulders first and then got her good foot down on the staircase. He supported her as they worked their way down the steps into Stygian blackness below. As they reached the base of the stairs, the kitchen ceiling collapsed completely, obliterating the space they had occupied moments before under a mass of splintered rafters and jagged two-by-fours.

At the bottom of the staircase they stood on a concrete floor in a full-height basement space. Jake peered through the nearly complete darkness, spotting the unfinished upright support posts and whitewashed concrete walls of a wide square basement that housed dozens of storage boxes, a washer and dryer, and an old oil furnace. A scary thought struck him. "Do you have gas appliances?"

"No," she replied. "They're electric, except the furnace. And it's got a buried oil tank.

"Good," he said. "So we probably won't get burnt alive."

She shuddered in his arms. "Don't say that."

"Sorry. Just thinking out loud."

"So, what do we do now?" she asked.

"That corner over there looks safest," he said, helping her toward the far side of the basement where the washer, dryer, and an old fashioned concrete mop sink offered a bulwark against anything coming down from above.

"Shouldn't we try to get out?"

A thick beam over their heads split open with a loud *crack!* Her scream and his yell of alarm combined in a weird harmony—but the beam held the weight above it. They retreated to the corner without further discussion. As they settled into the protected space between the washer and dryer, he glanced at the sagging beams and joists overhead. "Come on baby," he muttered nervously. "Hold together!"

***

"Iggy!" Noah called out a smashed window. "Iggy! Where are you?"

"He's gone," Amelia grumbled. She sat against the wall with her arms wrapped around her knees, casting an irritated glance at her brother. "You're never going to see him again."

"Don't say that!" Noah frowned at her petulantly, and then turned his back on her and crossed his arms to emphasize his irritation. Suddenly, his eyes widened as he looked out the window on the opposite side of the wrecked room. "Dad?" he asked in a voice whose tone changed from chiding to fearful in an instant. "Is the water rising?"

Seth got to his feet and glanced at their surroundings. "You're right," he murmured. "It *is* rising."

CHAPTER 22

Hans Clearidge had not moved from the pilot seat of Chinook 135. Nor had he dismissed his crew, who still occupied their seats as the big helicopter sat on the mud covered tarmac of their landing pad. Hans looked at his wristwatch and sighed impatiently. "Flight Control," he said into his helmet's microphone. "You've had us grounded for more than an hour. The sky is beginning to clear down south. Chinook 135 requests permission to take off. Over."

"Ah, we are still on weather hold," Flight Control replied.

"I don't give a damn about the weather!" Hans growled. "There are people out there who need us."

"That's still a negative, Chinook 135."

Hans switched off the comm link. And then he pounded a fist on his armrest. "I can't stop thinking about that help sign we saw!"

"I know," Ramon said. "But what are we gonna do? A weather hold is a weather hold."

"I can't bear just sitting here!" Hans replied through gritted teeth. He tilted his helmeted head back against his head support and let his shoulders slump. He was stymied.

"Permission to come aboard," a voice said through the Chinook's open side door.

Hans turned and stared at the speaker, a stocky but well-muscled man with a shiny, handsome, ebony face. He was wearing a blue-and-white U.S. Coast Guard uniform.

"Can I help you?" Hans said, his ongoing irritation leaking

through in his tone of voice.

The man cracked a grin. "Question is, can I help *you?*

"Help me how?"

"I heard you might have a river rescue coming up." The man straightened and fired a crisp salute. "Specialist Tyrell Collins, Rescue Swimmer, currently unattached."

Hans broke into a grin to match the newcomer's. "Well, consider yourself attached, Tyrell. And welcome aboard!"

***

High in the upper reaches of the Puyallup River Valley was a place where the main lahar, in its passing several hours before, had sealed off a tributary stream valley with a dam of muck, logs, and debris. And that stream valley, already partially filled with muddy black water from the lahar, had continued to fill with melt-water runoff from the mountain and with the deluge of rainwater as well. Under driving sheets of black rain, the impounded waters rose until they matched the height of the mud bank. At first only a small black stream came over the top, but as time passed it eroded the muck and debris that held it back. Finally, the temporary dam collapsed along its entire length, unleashing a gigantic moving wall of water, mud, and debris, which rushed into the main Puyallup River Valley and quickly swelled the already substantial floodwaters there with a new flashflood of black, churning death.

***

It had been nearly half an hour since Hans Clearidge had spoken to the Tower, and there still was no flight clearance. Tyrell Collins had gone and fetched his diving gear and stowed it and taken a seat aft, but no communication had come at all from Flight Control. Hans closed his eyes to allow himself to think. A while ago he had gotten a call through on his cell phone to his wife Rachel, who was at home with the kids in the suburb of Steilacoom. All were okay but frightened. Although the power was out, the house was intact and only moderately covered with ash and mud. Rachel had admonished him to be

205

careful. He had promised to be as cautious as he could under the circumstances. And then they had said goodbye.

Sitting idle in the pilot's seat, he pondered an unfamiliar notion. Depending on choices he made in the next several hours, that phone call, filled with statements of love to and from his wife and family, might be the last phone call they would share.

He shook his head violently to banish such thoughts. Out there in a crushed and flooded house was another family that was on the brink of their own last farewells.

"God damn it!" he said loudly. "That's it!"

He began flipping switches and adjusting levers on the console in front of him and others overhead. In response, the Chinook's turbine engines whined and revved up. The fore and aft rotors made *whup-whup* sounds as they came up to speed.

Out of the corner of his eye, Hans saw Ramon's helmeted, visored face looking at him sidelong. But Ramon wasn't complaining. Neither were Arlen, or Jason, or Tyrell in the rear compartments.

Hans pulled up on the thrust lever beside his left leg, increasing the power from the engines. The rotors beat a heavy tattoo—and the big Chinook lifted off.

McChord Tower came on the air immediately. "Chinook 135, you have no flight clearance!"

"I'm flying anyway.

"That's a direct violation of—"

"I'll violate your ass if you don't shut up!" Hans shouted as the Chinook, with turbines roaring, vaulted straight up into the dark but now rainless sky.

There were sputtering noises over the radio. And then McChord Tower came back after a long pause. "Roger that, Chinook 135. And... good luck to you!"

***

Noah Johnson stood to look out the window while the others huddled together for warmth. After a few minutes of gazing silently at their dismal surroundings, he said hoarsely, "Dad! I think the water is getting higher!"

"It's been rising for some time, son."

"Yeah, but not like this!"

Everyone got to their feet. With the squall line moving beyond them and late twilight suffusing the sky, it was easier to pick out detail in the wasteland around them. And one of those details was disturbing in the extreme. The shallow streams that had crisscrossed the muddy surface on all sides of the house had coalesced into one vast, moving sheet of black water. Where it moved past the few gable roofs that remained, it had risen from only two or three inches, to nearly a foot deep. The flow churned around the swamped edges of their sanctuary with increasing speed and force, making alarming sloshing and splashing noises.

"I don't like the looks of that—" Katy began but was interrupted by a shrill outcry from Amelia.

"Look there!" Amelia gasped, pointing through a window that looked up the valley. There were more cries and screams when the others saw what she had spotted. The wall-like face of a black mudflow was rushing toward them. The flow itself was only about a foot high, but it stretched entirely across the flat wasteland. And it was coming at them with terrifying speed.

For anxious seconds, there was nothing to do but watch disaster sweep toward them. When the surge washed against the remnant of the house, it smashed into the already splintered wall of the study and sloshed fresh splatters of cold mud over everyone and everything inside. Beneath the floor, more house timbers cracked under the new strain. The family watched in horrified dismay as the gable roof bearing their HELP sign collapsed into splinters and washed away.

Their sanctuary had diminished to just the octagonal study, which tilted at a steepening angle. Black water oozed through cracks on the low side and began flooding the floor. The family retreated to the highest point in the room as the muck advanced across the soggy carpeting toward them. The big desk slid on the wet surface and crashed into the lowest wall, splintering the wall more and allowing greater surges of black muck to well up into the already sinking structure. The family huddled against the opposite wall, trembling in terror as the slope of the floor increased and the noise of snapping timbers rose to a crescendo.

***

The windshield wipers of Chinook 135 smeared black muck from side to side, but could not keep it from interfering with Hans's search. He was certain from Ramon's GPS coordinates that they were now in the right area. But the HELP sign was gone. Nor was there any other indication of the whereabouts of the family that had waved to him in desperation hours before.

"Where are they?" Hans fumed. "Dammit, I remember them being right about here. Are we in the wrong place?"

He steered the Chinook in a tight circle, looking down and to the side. Out that clearer portion of the windshield, his vision was better—but he still saw nothing in the mud-washed wasteland that reminded him of the wrecked roofs he had seen before.

"It's getting dark," Ramon said. "Night is falling."

"You're right," Hans agreed. "Turn on the floodlights."

Ramon switched on the powerful lamps on the underside of the Chinook's fuselage. They seemed to help somewhat, brightening the dark landscape by a small but helpful increment.

As Hans continued to circle and stare downward, Ramon said, "I think maybe it's hopeless. The water's running pretty strong down there. They probably got washed away. And, did you look at your engine temperature gauges lately?"

"I know," Hans said without looking. "Turbines are running hot. Both of them. They've taken in a lot of ash and mud."

"Number two engine's got a real bad whine."

"I hear it."

"Maybe we should go home," Jason suggested from the

back. "No use getting ourselves…" He didn't finish the thought.

"One more circle," Hans said.

A lightning flash on the trailing edge of the storm lit the land brightly.

"There!" Hans cried, pulling the Chinook into an even tighter, spinning turn. He pointed down. "What's that right there?"

"Its a roof alright," said Ramon. "Looks kinda like the one we saw, but where's the sign?"

"Torn off or sunk, maybe."

"Yeah," Ramon agreed. "The water is getting pretty deep down there."

Torrents of black water rushed around the remnant of the house, which had shrunk to a tiny, cockeyed, octagonal island with a blackened roof and dark, raging currents on all sides.

CHAPTER 23

Inside their sanctuary, the Johnsons were unaware of the nearness of rescuers. The flood had deepened and accelerated until the rushing black waters where spilling through the window frame on the upstream side of the study and immersing them in a waist-high whirlpool of water—chest high to the children. Bella had broken free of Amelia's grasp and was swimming in aimless circles around the room among pieces of floating furniture. Darwin had clutched his way onto Katy's shoulder. Iggy was nowhere to be seen.

Outside, the torrent surged against one corner of tilted roof, sucking and pulling at it with tremendous power. Suddenly, with rending cracks and crunches, the roof was torn away from overhead. Accompanied by their screams, it cartwheeled in the grip of the current, splashed down, shattered to pieces, and floated away swiftly on the malevolent waters.

"Goodbye, my dear ones," Katy sobbed. She reached out to her children, now neck deep in the muddy maelstrom, and gathered them to her.

"Goodbye!" Amelia cried.

"Goodbye Mommy!" Noah wailed.

As mother and children hugged each other tightly, the only one not saying farewell was Seth. He stood apart, washed by water splashing over his shoulders, but staring straight up into the black sky overhead. His face was outlined in harsh white light. Suddenly he was in motion, waving both arms over his head frantically.

"Hey!" he cried, "Hey! We're down here!"

There was no need for him to call out or wave. Already suspended below the Chinook was a wire-mesh, rectangular, box-shaped rescue basket. Seated in it was Tyrell Collins, red helmet and life preserver on over his yellow, black, and orange rubber survival suit, harness strap buckled to the steel mesh of the basket. Jason Shen was lowering the basket and rescue swimmer toward them from the central cargo door under the Chinook, while Hans carefully kept the helicopter on an even plane and nearly motionless less than fifty feet above.

With the roof removed by the flood, the task of getting Tyrell to them was easier than it otherwise would have been. Deftly operating the hoist controls, Jason lowered the basket and Tyrell directly into the half-sunken study.

"Mother gets aboard first! Mother gets aboard first!" Tyrell shouted by way of greeting as the basket's wire mesh bottom splashed onto the whirlpool's surface and he quickly sized up the situation. He vaulted out of the basket and into the water, took a surprised Katy by one arm, tipped the basket and physically forced her over the edge. He swiftly arranged her in a sitting posture with her back against one end of the confining rectangular space, which was barely big enough to accommodate two adults. While the basket stayed semi-submerged at just the right level thanks to Jason's deft handling of the winch and Hans' steady flying, Tyrell barked, "Kids and pets next! Kids and pets!"

Without an instant's hesitation, Noah and Amelia clambered aboard the basket as agilely as monkeys. Amelia sat opposite her mother and Noah slid into Katy's embrace. It was a tight fit, and it got tighter when Tyrell gripped swimming Bella by the nape of her neck and unceremoniously tossed her, with a startled yip, in among the other occupants. Amelia clasped shivering Bella to her. Darwin, who had gone into the basket clinging to Katy, nuzzled himself between mother and son and stayed there.

"That's all for this load!" Jason cried.

As if to emphasize the urgency of the situation, the

downstream wall of the room crumpled and floated away in the flood. Without pausing to strap anyone in, Tyrell raised a hand and made a one-finger-up whirling motion with his wrist that signified to Jason to lift the basket and bring its occupants up. With the jerk of an engaging gear, the hoist raised the overly full basket, dripping with muddy water, and quickly lifted it out of the shattered room. The roar and thump of the rotor blades increased in volume as the twin turbines strained to support the new, heavier cargo.

"Wait!" Noah cried as the litter rose past the remnants of the room's broken walls. He leaned far over the side and reached down, crying, "Iggy!"

The lizard had reappeared high on a splintered two-by-four upright. With his self-preservation instincts running strong, the agile little creature leaped through the air and caught hold of Noah's muddy shirtsleeve. Simultaneously, Noah shrieked as he lost his balance and plunged over the rim of the litter. Fortunately for him, big sister Amelia reacted quickly. Leaning out herself, she caught Noah by the belt and pulled him back. Katy screamed in shocked surprise, but got a hand on Amelia and helped pull her, Noah, and Iggy back to safety inside the rim of the basket. Then, weeping with relief, she made sure they were all settled in securely and hugged them as a group. Meanwhile, the basket rose toward the hatch in the belly of the Chinook.

When the basket reached the Chinook, Ramon and Arlen guided it inside, and then wrangled it onto the corrugated metal decking beside the hatch. Quickly, they moved their cargo of survivors out of the basket and belted them into seats on both sides of the rear of the helicopter. Once Mom and kids were settled in with pets in arms, the crewmen moved the basket back into the opening and Jason used the hoist controls to lower it toward the house. As he did so, Arlen, who was scanning the dark scene below, murmured, "Oh-oh."

Below them, the house was vanishing piecemeal.

Another wall peeled away, leaving only one jagged remnant standing. A strong surge of muddy water flooded into the study where Seth and Tyrell waited chest-deep in the bone-chilling wash of melted ice and sulfurous muck. Around them, the last of the strained two-by-fours groaned under the pressure of the torrent.

With a final horrific cracking and rending sound, the remaining walls gave way. Without any further hindrance, the floodwaters overwhelmed both men and swept them away. Seth was near his now floating desk and as the current drove it downstream, it swept over him and bore him under the surface. With the massive weight of the desk pressing him down, Seth choked on mud in his nose and throat. All but certain he was about to die, he nevertheless thrashed and kicked and struggled to get out from under the desk. When he somehow miraculously got free and broke the surface of the water, he clutched his way onto the top of the desk and held on, gasping and sputtering for breath. The huge piece of woodwork that had nearly drowned him now became a life raft of sorts, although one that might overturn at any moment in the turbulent current that quickly swept him away from the remnants of the house and the Chinook. The helicopter's lights were quickly a hundred feet upstream and shrinking with distance as the current bore him away into what was now the darkness of night.

"Help!" he cried weakly in the direction of the lights. "Help!" he shouted again, though he knew his voice couldn't be heard above the thumping of the rotor blades.

Inside the Chinook, Hans was desperately glancing around as he held the helicopter rock-steady above what had been the wreck of a house, but now was just an upwelling on the surface of a raging flood of black water. "Where are they?" he cried in frustration. "Where did they go?"

"There!" Ramon suddenly cried, pointing down and to the right. "I see Tyrell's suit!"

Hans banked the Chinook tightly and was rewarded by the

sight of Tyrell's bright red, yellow, and orange survival suit illuminated in the Chinook's floodlights.

Tyrell was swimming strongly across the current, as if intent on…

"And there's the guy!" Ramon cried as Tyrell reached Seth and grasped him by an arm just as a surging wave swept him off the desk. The two men now floated in unison on the current while Tyrell secured them together with a strap.

"Lower the basket!" Hans ordered.

"Already on its way!" Jason replied over the intercom. "Move five feet right, sir. That's it. Basket's in the water, right on target! Both men are getting in. Hoisting now!"

Within minutes, the basket was inside the Chinook, Seth and Tyrell were belted in, and the helicopter was hurrying for home base. Hans glanced back at Seth, now wrapped in warming blankets. "Welcome aboard, sir!" he called. "Glad you could join us. We'll have you on solid ground in just a few minutes."

He gave the family a big broad grin, which they returned with expressions of relief, astonishment, and gratitude on their muddied faces. Hans had no more than a moment to acknowledge their appreciation before the number-two turbine sputtered, sending a shudder through the aircraft and dipping the nose down steeply. He turned back to his controls and straightened the aircraft out again. "Have you on the ground," he muttered to himself as his grin turned to an expression of concern, "one way or the other."

The temperature gauge of number-two turbine was giving an impossibly high reading.

CHAPTER 24

The gentle *slap-slap-slap* of water lapping against the side of the dinghy woke Carlie. The light of a clear dawn greeted her eyes. She had passed the night huddled on the hard floor of the bow of the little boat, with little to comfort her but an old square seat cushion under her neck and the blue tarpaulin that Jimmy had rigged over the gunwales as a cover against the cold breezes of the night. The mountain had rumbled long past dark, but it was quiet now. When Carlie stirred, Jimmy stirred as well. He rose from where he had been curled up at the stern and untied the tarpaulin cover and pulled it aside. They both got up and sat on their seat planks and looked around. The boat rocked peacefully on calm water. They had drifted clear of the logjam by a hundred yards or so. The sky above was clear, although slightly hazy with dust. Dazzling sunlight came from the east. The mountain was still shrouded in gray but the cloud had settled from its stratospheric heights of the day before into a long, low bank of dust that obscured the volcano—or what was left of it—from their view. Rising from the center of the dust pall was a hint of activity, a puffing white steam cloud that rose several thousand feet but then dissipated without leaving much new ash in the air.

Jimmy folded the tarp and stuck it under a seat. "Tacobet, she's calmed down this morning," he said. "Seems like she's finished her little temper tantrum."

"Little?" Carlie questioned.

Jimmy shrugged. And then he changed the subject. "Want some breakfast?"

"Sure," Carlie replied. "What have you got?"

Jimmy reached under a seat and pulled out a half-fileted salmon. "More sushi."

"I'm starved," she said.

He took out his pocketknife and began cutting strips for both of them.

"And after we eat?" she asked, savoring the still-fresh taste of the fish.

"Oh. I suppose we could row to shore. It don't look too far off. Maybe a mile."

***

At Joint Base Lewis McChord, a National Guard unit was serving pancake breakfasts to survivors and refugees. In a wide parking area adjacent to the helicopter field, they had set up a mobile kitchen under a large Army-camouflaged tent cover. Lines of people, many wrapped in Army-green emergency-issue blankets, were served paper plates full of pancakes topped with real butter and syrup, with home-fried potatoes, sausages, and scrambled eggs added on the side, as well as fruit salads, orange juice, milk, and coffee.

The Johnsons were seated and eating at a metal foldable table with foldable benches. They and their pets had spent the night in a nearby hangar that had been converted into a vast bunkhouse with cots and mattresses laid out in rows with Army-green blankets and white sheets and pillows.

Bella sat attentively at Noah's side, hoping for another in a succession of tidbits from his plate. Darwin stood on the tabletop, tail high and purring while he accepted bits of sausage from Katy. Iggy, tied by a string onto Noah's shoulder, eagerly gulped bites from a slice of watermelon Noah offered to him.

Seth, heartily eating a second helping of pancakes, turned to watch a helicopter lift off from the airstrip. He sipped some coffee from a paper cup and then raised it as if in a toast to the big Chinook. "I'll bet that's Hans Clearidge," he said. "Those guys have been coming and going all night and all morning. He's one hell of a pilot."

"He's my hero," Amelia said sincerely.

Seth turned to look at Katy, sitting beside him, and his smile faded. "What's the matter, Hon?" he asked.

Her mouth crinkled at the corners with suppressed emotion. Her chin dimpled in anguish. "What's going to become of us?" she blurted. "Where will we live?" Tears came into her eyes.

Seth put a comforting hand on her shoulder. "That's what we have insurance for, Dear."

"I don't think it covers flood damage."

"It wasn't a flood," Amelia said helpfully. "It was a volcanic eruption."

Katy shook her head, closed her eyes, and squeezed out the tears. "I don't think it covers that either."

"Maybe we'll get help from those government disaster folks," Seth said soothingly. "Who are they? FEMA?"

"Yeah. FEMA." Katy blotted her wet eyes with a napkin and struggled to regain her composure. "Maybe they'll help us."

***

Governor Long sat at the podium table sipping a cup of coffee. It was perhaps the two-dozenth cup since her vigil had started the previous afternoon. She was talking with Rudy Jones, Howard Gage, and Don Rutledge, who had endured with her an all-night marathon of ad-hoc meetings, conference calls on shaky phone lines, and decision-making in the absence of detailed information. Now in the calm of morning, they had paused in a lull between teleconferences to observe the mountain that was—or at least had been—so prominent from the lofty windows of the Columbia Center tower. What remained of it was now becoming visible as the dust and ash dissipated. Two thirds of the mountain had vanished into mudflows and an ash cloud that was spreading across much of North America. In place of the peak was a jagged-rimmed caldera several miles wide. From unseen sources inside, white columns of steam billowed into the hazy blue sky.

THOMAS P. HOPP

An aide approached. "Governor," he said. "Your limousine is waiting."

She set her coffee cup down. "Well, gentlemen," she said to Jones, Gage, and Rutledge, "it has been—an experience."

They nodded in thoughtful, exhausted silence.

The aide said, "Use the Fifth Avenue exit when you go down. It's on the uphill side of the building. The Fourth Avenue exit is lower and, well, it's flooded with mud."

"And my airplane?"

"Just arrived up north at Payne Field in Everett. They'll get you back to Olympia before noon."

"How is dear old Olympia, anyway?"

"Not too badly affected. About half an inch of muddy ash on the ground, but the city is in pretty good shape. Traffic is moving. Power is on."

"Good. We're going to need a reliable infrastructure."

She turned to the others. "Now, I know Howard Gage will be flying with me. That will get you halfway home to Vancouver, Howard. But what about you, Rudy and Don? Either of you need a lift? We'll be driving in your direction when we go to Payne Field."

"No thanks," Jones replied. "I've got a car downstairs that made it through the flood in the garage okay. I'll find my way back to the FEMA offices."

"And you, Don?"

Rutledge turned and gestured at the telescopes still trained on Rainier. "I think I'll hang around here awhile longer, if nobody minds. This is a scene I don't want to forget."

"I doubt any of us will."

The waiter DeWayne approached with a coffee serving pot in his hand. "Anyone want another refill?" he asked.

The Governor held out her cup and he topped it off.

"You've been with us the whole time, haven't you?" she asked him.

He shook his head in the affirmative. "Normally it's just a job," he said. "A pretty nice one. But the last couple of days, it's been my chance to help everybody. Even if it was just

218

keeping you guys fed and loaded up on coffee."

"Everyone has a role to play," said Long. "And you have my undying gratitude." She opened her purse, took out a wallet, fetched out five twenties, and offered them to him. "A nice tip for your troubles."

DeWayne waved it off. "No thanks. I wasn't working for a tip this time."

The Governor stood. "And it's exactly when you aren't trying to earn a tip that you should be given the biggest tip of all. Now, as Governor of the State of Washington, I hereby order you to take it." She shoved the tip in his shirt pocket.

He grinned and let the money stay in its place.

She smiled back pleasantly, but the smile faded when she spotted another of her aides talking on a cell phone. She went to the young man and asked, "Got that death-toll estimate yet?"

He shook his head in the negative. "Nothing solid yet. There were at least a couple hundred thousand people living and working in the paths of those floods."

Long's face went red. "But it couldn't have been that bad, could it?"

"I'm pretty sure it won't be," Jones said, having followed her with Rutledge and Gage. "Plenty of people heard your early warnings in the last few days. Those who responded quickly got to safety in plenty of time."

"But our warnings weren't dire enough," she murmured. "I should have declared martial law and forced everyone out of the valleys. I feel personally responsible."

"You were in the process of responding," Jones said.

"If only I had been more forceful."

"You would have encountered more forceful resistance. Remember, we started yesterday morning with some pretty strong arguments from those community and business leaders."

"Until the mountain exploded," Gage observed.

"That's true," Long murmured. "But I still don't know how I'll forgive myself for the people who have died." She grew more red-faced.

"Acts of nature are nobody's fault," said Rutledge. "You were doing your best. That's all anyone could expect of you. The mountain didn't give us enough warning. There should have been weeks of premonitory quakes. This is one for the record books."

"In more ways than one," Long said. She looked out over the ruined landscape of the Duwamish Valley.

"People on the hills are okay," the aide on the phone continued, "except those closest to the mountain, in the direct blast zone. But that's a pretty sparsely populated area."

"But anyone who didn't evacuate the river valleys—" Long began but choked on the thought.

"Not so good," the aide finished for her. Then he turned his attention back to the phone he still held to his ear. "What's that?" he said. "Estimated between twenty-five and fifty thousand dead?"

The Governor gasped.

Jones' eyebrows went high, but he said thoughtfully, "That's nowhere near as bad as I was expecting."

Rutledge agreed. "Maybe that's because it was Sunday and people were at home rather than at work. The suburbs are mostly on hills and industry is—or was—in the valleys. If it had been a workday, it might have been far worse."

"But fifty thousand dead!" The Governor had begun to tremble visibly. "That's a horrific death toll. Where will we bury them all?"

Rutledge shrugged. "I think nature has taken care of that for you."

She looked at him in astonishment for a moment. And then she closed her eyes and let out a long sigh. "Oh, my Lord," she said.

"The time for recovering bodies and death tallies will come later," Jones asserted. "Right now we should focus on the living."

"Of course, you're right," Long agreed. "The dead can wait. The living need us now."

DeWayne was at the window again. All four stepped near and joined him in looking almost straight down. There were still crowds stranded in the stadium, but enterprising rescuers had commandeered planks and boards from a construction site and laid down a causeway from the stadium that snaked over the mud to reach solid pavement on the hillside streets of Seattle.

As they watched lines of people walking to safety over the plank path to a point not far from the base of the Columbia Center, Rutledge murmured, "That's a game day they'll never forget."

Jones stared out at the ravaged landscape with his fists on his hips. "It's going to take *decades* to pick up the pieces," he said. "My office will be swamped."

"Speaking of swamped," said the Governor, "How *are* FEMA's offices? They're awfully close to the north end of Lake Washington. That tidal wave—"

"They're fine. I've already had a dozen calls this morning. Everybody is in and the team is going into action—everyone except, well, a couple of folks not reporting. But the office is intact. The tidal wave didn't reach that far into Bothell. It must have dissipated along the Lake Washington shoreline."

***

Lake Washington's waters, like those of Puget Sound, had settled after the passing of the tidal waves. With nothing more than a light summer breeze ruffling the surface of the water, small waves slapped against the concrete side of one lone section of the Interstate 90 floating bridge that had managed to stay afloat. On the roadway atop the rectangular pontoon, several dozen trucks and cars sat immobile while their drivers and passengers wiled away the time until some form of rescue would reach them.

Some shared breakfasts made from emergency food they had brought with them packed in coolers. Some sat in their vehicles listening to radio news reports. Others wandered from vehicle to vehicle engaging in idle conversations or mooching

USB charges for heavily used cell phones.

The pontoon had drifted under the influence of the light wind. Overnight, it had become stationary when it touched bottom just off the eastern shore of Medina. Some of the stranded people had gathered at the near-shore railing to gauge the distance to land—about fifty yards. Others were more interested in gawking at the wave-wrecked mansions along the beach.

"I think that's the Gates Mansion," one onlooker said, pointing at the place directly in front of them, which had weathered the wave's assault much better than most.

"It *is* the Gates' place," said another. "I saw it on a boat tour. But the docks and the beach house and some of the trees are gone."

Uphill from the shore, the modernist mansion was in good shape, blessed by just sufficient elevation to keep all its wood-finished wings intact. A man and woman stood looking down from the railing of a deck high on the main portion of the mansion.

"That looks like Bill Gates right there!" said the first man. "And Melinda!"

When the man and woman, who were indeed Bill and Melinda Gates, saw them pointing and looking, they turned to go inside. Bill offered a friendly farewell wave.

"It'll take a whole new Gates Foundation to fix this town," said a woman watching with them.

"These guys over here weren't so lucky," said another man. He pointed to the south, where little remained of what had once been a proud lakeshore estate. Only its concrete foundations and the upright wooden pilings of its dock still stood. "They built that one a little too close to the water. I wonder if *they* survived?"

Unnoticed below them, a single pink visor cap floated in the water lapping at the base of the pontoon.

***

The roof of Sophie Minto's house had collapsed so symmetrically that it formed a neat cap atop the annihilated dwelling underneath. A thick layer of muddy black ash still coated the roof and the broken chimney. The surrounding neighborhood was in no better condition. Many houses had collapsed completely or were in varying states of collapse from heavy loads of wet ash. Several were burning with no one to fight the fires. People were nowhere to be seen. They had either fled or were hunkered down—or were dead.

At the back of what had been Sophie's house, there was a concrete-walled stairwell that led down to the basement. It was nearly filled with shattered wooden beams and light-blue cedar siding planks. From under the pile came the sound of splintered wood splintering further. This morning, the force to move the wood did not come from above. It came from within the basement. Hands inside were working at the pile of wreckage with determination. One after another, split beams and posts were removed and drawn inside. Then, accompanied by a man's groan of exertion, a small opening appeared in the pile. A hand appeared from underneath the wreckage and pushed away a slab of what had been the house's plywood framing.

Jake Swanson's head emerged from this new hole. He looked around briefly and then disappeared. After a moment, Sophie's head emerged. With Jake's assistance from below, she snaked her body out the tiny opening and climbed up and out of the wreckage on the concrete staircase. At the top, she stood, balancing on one leg, in the open space of what had been her small backyard patio. The yard was covered smoothly in thick, black, wet, and glistening mud. Sophie had changed from her dusty sweats into a relatively clean shirt, pants, and pair of socks she had found in a hamper near the washer. A hiking boot on her right foot was already covered over its top with black goo. Her left foot, which she kept elevated above the mire, was wrapped in a sock she had stretched over her cast. Her crutches were lost somewhere inside the flattened house.

Jake emerged and helped her steady herself. He looked

around. "Weather's improved," he said impertinently, looking at the hazy sky.

"You've got a way with words," she said. "What do we do now?"

He shrugged. "We could wait here for help, but that could be awhile. Days, maybe." He glanced around further, pausing to note dozens of billows of smoke going up from houses burning near and far.

"I'm really getting hungry," she said. "You got a better plan than just standing here?"

He wiped dust from his beard and knit his brows in thought for a moment. "My place was shedding dust off its roof when I left. I'll bet it's still standing. There's food in the cupboards and fridge. We could go there."

"How far is it?"

"Too far for you to walk," he replied. "But my pickup isn't too far away. Maybe it won't stay stuck if I turn around and go downhill. I could drive us home."

She shrugged. "I'm game, I guess. Let's get…hobbling."

He put an arm around her waist and supported her as she limped, one-legged, through the slippery muck.

CHAPTER 25

Hans Clearidge flew Chinook 135 dangerously close to the ground, moving under a low-hanging marine cloud layer that had drifted in and obscured the Cascade foothills. That left only the ravaged Puyallup River Valley floor visible below him.

"You see the Orting Fire Station?" Hans said into the microphone of his flight helmet. "We should be right over it."

"Nope." Ramon Diaz leaned forward in the copilot's seat and scanned the flood-washed landscape, searching for one of a few buildings that had survived. The fire station's planners had wisely located it just far enough above the valley floor to spare it the destruction that had been visited upon its community. But the low clouds and unfamiliar new landscape were making Chinook 135's final approach nightmarish.

"Keep looking," Hans said. "It's got to be here somewhere. I don't want to turn back empty-handed. Eighteen survivors, most with only a low-grade injuries—the worst is a woman with a day-old broken arm. But we promised to get them all, and get them we will."

"Fly safe, sir. If they've lasted this long, they can wait a few more minutes."

"I'm getting all turned around under this cloud layer. I wonder if we can get above it and reconnoiter by identifying some local foothills?"

"It's worth a try."

Hans pulled the thrust lever and the Chinook began to climb into the cloud layer. All was gray for a time and Hans flew by instruments mounted on the panels in front of him.

Eventually the sky cleared to blue above and white below as they got above the marine layer. Here and there, the tops of foothills poked up from the white cloud deck. To the north and a half-mile away was a snag-lined ridge that ran up to a peak among Rainier's foothills. Hans decided this peak would be a good choice for getting a GPS fix on their position. He turned the Chinook toward it.

Ramon suddenly cried out, "Madre de Dios! Look at that!"

To the east of them ran a longer, taller ridge that was the newly lowered summit of Mount Rainier. Its jagged crest ran along the horizon for several miles, approximately at their level. Something could be seen through a low gap in the ridge—something that shimmered in the bright sun of a cloud-less and ash-less day at their high altitude.

Hans took the Chinook up a few hundred feet more and banked toward the mountain. As he approached and then crossed the ridge, his helmet's headphones registered Ramon, Arlen, and Jason all crying out in amazement. From this new perspective, hovering several hundred feet above the rim, they looked down into what had once been a stupendous caldera of volcanic heat and violence. But in the time since the mountain's rage had subsided, rainfall and the last of the melting snowfields had combined to partially fill the crater with a circular lake more than a mile across.

"It's a whole new Crater Lake!" Ramon exclaimed.

Around the lake's perimeter were dozens of boiling geysers and steam vents. And entirely within the lake but offset to one side, was a black cinder cone that had risen from the lake bottom. It was still spouting twin fountains of red-hot lava, the outfall of which spattered down its slopes, slowly building up the island with glowing volcanic bombs and tumbling, smol-dering boulders.

"I wouldn't believe it if I wasn't looking at it with my own eyes," Ramon murmured like a mesmerized man. "We should get this on video."

"I've already got the nose camera on," Hans said, grinning. "This is once-in-a-lifetime stuff."

The lake water was reddish brown and its sulfurous stench pervaded the Chinook, but the scintillation of sun glinting on the lake's surface lent it a terrible beauty. Hans rotated the Chinook in place to give its camera—and crew—a full 360-degree pan of the fuming caldera. Then he turned the aircraft back the way it had come. "All right," he said, "we've got a mission to accomplish."

As he flew toward the foothill where he intended to resume his quest for the fire station, Arlen called out, "Hey guys! What's that? I mean, who's that?"

"Say again?" Hans asked. He didn't think he had heard Arlen correctly.

"Right below us!" Arlen exclaimed. "Walking down the ridge. Two people!"

"All the way up here?" Hans asked in surprise. "That's imposs—" He stopped in mid-sentence, struck by a thought. "You got our location on GPS, Ray?"

"Yeah. We're... let's see. We're right over..."

"Burnt Mountain?"

"Yeah. We're over the ridge running down from the peak, about a mile down. How did you know that?"

"Because I think I know who those people are."

The mountain ridge road had been blown almost clean of ash by hurricane-force winds that had been drawn in at the base of the towering plinian clouds during the height of the eruption. That fierce updraft of cooler air amid the maelstrom of volcanic outbursts had been the determining factor in the seemingly miraculous survival of two people who now plodded through ankle-deep ash, which had retained sufficient heat to bake away the moisture of the previous evening's rainfall. Both survivors were covered in dust from head to foot. In places where the ash had piled into drifts despite the gale, they waded rather than walked through drifts of pumice pebbles and dust that were at times nearly knee deep and so hot as to all but bake their feet inside their hiking boots. The agony of placing each footstep into these drifts was compounded by the pain of weeping sores where their bare shins contacted the hot dust. Both knew they were lucky to be alive at all, but neither cared to talk much about it. Speaking brought the added agony of choking and gagging on dry ash that rose on the breeze and coated their throats and burned their nostrils and sinuses. There was nothing to be done but silently pray that they might, somehow, against all that opposed them, make their way to lower elevations by plodding down what had been a logging road but was now little more than two wheel ruts filled with ash.

The smell of sulfur was as pungent as if they were walking through the brimstone stench of hell and, in a sense, they were. The forest had been devastated by the eruption and subsequent gales. Scorched, downed trees with ash-laden branches lay across the road at frequent intervals, forcing them to climb over or detour around. At random intervals, wind gusts would stir the fine dust that was everywhere, causing them to endure more coughing and choking.

"Andy—" Lexi Cohan wheezed, "I don't know if I can go on much farther."

Andy Hutchins didn't reply. Breaking a trail through a particularly thick drift of ash a few paces ahead, he hadn't the strength or inclination to turn and look at her. His entire energy was being expended just putting one foot before the other and pressing on against the resistant mounds of hot ash. He had long since abandoned conscious thought and was operating on the simple, instinctual urge to survive by walking down the ridge for as long as his strength held out. And that might not be much longer. There was an intense ringing in his scorched ears. And now an odd sound broke into his numbed, dull, exhausted mind. It was a repetitive thudding. As the thudding grew louder, Andy thought he might be having some sort of heatstroke. He stopped in his tracks and stared around himself in dizzy confusion. And then he looked up—and let out a hoarse shout of disbelief.

It took only a matter of minutes to lower the rescue basket and fetch the two survivors up and into the Chinook.

"I thought it was you!" Hans called back to them after Arlen and Jason helped them get belted into two rear seats and gave them bottled water to clear their parched, dusty throats.

"I can't believe you came back for us," Lexi called over the rotor roar. A smile of immense relief cracked the caked dust on her sooty face. Her clothing showed signs of scorching, as did the skin of her arms and legs, reddish and swollen where volcanic heat had stopped just short of cooking her.

"Better late than never," Hans replied, holding a headphone aside so he could hear her.

Andy, similarly scorched but otherwise unharmed, grinned almost from ear to sooty ear.

Hans asked him, "How did you guys ever survive all that?"

Andy took a deep, long pull from a water bottle. "As bad as that first blast was, it split around the sides of Burnt Mountain. It didn't hit us full-force. We were both knocked down— knocked out—but we came to pretty quick and we got into some forest fire fighter emergency shelter blankets."

"We stayed there the whole time," Lexi said. "The first ash fall partly covered us, and that helped protect us."

"Two more pyroclastic surges came after the first one," said Andy.

"And each was worse than the one before," Lexi added. "We almost choked to death a couple of times. But we just lay there and kept close to each other."

"And prayed," Andy concluded.

"You guys are gonna have to write a book!" Hans said, grinning. Then he reassured them, "We'll get you guys down to Madigan Hospital to have those burns looked at. But first, we've got some other passengers to pick up on the way back, if you don't mind."

"That's fine," Andy replied. He settled back and put an arm around Lexi's shoulders. They leaned their weary heads together.

Hans transitioned the Chinook to forward flight and resumed his course away from the caldera.

High above and to the west of the helicopter and the mountain, the Washington State Patrol Super King Air twin-engine aircraft cruised southbound at 6,000 feet, en route from Payne Field in Everett to the Olympia Regional Airport, piloted by Officer Claymore. Governor Long and a half-dozen of her staff lined the windows, staring down at the ravaged landscapes below.

"So this is what Armageddon looks like," Long said to those nearest her as the airplane's seemingly slow movement over the landscape revealed one calamity after another. Where bustling suburban communities and dozens of small towns had stood before, the valleys were surfaced with black mud criss-crossed by interwoven shallow stream channels—remnants of the lahars that had knocked thousands of houses and businesses flat and overlaid their foundations with deep deposits that were solidifying into new, solid, encasing ground. "Oh!" she murmured. "What a terrible loss of life. And property. And history!"

"A lot of people got away," an aide remarked. "After our first warning."

"But a lot didn't," the Governor said morosely.

As the plane flew on, skirting the crater, its height afforded those onboard the unforgettable sight of the new primordial landscape within the caldera itself. Dozens of columns of white steam towered up as high or higher than the aircraft. Some low areas within the caldera hosted new hydrothermal vents rivaling Yellowstone's boiling cauldrons, smoking sulfur-yellowed fumaroles, and iridescent multi-colored pools. Geysers shot spouts of steaming water hundreds of feet into the air. The black cinder cone—a mountain-within-a-lake-within-a-mountain—gushed a red-orange lava flow that zigzagged down one flank and flashed into steam upon entering the reddish-brown waters of the lake.

The King Air's engines throttled back.

"Everyone please be seated," copilot Reed announced over the loudspeaker. "Please fasten your seatbelts for the descent into Olympia. We'll have you on the ground in about twenty minutes."

"And then our work really begins," Long said to Howard Gage, who was buckling in beside her. She shook her head slowly, still gazing out at the devastated landscape. "I never dreamed my time in office would involve such an incredible catastrophe. I had my sights set on…" she stifled a sob. "So many better things."

Gage patted her forearm sympathetically. "Fate deals the cards," he said. "Sometimes your only option is to play a positive role in setting things right again."

She nodded. "And as quickly as possible. But I'll need a lot of help."

"Rudy Jones ought to be at the FEMA Operations Center soon, if he isn't there already. And Camp Murray has confirmed we've got four-way satellite communications up and running between Olympia, our Vancouver offices, FEMA's people in North Seattle, and Washington DC. You've got the tools you need to complete the rescue and recovery phase and then start patching things up right away. As to my role, I can tell you the seismic profile of the mountain looks much better. Almost back to baseline. I really think this event is over."

"I hope you're right," the Governor said, patting his hand, which lingered comfortingly on her forearm. "But either way, I'd better be ready for a lot more long days and sleepless nights."

He opened a laptop computer and set it on his tray table. "I've been keeping an eye on the National Weather Service's ashfall maps," he said. "I think you should look at the latest." His screen presented a strikingly colored map of the Pacific Northwest, with state and county boundaries outlined in black and a color scheme reminiscent of a Doppler radar rainfall projection. Stretching from an origin point around Mount Rainier and crossing the entire region was a swath of red in a sausage shape that arched north and then east across the map. As with a rain map, a core of red was surrounded by a spectrum of colors ranging through orange to yellow and green.

"Is that the ash cloud?" Long asked.

"No," Gage said grimly. "The cloud has moved on. It's already approaching the East Coast and will soon be headed out over the Atlantic Ocean toward Iceland and Europe. What you're looking at is something much worse. It's the ash cover left on the ground after it passed."

Long closed her eyes and slowly shook her head. "I don't think I want to hear this, but go ahead. How deep is it?"

"The red part in the center is... well, it's pretty awe inspiring. From six inches to over a foot deep."

Long gasped. "But that stretches from Rainier all the way into Montana!"

"Some major towns and cities were right in the path. Ellensburg, Wenatchee, Spokane, Coeur D'Alene, Missoula—they're all covered pretty deep."

"We've got to expand the disaster declaration to include the whole state!"

"Pretty much. The Olympic Peninsula, the coast, and the southern border of the state are okay, but yeah, most of the state is a wreck. Not to mention Northern Idaho and Western Montana. If they haven't lost their power, water, and sewer systems yet, they will soon."

"How bad is the orange area the surrounds the red?"

He glanced at the map's legend, reading while tracing a line with his fingertip. "From two to six inches. Pretty bad."

Long quickly glanced around the map. "That includes most of Tacoma and a couple dozen major municipalities."

He nodded. "They are in big trouble too."

"And the yellow?"

"One to two inches."

"And the green?"

Anywhere from a dusting up to an inch."

"But that's a huge area. The green even covers parts of Olympia, and all of Seattle."

"And then it fans out to cover most of Washington State, Idaho, and Montana. Southwestern British Columbia and Alberta, Canada, too."

"Unbelievable. The economy will be in shambles. The farmlands of Eastern Washington—"

"Some of them are buried too deep to till, maybe for years. But farmers are resourceful people. If they can get it turned under, ash is a wonderful fertilizer."

"Forestry lands—"

"Ash makes good fertilizer there too. But lay it on too thick and it smothers the life out of trees. Chokes their roots. I suspect some areas will benefit and some will the killed. And as with Saint Helens, there is a huge area where the blast blew down every tree in the forest. But just like back then, the logging industry will find a way to salvage much of that timber."

"The hydroelectric dams on the Columbia River, and the commercial waterways—"

"Some will silt up pretty badly. So will some municipal sewer systems."

Her cheeks and neck had been reddening as they talked. Now she covered her face in her hands and burst into tears. He put a comforting hand on her shoulder and, after a moment, she regained her composure and fished a Kleenex out of her purse to dry her eyes.

"At least there are a few bright rays in all this darkness," she said, wiping away a drip from the end of her nose. "The Microsoft, Amazon, and Google campuses have escaped almost unscathed. They've got some ash cleanup to do, but that's about it. Boeing's Everett plant is fully functional, even if their Seattle and Renton facilities are not. Starbucks' headquarters is an island in a sea of muck right now, but it's still standing. Those companies represent a pretty powerful economic force still in operation."

He nodded his agreement. "Washington State may be severely damaged, but we're far from non-functional. You should take heart that you will be leading one of the greatest recovery efforts the world has ever seen."

"Thanks," she replied. "And you're right. I've got to develop a positive attitude from here on out. And I will."

"If it's any comfort, you should know that most of the East Coast of the U.S. is expected to experience twilight at noon tomorrow and at least a dusting of ash."

"Why would I take any comfort in that?"

"Because the bureaucrats in D.C. and the financial people in Wall Street are discussing ways to help clean up this mess. If anyone there doubts we've got a serious problem, the darkness and the grit in their throats ought to dispel any illusions."

DeWayne Pettijohn's apartment building was an older, dark-brick, four-story walkup in a usually boisterous LGBT-dominated neighborhood a few blocks east of Broadway on Seattle's Capitol Hill. Gusty breezes that drove whirlwinds of fine ash into the air had forced local denizens to retreat indoors.

"That's a parking space right there," DeWayne said, pointing at a space just behind where Jones had double parked to let him out in front of his building's entry. "Would you like to come in for a few minutes?"

Jones shook his head. "Not today" he said. "I just inherited the biggest cleanup job in the history of civilization. My boss already has our offices up and running at a fever pitch. They need me on site as quickly as I can get there. I've got a massive workload waiting for me, mustering supplies from all across the nation. Pre-fab housing, portable drinking-water purification installations, cleanup vehicles, an army of dump trucks to carry away the ash, and enough food and clothing for hundreds of thousands of people."

"Man!" said DeWayne. "I thought I went through a lot serving food and coffee to you all. But you've really got it bad."

"It's already been an emotional rollercoaster ride. I could use… a hug."

"Me too," DeWayne said.

They embraced. "Let's keep in touch," Jones murmured. "Okay?"

"Okay."

***

Jimmy Finch had set the oars in the dinghy's oarlocks and then he and Carlie had taken turns rowing for shore. The currents had carried them south of the main Nisqually River delta, and as they came inshore, it became clear that the river mouth had divided into a maze of new channels, sand bars, and muddy banks that would be impossible to land upon if they wanted to avoid sinking to their waists in muck. Instead, they made for what looked like a decent landing site farther south on a rocky beach at the public boat launch at Nisqually Head, where the park buildings, pier, and concrete boat launch had been swept by the tidal wave but not washed away completely. Jimmy took over at a point where the current of the incoming tide was moving upstream in one of the larger channels and his stronger, more practiced hands were needed on the oars to keep the boat from being drawn into the mud-banked waterway.

Carlie tried for the umpteenth time to get an open line on her cell phone, and finally succeeded. She reached her parents in Yelm with the miraculous news of her survival, and got a report that they too were safe, although their home needed a thorough shoveling off of several inches of ash that had covered both house and yard.

She next tried the Nisqually Tribal Center and got Verna Finch on the line. Verna informed Jimmy that she was fine, while constantly weeping great sobs of joy at his unexpected survival. "You old coot!" she cried. "I knew you were too tough to die!" She further informed him that the great majority of Nisqually Tribal people were safe and sound, having evacuated the riverside village and Frank's Landing as the tribal council had insisted.

"We're all staying at the Tribal Center and the Red Wind Casino. You get your old bones back here so's I can give you the biggest hug of your life! You hear me, old man?"

After goodbyes, Jimmy handed the phone back to Carlie and rowed on. As they approached the beach at Nisqually Head, a Fire Chief's red SUV appeared at the landing with red lights flashing and two men got out and began inspecting damage to the buildings and the pier. When one of them spotted the dinghy coming in, he waved. Carlie returned the gesture excitedly.

Jimmy said, "I guess maybe we can hitch a ride home with them."

Carlie nodded, and then said somberly. "My folks said they went to my house looking for me and the place is okay. But your house…"

Jimmy paused with oars up at mid-stroke and thought a moment. And then he laughed fatalistically. "I suppose my house is out there floating around with the icebergs."

"I'm sorry. You probably lost everything."

"Yeah." He lowered the oars to float at the sides of the dinghy, and then he thought some more. "But there wasn't too much to lose. We lived in another old house before that one. Burned to the ground while we were away one day. Electrical fire, they said. Lost all our treasures then. Not so much to lose this time. We'll get by."

Carlie said, "I doubt either one of us will ever see our cars again."

"Not much of a loss for me," he said with a chuckle. "But I'm gonna miss Franks' Country Store. I hope they rebuild it. And our house was a crummy old place. We're probably better off without it. Now maybe we'll get some money to build a new one—from the state maybe, or from the casino. Either way, we'll be better off."

"Build on higher ground," Carlie suggested.

"Oh, I don't know," he said. "I gotta be near the river. I'm a Nisqually, don't forget." He pointed up the channel they had just passed. "River sure looks different now," he said.

She smiled at his Native American understatement as she glanced around at the flood-washed and mud-covered landscape.

"That there channel," Jimmy said, "is a whole new river mouth. Didn't used to be here before."

"I thought so," she replied.

"Used to all be forest along here. Tall trees. Now they's all gone. 'Cept for them stumps."

Carlie glanced around at dozens of snagged off stumps jutting from mud banks on either side of the channel.

"But those trees, they'll grow back," Jimmy said. "Nature heals herself. 'Specially when she gets people out of the way. Look. There's a few live twigs poking up outta the mud. Even a couple with leaves still on 'em."

"You're right," Carlie said. "The trees will come back okay. But I'm thinking about the salmon run. I guess that has been... destroyed. Exterminated."

"Oh, I don't know." Jimmy looked even more thoughtful. "This year's run, maybe so. But the salmon people, they's used to volcanoes. They already learned how to deal with them a long time ago." He took another pull on the oars. Gently, under his breath, he began to sing, "Hey-ah-hey-yo-ay-yay."

"I don't get your meaning," Carlie puzzled. "The salmon run must have been killed completely. It's extinct now. Isn't it?"

He shook his head negatively with assurance and rested his oars. "You see. Salmon go out to sea and stay there for a couple of years."

"True," she said.

"Our legends say they live in the Village of the Salmon People, under the ocean, till it's time to come back to the land. So there's two or three years worth of them out there right now. They'll come along when it's time for them to come home."

"But look at this watershed," Carlie persisted. "It's utterly devastated. There's nowhere for them to go. Nowhere to spawn."

Jimmy shook his head again. "Look there," he said, nodding at a bar of small rocks and pebbles that ran beside the river channel for several hundred feet. "All they need to be happy is a gravel bar like that one, as long as it's underwater so they can lay their eggs. I expect the flood left plenty of gravel bars upstream. That one looks a little muddy. But they'll all be washed clean next year by the winter rains. Then the salmon will come like they always do. And they'll lay their eggs and then they'll die, just like they always do. And their bodies will nourish the land."

"I'm glad you're so optimistic," she said.

"'Course I am. And all this gray muck?" He passed a hand across the view of the mud-caked delta. "It will be green again with squallie grass like it was in the old days. All them dikes the pahstud pioneers put on this delta, they's all gone now. Pretty soon, everything's gonna be back to normal. Back to the way it was before pahstuds came here in the 1800s."

"I guess that's a good thing."

"It's like our elders taught us. Everything happens when it's s'posed to. That's called living on Indian Time. The Salmon People will come back here when it's time." He smiled smugly at his little soliloquy, and then he resumed his slow rowing and his singing.

"You know," Carlie said after a minute. "You've got me believing it *will* be all right."

"Yep," he said, taking another pull on the oars. "Everything that needed cleaning just got washed by and Tacobet's nourishing waters—with the help of Dokwebalth the Transformer."

"But you can never really go back to the old ways."

"No, I suppose not. But Shuq Siab says it's time to start over. This time, he's sayin' respect the land. This time, he's sayin' respect the salmon. This time, he's sayin' respect Tacobet—or she'll do it all over again. But now there's a new chance for salmon and animals and people to live together." He pulled on the oars again. "Your situation ain't so nice, though, is it?"

"Oh, I'll be alright," she said. "Once I get home and get my yard cleaned up."

"I didn't mean that," Jimmy said, smiling wryly. "I meant, it seems like Dokwebalth sent you all the bad luck and changes."

"How do you figure? After what we survived, I feel lucky."

"Yeah. I suppose so. But now you've got nothing to do."

"What do you mean?"

"Unless I'm wrong," he said, cracking a wider grin. "There ain't no pollution around here for you to monitor no more. No DNA damage to check up on either. It's all washed away." He pointed across the new mudflats to the river bluffs on the north side of the delta.

She raised a hand to shield her eyes from the bright sky and scanned the base of the bluffs.

"Remember?" Jimmy asked. "There used to be some old docks and ditches there, where the ammunition plant used to be. That's where they used to dump all their chemical waste in here."

"My, my," she murmured. "The docks are all swept away. Nothing there now but river banks."

"Nature takes care of herself," said Jimmy. "Dokwebalth just helped her along this time. He used Tacobet's waters to wash all that pahstud poison right out of the river. It's gone for good. And, look at this here sand bank next to us. See where a river otter mamma and her pup have hauled out there? They probably got washed out to sea like us, but now they're already back, and they got here before us. And what's that they're fussing with? Looks to me like they've got themselves a big fish. A flounder, maybe. How about that? Nature takes care of her own."

He took another pull on the oars and began singing his Indian song again.

Carlie thought the song's melody was, if not joyous, then at least hopeful. She smiled at the Fire Marshal who had come to the tide-line to meet them as they neared the shore.

With a last pull on his oars, Jimmy ceased his song and let the boat nose onto the barnacle-coated cobblestones of the beach. The Fire Chief came to assist in pulling the boat ashore. As he bent and took the bow line, he asked half facetiously, "You two been fishing?"

"Sure have," Jimmy replied, inclining his head at the salmon catch, one of which had been reduced to little more than a skeleton by their repeated feasting.

***

The news helicopter, Chopper Twelve, was airborne again after being grounded more than a day for safety reasons. As it moved over the devastated lower Duwamish River Valley south of Seattle, the video feed showed the reporter wearing his headset and microphone.

"Matt Ziegler reporting from above what used to be Seattle's main industrial area. Amanda, we are witnessing something amazing here—a miracle on the banks of the Duwamish River."

"Fill us in," Amanda replied from the anchor desk.

The video feed switched from Ziegler to the nose camera's view of the mud-ravaged landscape below. "We have been seeing devastation here in the lowland portions of Seattle that is comparable to the almost complete destruction of the Tacoma lowlands. But a one-in-a-million chance has spared one special building right below us."

The camera view swung to a long, slant-roofed wooden structure at the base of a tree-clad hillside, situated where the unharmed forest slopes met the lahar-washed bottomland.

"The Duwamish Tribal Longhouse building," said Ziegler, "still stands here on its little postage stamp of land. And it almost seems as if the mudflow was magically kept from harming it."

"That's amazing," Amanda said. "Can you explain to our viewers what happened?"

"Affirmative," Ziegler replied. "Apparently, a long railroad train was parked on the tracks that run past the longhouse. It was a freight train loaded with two-tiered stacks of shipping containers filled with Japanese automobiles. When the lahar hit, the train was knocked off its tracks but the debris flow sort of coiled everything right around the longhouse. All those containers acted like a dam, which deflected the lahar. It flowed right past this place without touching it. Now the longhouse is the only structure still standing in the entire area. Everything else in this part of the valley has been swept away."

The video image of the longhouse rotated slowly as the

chopper circled and Ziegler explained further. "Here's something else that's interesting, Amanda. After the mudflow passed, the Duwamish River went back into its original channel. That includes the old oxbow river bend that loops past this spot, which was once Chief Seattle's village. There was an old industrial district here, but every trace of those buildings has vanished. All the dredged-and-filled industrial land has—well, it has just been swept away. And the natural bend of the river has been put back in its place."

"That's amazing Matt. It's almost like divine intervention."

"Yes, Amanda. Like the tribe has some mysterious influence with the forces of nature. Some transforming principle."

"I am reminded of something," Amanda went on. "As our viewers may recall, we covered a related story recently. The Duwamish People received word just a few weeks ago that their appeal for federal recognition as a tribe was denied yet again."

"Do you think the mountain is showing its support for them?" Ziegler suggested.

"That's hard to believe, Matt."

"But it's also hard to explain the longhouse's survival when everything else was destroyed. It's as if the tribe's appeal to a higher authority here on earth wasn't working, so an even higher power than the U. S. Government took action. Maybe the native spirits in Mount Rainier are sending a message that the Duwamish Tribe should be recognized."

"I don't know about that," Amanda replied. "But it's clear from the miraculous survival of their longhouse that somebody up there likes them."

***

A dusty field adjacent to the hangar at Lewis-McChord airbase had become home to several hundred camping tents of varying sizes, colors, and models. Most were camouflage-green and tan, befitting their normal use in the Army National Guard's field training maneuvers. They had been hastily but effectively set up by teams of soldiers working through the night. Families like the Johnsons, victims or refugees who had escaped the mountain's wrath, were assigned to the seemingly too-small places of shelter, but had little choice to do otherwise. Evacuation routes by land were cut off to the north and south of the base by lahar flows in the Puyallup and Nisqually river valleys. But the Army had provided as much aid and comfort as was possible under the circumstances. There were even field shower tents where they were able to get clean before retiring to their cots and sleeping bags for the night.

At mid-morning, Noah sat under the entrance flap of the Johnson's tent, holding little Iggy in his hands. "Dad," he said. "Iggy feels all cold."

Seth had been standing beside the tent wearing an aimless, weary expression. He leaned and felt the lizard's back. "He does feel a little cold, son. The air got pretty chilly last night."

"He needs to go home to his cage," Noah said, pouty-faced. "It's got a warm rock and an infrared light for him. But it's gone!" He began to cry softly.

"We'll get him a warm home real soon," said Katy, who was siting on a folding chair nearby.

"How soon?"

Katy looked to Seth questioningly.

He shrugged his shoulders and shook his head slowly. "I don't know exactly."

Noah began to cry out loud. "Will things ever be all right again?" he bawled.

Katy went to him and began stroking his hair and comforting him. "Yes, of course things will be all right," she said softly. "That's what you have a mom and dad for. We're going to make everything all right."

"How are you going to do that?" he wailed.

"We'll get a brand new home." Katy said, wiping tears from Noah's cheeks. "Won't we, Seth?"

"Yes, we will. And it will be up on a hill, I can promise you that."

"A real tall hill," said Amelia, who was feeding Darwin bits of breakfast sausage through the screen of a transport cage while Bella sat nearby, wagging her tail and hoping for a treat.

Being among the earliest tenants of the refugee camp, the Johnsons had been issued a tent near the hangar, where food services and other amenities were located. Seth glanced over and spotted a familiar man sitting at a table in the hangar's open space, sipping a cup of coffee. He excused himself from Katy and the kids and went to the man. He and held out a hand, and Hans Clearidge stood and shook it, giving him a tired but genial smile.

"Good morning," Clearidge said. "Did you get a good night's sleep?"

"Good enough," Seth replied, "considering there were four people and three animals in one tent." After a pause, he added, "I didn't get a chance to thank you."

"Just doing my job," Hans said.

"That may be the way it seemed to you," said Seth. "To me it seemed like you came straight down from heaven."

Katy and the kids joined them. Their appreciative gazes and words of praise soon had Hans wearing an embarrassed smile. Pink color suffused his cheeks.

Seth clapped the big man on the shoulder. "We'll never forget you."

The others nodded their agreement.

"I'll never forget you guys either," Hans replied. "That was about the wildest rescue I ever took part in."

"You must be exhausted," Katy remarked, looking him in the face. "You've got dark circles under your eyes."

He nodded. "I haven't been getting much sleep lately. But that'll change pretty soon. The President has ordered a massive relief effort. What I hear is, every Army and Air National Guard unit in the western U.S. is sending all available helicopters ASAP. And the Navy is mustering a flotilla of ships from up and down the west coast. Some of them are on the way already, including an aircraft carrier loaded with helicopters."

"They've got a huge task ahead of them," said Seth.

"And they know it," Hans agreed. "First, we've got to get

the rest of the stranded people out of the remote areas. Then, we'll get food, water, and supplies to communities that are cut off from highway transport. We're talking hundreds of helicopters with rotating crew assignments so they can work 'round the clock." He paused and looked into the distance to the south. "Here comes a pretty big formation of Chinooks right now. Probably up from Oregon or Northern California."

On the far horizon, several dozen dark dots grew and began to take on the forms of Chinooks, accompanied by the distant thumping of their rotor blades.

After a moment Hans asked, "You guys got a place to stay?"

The Johnson's faces all fell at once. Seth shook his head. "Not yet. Maybe in a couple more days. We've been calling around when we can get an open line. We had an offer from Katy's cousin up in Lynnwood but I don't know how we would get there. Our car is buried in mud and the freeways are washed out anyway."

Hans thought a moment. "I think I could talk Rachel into letting you guys stay at our place for a couple days until you can find a more permanent spot. It's not far from here. We've got a guest bedroom with its own bath. Might be a little crowded for four people and three pets but—"

"That would be great," Katy said. "If Rachel doesn't mind."

"We'll never know until we ask." Hans took a cell phone from his pocket and began making a call. The family's faces lit in anticipation. "Besides," Hans said while waiting for the slow service to put the call through, "we've got lots to talk about."

"We do?" Seth responded.

"Yeah. For starters, I'd like to know how you kept that lizard with you through it all."

Noah grinned, stroking little Iggy, who clung to his forearm for warmth.

***

When Jake and Sophie reached his pickup truck, he helped her into the back where she had sat before and they got her mud-smeared, casted foot up on the bench with a shopping bag under it. He got into the driver's seat.

"Whew!" she exclaimed once she caught her breath. "That was a long hike on one leg."

"The ash has dried a little bit," Jake said as he put the key in the ignition and fired up the engine. "I think I might be able to drive out of here without someone having to get out and push. Hint, hint."

"Very funny," she said.

While he let the engine warm up for a moment, she glanced out her mud-streaked side window. At a house nearby a man had leaned a ladder against a sagging section of roof and climbed up to shovel inches of wet ash off it.

Suddenly she burst into tears.

"What's the matter?" Jake asked, turning and putting a hand on her good knee.

"I feel so sorry for all the people. They've lost their homes—or their lives! So many of them."

"I'm sorry too," Jake concurred.

"And those other people on our climb. You lost your partner on the very first day."

Jake's face pinched with pain. "Hari was my best friend—" Choking emotion kept him from saying more.

They sat silently for a moment as the engine rumbled. When the man on the roof saw Sophie looking his way, he gave her a friendly wave and a smile that seemed too chipper for a man faced with so daunting a task. Then he went back to his work. The roof wasn't sagging as much as it had been.

She said to Jake, "I just had a thought, for what it's worth. Our team was the last to reach the summit of Mount Rainier—forever."

"That's something, I suppose," he said rather bleakly. And then he leaned far back into the crew cab and kissed her on the forehead. She turned her face up to his and he responded by kissing her on the lips. They hugged, and tears that squeezed from the corners of her eyes rolled down her cheeks.

He settled back into the driver's seat. He turned the wheels to go back down the hill, and when he put a light foot on the throttle, the four-wheel drive grabbed and pulled them through the wet ash. In a moment, they were on flat streets again and headed for the safety and comfort of Jake's home.

Please Write A Reader Review

If you enjoyed *Rainier Erupts!* please write a reader review on the website from which you obtained the book. Reviews and star ratings help other readers find great books, and they help authors get the word out about their stories. Simply go to this web page: www.thomas-hopp.com/blog where you will find a link to a page with all my books listed in every format.

Thanks! —Tom Hopp

ABOUT THE AUTHOR

Thomas Patrick Hopp writes science fiction and mystery/ thriller novels that make use of his background as a scientist and scholar of the natural world. His stories have won multiple literary awards and gained him a worldwide following. He is an active professional member of both the Mystery Writers of America and the Science Fiction and Fantasy Writers of America. Before he took up writing Tom was an internationally recognized molecular biologist. He discovered powerful hormones that strengthen the immune system and helped found the multi-billion-dollar Seattle biotechnology company Immunex Corporation. He advised the team that created Immunex's blockbuster arthritis drug Enbrel. He innovated techniques for analyzing protein molecular structures. He developed the first commercially successful nanotechnology device, a molecular handle for manipulating molecules at the atomic level. This product has been used in molecular biology labs throughout the world to study human cells and every major microbe known to science.

Tom's mystery stories follow Dr. Peyton McKean, a super-intelligent sleuth known as "The Greatest Mind Since Sherlock Holmes." Like the author himself, Dr. McKean is not so much a user of DNA tests as an inventor of DNA tests. Viruses, microbes, and evil geniuses form the core of his opposition. Dr. McKean possesses tremendous intellectual power, but often must back it up with daring feats that would challenge James Bond. Tom's Dinosaur Wars books have been described as "Star Wars meets Jurassic Park." Featuring laser-blasting space invaders and huge beasts revived from Earth's past, these tales follow Yellowstone Park naturalist Chase Armstrong and Montana rancher's daughter Kit Daniels as they struggle to survive in a world where dinosaurs live again. These exciting science fiction adventures are suitable for all ages and both genders.

ACKNOWLEDGMENTS

I would like to thank David Galvin, an avid mountaineer who has reached Mount Rainier's summit six times, for his excellent advice regarding the experience of climbing the mountain and the techniques involved in getting to the top. I would also like to thank Kathleen Johnson for her personal recollections of the day she fled her home in Kelso as a lahar bore down upon it from the eruption of Mount Saint Helens. She has my gratitude for her help and my sympathy for any old hardships her retelling may have brought to mind. Karin Rogers recalled ominous clouds and ash that covered Pullman while she was attending Washington State University. Carson Odegard described watching Saint Helens explode from Portland, Oregon and subsequent problems with ash blanketing the city three inches deep. Cameron Thompson got a too-close-for-comfort view of the eruption when the Washington State Patrol stopped him first in a miles-long line of vehicles jamming Interstate 5. He watched whole forests of logs wash under the Toutle River Bridge carrying crushed homes away while thunder and lightning exploded in ash clouds looming overhead. Greg Gilson recalled his desperate trek from the Tatoosh Wilderness when a mountain hike turned into a dust-choked retreat to a car covered in ash six inches deep at the trailhead. I also want to acknowledge James Weatherill for giving me the benefit of his lifetime of experience flying Chinook helicopters in the Viet Nam War and in peacetime pursuits as well. His book *The Blades Carry Me* is a touching and deeply insightful record of one man's experience of war and his wife Anne's long and difficult wait at home. Finally I would like to gratefully acknowledge the help and support of the Duwamish Longhouse Museum where I have had the good fortune to receive training in the Lushootseed language as well as many opportunities to meet with cultural leaders and learn at least a small portion of the traditions, history, and folklore of the people who have long inhabited the shores of the Whulge, or Salish Sea, which we pahstuds call Puget Sound.

OTHER BOOKS AND STORIES BY THOMAS P. HOPP

The Dinosaur Wars Series

Earthfall
Counterattack
Blood on the Moon
Dinosaur Tales

Peyton McKean Mysteries

The Smallpox Incident
The Neah Virus

Short Stories

The Treasure of Purgatory Crater
A Dangerous Breed
The Re-Election Plot
The Ghost Trees
Blood Tide

Visit the Author's Official Web Site

www.thomas-hopp.com/blog

To keep informed of new publications by Thomas P. Hopp, you can join his mailing list at the site above. Or you can find links to purchase all of his books and stories in any format at: www.thomas-hopp.com/LandingAllTitles.

Made in the USA
San Bernardino, CA
17 April 2016